FAIRY WINGS

BOOKS BY E. D. BAKER

The Tales of the Frog Princess:

The Frog Princess
Dragon's Breath
Once Upon a Curse
No Place for Magic
The Salamander Spell
The Dragon Princess
Dragon Kiss
A Prince among Frogs

∾

The Wide-Awake Princess

∾

Fairy Wings
Fairy Lies

FAIRY WINGS

E. D. BAKER

BLOOMSBURY

NEW YORK BERLIN LONDON SYDNEY

First published in the United States of America in May 2008 as *Wings*
by Bloomsbury Books for Young Readers
Paperback edition published in September 2009
This edition published in February 2012
www.bloomsburykids.com

For information about permission to reproduce selections from this book, write to
Permissions, Bloomsbury BFYR, 175 Fifth Avenue, New York, New York 10010

The Library of Congress has cataloged the hardcover edition as follows:
Baker, E. D.
Wings / by E. D. Baker. — 1st US. ed.
p.   cm.
Summary: When Tamisin finds out that she is half fairy, she decides to find out more
answers directly from the fairies themselves, including her mother, the fairy queen.
ISBN-13: 978-1-59990-193-0 • ISBN-10: 1-59990-193-5 (hardcover)
[1. Fairies—Fiction.] I. Title.
PZ7.B17005Wi 2008   [Fic]—dc22   2007023553

ISBN 978-1-59990-756-7 (*Fairy Wings* edition)

Typeset by Westchester Book Composition
Printed in the U.S.A. by Quad/Graphics, Fairfield, Pennsylvania
2 4 6 8 10 9 7 5 3 1

All papers used by Bloomsbury Publishing, Inc., are natural, recyclable products
made from wood grown in well-managed forests. The manufacturing processes
conform to the environmental regulations of the country of origin.

This book is dedicated to Ellie for being my sounding board and my first reader through all the versions I've written over the last three years, to Victoria for believing in me and for her clarity of vision, and to Kevin for being my technology and athletics adviser.

PART ONE

Chapter 1

Tamisin Warner first saw real goblins the Halloween she was eleven. She had gone trick-or-treating with her mother, her little brother, Petey, and her best friend, Heather. The evening had begun ordinarily enough, but it didn't stay that way for long.

"I can't believe my mother made me wear this stupid costume," Heather had complained as one of her paper leaves fluttered to the ground. After rearranging the trash bag so her neck was centered in the hole, she frowned and tried to smooth another loose leaf. "Who ever heard of dressing up as Autumn for Halloween? I wish I had a costume like yours. I've never seen such a pretty fairy princess costume before."

Tamisin glanced down at the blue petal dress her mother had helped her make. Even with all the sewing, the dress had taken less time than the silvery wings, which drooped no matter what Tamisin did with pins and duct tape. "Thanks. I tried to make it look real."

The girls started toward the next house while Petey

and his mother trailed behind. "It's getting dark," said Heather, hitching up one side of her trash bag to reach into her jacket pocket. Pulling out a slim flashlight, she aimed the beam at the porch, letting the light rest on the carved pumpkins and bundled cornstalks by the door.

"We can't go there," said Tamisin, aiming her own flashlight at the front of the house. "They don't have their lights on. It looks like nobody's home."

"I'll race you to the blue house then!" Heather announced as she took off down the street.

Tamisin was following her friend when something moved in the beam of her flashlight. She paused in the front yard of the empty house, letting the light play across the space between the two houses. There it was—a small figure no bigger than Petey emptying a trash can onto the lawn. When it laughed, it sounded like a child, but its body was more like an animal's with a hunched back, a long, puffy tail, and legs that bent the wrong way. The creature was laughing when it reached into the garbage and flung banana peels and eggshells over its shoulder. It was laughing when it climbed into the trash can and rolled across the yard until it banged into a tree. It was still laughing when it crawled out of the can shedding coffee grounds and scraps of greasy paper towels. But when it stood up and turned around only to have Tamisin's light fall full on its masked face, the little creature shrieked like a siren and flung its furred hands into the air, its mouth wide open in surprise.

And then it was gone, leaving Tamisin unable to believe what she had seen.

"Are you coming or what?" Heather called from the front steps of the blue house.

"Did you see ... No, I guess you wouldn't ... Yeah, I'll be right there," Tamisin answered, torn between going after the little creature to see if it was real and joining her friend.

They visited a few more houses before meeting up with Tamisin's mother and Petey across from the school. While her mother tried to persuade Petey to wait to eat his candy, Tamisin watched the passing trick-or-treaters. Children dressed as superheros, pirates, and ghosts ran from house to house, leaving their parents standing on the sidewalk. She heard her older brother Kyle's voice when he ran by with two of his friends, but he pretended that he didn't know her. All three of the boys were dressed as aliens with rubbery masks and blue coveralls. A child dressed as a fire hydrant and another dressed as a candy bar hurried past with a little girl in a pink dress following only a few feet behind. Tamisin caught a glimpse of her face, which looked much older than her size suggested. Even stranger were her little twitchy nose and mouselike ears.

"Did you see the girl with the mouse nose?" Tamisin whispered to Heather. "Did you see the way it moved? It had to be real!"

Heather laughed. "You're so funny, Tamisin!"

Tamisin sighed. She should have known not to try to tell Heather what she had seen. Heather had been her best friend since kindergarten. She was someone Tamisin could tell the really important things to, like when she got a bad grade on a test or how she felt about having a baby brother, but there were certain things Heather didn't understand.

A group of children passed them on the sidewalk. Tamisin and Heather hurried after them, while Petey and her mother tried to keep up. One of the boys in the group was dressed as a cowboy with a ten-gallon hat and boots that looked two sizes too big. He was clomping along, talking excitedly with his friends, when an impossibly long arm reached out from under a car and tripped him. His friends immediately gathered around, teasing him about his oversized shoes. No one except Tamisin seemed to have noticed the arm and the six-fingered hand that grabbed some of the candy that had spilled from the boy's plastic pumpkin when he dropped it. Only Tamisin seemed to hear a deep voice laughing under the car as the boy scowled and got back on his feet.

"Watch your step, kids," said Tamisin's mother. "The sidewalk is uneven."

Tamisin was wary now; creatures that no one else could see were playing pranks on people. If she hadn't seen the arm trip the boy, she might think that she'd imagined it, but it had suddenly become more real. Although she'd been trick-or-treating on Halloween for as long as she could remember, she'd never seen anything like this before.

With Heather at her side, Tamisin climbed the steps to the next house. Neither the smiling face of the woman at the door nor the piece of candy dropped in Tamisin's bag made any impression on her. There were things in

6

the dark, things that she'd never seen before, except . . . maybe she had. The creature with the legs that bent the wrong way, the long skinny arm that looked more like a hose than the limb of a body . . . Both reminded her of creatures she'd seen in a nightmare—*the* nightmare—the one she'd had for as long as she could remember. It was enough to wake her up at night. It was enough to make her afraid to step off the porch.

She was about to tell Heather that she wanted to go home when Petey shrieked and began to cry. Tamisin felt safer inside the crowd, but if her little brother needed her . . . Moving against the current of children, the girls found Petey seated on the ground, his chubby legs splayed out in front of him. He was hiccupping around the two fingers crammed in his mouth, his face tear-streaked and flushed. Their mother was kneeling beside him, inspecting his bloodied knee. Glancing up at the girls, she said, "He'll be fine. He tripped on the sidewalk. I knew it was uneven, but he insisted on walking."

Alarmed, Tamisin looked up in time to see something shiny glint in the shrubs, then suddenly disappear. The sound of voices made her turn. A group of children stood under the street lamp on the opposite corner. She would have given them no more than a quick glance if she hadn't been struck by the costume that the tallest child was wearing. He looked like a lion with a furry ruff around his head and what looked like fur on his face, but after a moment's study, she began to wonder if it was a costume at all. And as for the rest of the children—the longer she looked, the less they looked like children. One had droopy ears that dangled below his collar. The boy standing beside him had small rounded ears on top of his head. A third had teeth that curled over her lower lip when she closed her mouth. There were others with too many joints in their arms or a sheen to their skins that made Tamisin think of scales.

A skinny almost-boy with a pointed face and dark, tiny eyes like a rodent seemed to be in charge. His movements were quick and furtive as he took eggs and rolls of toilet paper from an enormous sack and passed them to the others. When those ran out, he gave them buckets into which he poured liquid, gloppy mud.

Heather had crouched down beside Petey and was trying to distract him with the candy in her bag. "What are you looking at?" she asked when Tamisin didn't join her.

"Nothing," said Tamisin, not wanting to be laughed at again.

The rodent boy looked up at the sound of her voice. His eyes met Tamisin's in an unblinking gaze that made her heart start to pound and her mouth go dry. Turning his head to the side, the rodent boy said something to his friends. In an instant they all stopped what they were doing to stare at Tamisin. They didn't look at her the way ordinary children did, as if seeing what she looked like or what she was wearing; they looked at her the way a cat might a mouse or a fox a hen in an appraising, "I'm hungry" sort of way. If she'd been frightened before, Tamisin was terrified now.

While her mother fussed over Petey, Tamisin backed away one slow step at a time. The eyes of the not-quite-children stayed on her even when Petey whined and fretted. "Run!" her mind shouted, yet she couldn't just abandon her family. As she moved farther away and the strange children didn't look at anyone but her, Tamisin realized that her family wasn't in danger. She was.

Tamisin ran, clutching her bag to her chest where her fist could feel her heart racing. She heard her mother calling to her, but the creatures were so close that she didn't dare stop. Over the tap-tap-tap of her shoes on the sidewalk, she heard the slap of bare feet, and a thud-thud, thud-thud that might have been hooves. She had a painful stitch in her side when she slowed to glance behind her. Her pursuers were spread across the street, some loping on all fours, others scurrying on two, but none of them running quite the way humans do. When she saw a girl's fangs glistening in the glow of a streetlight, Tamisin ran faster, barely clearing the back bumper of a passing car.

Too frightened to think, she ran past the library, a store, a gas station, and a small park with a playground, and still she could hear them behind her. Then they began to call out, sounding like wild animals, cackling and hooting, growling and bellowing. She couldn't stop now. If she did, she knew that something horrible would happen.

The wind began to blow, slowing her down and whipping twigs and leaves at her and her pursuers. It had grown late; most of the trick-or-treaters had gone home. And still Tamisin ran with aching legs and lungs that felt as if they were on fire. When she stumbled on a curb and fell to her knees, her pursuers howled with delight. Then suddenly, out of the clear night sky, a bolt of lightning struck a tree behind her while thunder shook the ground. The tree burst into flames and Tamisin clapped her hands to her ears, only vaguely realizing that she'd dropped her bag somewhere along the road. In the light of the fire she could see her hunters; they were so close that she was sure they could have caught her if they'd wanted to.

It occurred to Tamisin that they were toying with her. Rather than frightening her even more, the knowledge made her angry. She ignored the sting of her scraped knees as she turned to face them. They gabbled and snickered at her, padding closer on their inhuman feet. The closest ones were almost near enough to touch her when another bolt of lightning hit the street in their midst, and the air boomed with thunder. Temporarily deafened, she could no longer hear them, but she saw the look of terror in their eyes as they scattered, fleeing back the way they had come.

Wishing that the odd, rainless storm would go away, Tamisin waited for the next bolt of lightning to strike. When it didn't, she ran down the cross street, not wanting to see if the almost-children would come looking for her again. Finally, exhausted and footsore, she was relieved to see a familiar street sign. As she turned down the street and began the long trudge home, Tamisin vowed never to go trick-or-treating again.

Chapter 2

A few years later . . .

Tamisin swiped her tongue over her teeth as she lowered the rearview mirror. She hated visiting the dentist's office, but she had to admit that her teeth felt and looked a lot cleaner. Turning away from the mirror, she glanced out the window of her mother's minivan while she thought about her upcoming audition. Normally she would have used an afternoon dentist appointment as an excuse to skip school for the rest of the day, but the auditions for the school dance group were slated to start right after the last class period and she definitely did not want to miss them. The group was hard to get into and . . .

Her mother slammed on the brakes, narrowly missing a large animal that had darted across the street and into the hedge on the other side. "Did you see that?" Janice Warner asked, her knuckles white as she gripped the steering wheel. "That dog came out of nowhere. I don't understand people who let their pets run loose. I could have killed it!"

Tamisin's heart was racing as she studied the still

11

rustling shrubs. She had seen enough of the creature before it disappeared to know that it hadn't been a dog. True, it had been running on all fours, but its face was human, or nearly so, and it had been wearing brown pants and a baggy shirt. As her mother stepped on the gas pedal, the face reappeared framed in the leaves of the hedge and watched the car as it moved off. The slightly bulbous nose and close-set eyes looked human, although the long, flopping ears would have looked more appropriate on a cocker spaniel. Another face appeared beside it, smaller than the first, with curly white fur covering its human cheeks and chin. It too was watching the passing cars and was turning toward her when Tamisin forced herself to look away. They were the same kinds of creatures she'd seen before, only this time she knew better than to let them know it.

"A penny for your thoughts," her mother said as they waited at a stoplight. "You're being awfully quiet. If you're worried about your audition, you shouldn't be. I'm sure you'll do just great. You're a wonderful dancer."

"Hmm? Oh, sorry," said Tamisin. "I'm not worried."

At least not about the audition, she thought. A few years before, the creatures had chased her down this very same street. She hadn't seen them since then. If they were back, why now and why had they been gone for so long? All the fear of that long-ago night had come back, leaving her unable to think about anything else.

At the dance audition, as she stood in line waiting for her turn, she hardly noticed the girls around her chattering about the butterflies in their stomachs and how much they wanted to get in the group. Tamisin took deep, even breaths, hoping to slow the racing of her heart. Her nervousness had nothing to do with dancing and everything to do with what she might see once she walked out the school door. Why were they back now?

At least Heather was with her, more to support Tamisin than because she really wanted to dance. The audition wasn't very long; each girl would get only a few minutes to show what she could do. Even so, the line seemed to be taking forever to move. Then it was Tamisin's turn to go into the room and stand in front of Miss Rigby and the senior members of the dance group. Once the music she had selected began to play, Tamisin forgot all about the creatures and what she would do if she saw them again, letting her desire to dance take over.

Although Tamisin had never taken any formal lessons, she had always enjoyed dancing. Years earlier her family had gone camping in a state park not far from their home. She had been asleep in the tent with her parents and brothers when she woke to the sound of music. Whatever was creating it didn't sound like anything she had heard before, but it was enough to make her wriggle out of her sleeping bag and crawl out of the tent.

The music drew her to the lake, where the silvered reflection of the moon rippled on the surface. Shivering in the crisp night air of autumn, she stood at the edge of the lake with the cold water lapping at her bare toes. The music was soft and sweet with a hypnotic quality that made her take one tentative step, then another. Before she knew it she was dancing, her feet keeping time to the melody, her arms swaying, reaching to the perfect circle of the moon overhead. She twirled, so light on her feet that she felt as if she were floating, the music carrying her in ever more intricate steps.

And then they came, a few at first, bright sparks that darted around her in an imitation of her dance. Anyone else might have thought they were fireflies, but she saw their tiny faces, dresses the colors of flowers, wings so bright that they hurt her eyes, and arms that gestured just as hers were doing.

The music grew louder, carrying Tamisin with it, filling her ears and her mind and leaving no room for questions. She danced with the moonlight shining on her face as the little creatures gathered around her, dancing as she danced, moving as she moved. Some broke away long enough to brush her cheeks with their feather-light wings and touch her nightgown as if she, and not they, were something special and worthy of awe. Entranced, Tamisin would have danced all night if a beam of light hadn't swept across the campground to center on her. As the light touched her face, the music faded and the sparks of light fled into the night, leaving Tamisin alone and shivering.

"There she is," announced her big brother, Kyle. "Dad, Tam is being weird."

"That's enough of that, Kyle," said her father, who had come looking for Tamisin. "Sweetie, what are you doing?"

"I was dancing with the fairies, Daddy," Tamisin replied.

"Girls!" said Kyle as he turned and headed back to the tent.

A month later, Tamisin was home in bed when the same feeling came over her again; once again she was unable to resist. Slipping out from under her covers, she padded barefoot out of her room and down the carpeted stairs. A turn of the dead bolt and the back door was open. The moonlight touched her face and the feeling became so powerful that her body swayed as if in a strong wind. Raising her arms over her head, Tamisin danced just as she had the last time there had been a full moon. She knew the twinkling lights were coming even before they appeared.

It happened again the next full moon and the one after that. It wasn't until two months later that Tamisin's parents learned that she was dancing in the moonlight in their very own backyard. They agreed that she must be sleep walking and put her back to bed. When they talked to her about it the next day, they seemed more concerned about the swarm of twinkling lights they'd found surrounding her than they were about her actual dancing. Within a week they had had a security alarm installed so they'd know if she opened the door after dark. Now they knew when she went outside, but that didn't stop her from going. When she continued to dance every month on the full moon, they installed new locks that she couldn't open. She danced inside that first night, twirling in the kitchen and through the living room, bumping into a coffee table, knocking over a floor lamp, and acquiring a set of bruises. Her parents finished off the room in the basement, creating a safe place for her to dance. They still didn't understand why she had to dance when she did, but they seemed pleased that at least the strange lights could no longer reach her.

Tamisin soon began to dance whenever she could—after school, on weekends, and at night. She danced because she was able to lose herself in the music, almost as if she were entering another world. If she closed her eyes, she could imagine herself there, but she didn't dare close her eyes for the audition.

Trying out for the school dance group was the first time she'd ever danced in front of someone who wasn't a friend or relative. Most of the girls trying out were older than Tamisin. Juniors and seniors seemed to think of it as their organization, although there wasn't any rule about it. Four seniors already in the group were seated on a row of chairs at the side of the stage beside Miss Rigby when Tamisin walked through the door. All four looked bored, as if they were already certain that she was about to waste their time. Although she hadn't been nervous before she walked on stage, her hands began to shake and her stomach felt odd. It helped that Miss Rigby gave Tamisin an encouraging smile when she told them her name and handed them her CD.

The music was simple, but it was one of Tamisin's favorite pieces and she danced to it often. She didn't dance the way she did under a full moon, but some of the steps were the same, and her movements were fluid and graceful, even though she felt odd performing in front of people she didn't really know.

When the music stopped and she saw how the seniors beamed at her, Tamisin could feel the heat of a fierce blush creep up her neck and turn her cheeks pink. Smiling until her face hurt, Tamisin nodded at the judges and left the stage. She'd kept telling herself that she didn't really care if she got into the group; she danced for herself, not for others, and could do it in the basement as easily as anywhere else, but of course she really wanted to get in.

She was waiting for Heather to finish her audition when Tamisin's least-favorite classmates, Kendra and Tiffany, walked by.

"Have you seen the new boy?" asked Kendra. "He is so hot!"

"His name is Jak," said Tiffany. "I saw it on his notebook when he was at his locker. He spells it J-A-K."

"Where is he from?" Kendra asked, ignoring Tamisin, who had to step aside to get out of her way.

"I don't know, but I hear he has loads of money."

Heather came out of the door to the auditorium. "Well, so much for that."

"How did it go?" Tamisin asked.

Heather sighed and ran her fingers through her short brown hair. "As well as could be expected, considering. I was so nervous that I bumped into the door on the way in. Those girls laughed at me before I'd even started and then I couldn't get my feet to match the music. I know I blew it, but that's okay. I'm thinking of trying out for girls' basketball and a lot of the practices would be at the same time."

"But you're shorter than I am," Tamisin said, laughing. "Do you think the basketball coach would take you?"

Heather shrugged. "I'm small, but I'm fast. My father says I have a mean hook shot. It's going to be interesting to see who gets in the dance group though. They take only the very best, and that, Tamisin, is you!"

The next morning Tamisin pretended that she wasn't interested in the results, but Heather insisted that they find out right away. While Tamisin waited by the drinking fountain, Heather joined the group of girls examining the list next to the office door. Voices rose and fell as girls pushed their way to the front, then retreated, a few of them smiling, but most looking disappointed.

"Did you make it?" asked Tamisin when Heather came back a few minutes later.

"Of course not," said Heather. "But you did! You're the first name on the list!"

"You're kidding me!"

"I told you that you would. We should do something to celebrate."

The bell rang in the hall; they had five minutes to get to first-period class and their classrooms were at the other end of the building.

"Race you there!" said Tamisin.

Laughing, the two girls clutched their backpacks to their chests and dashed down the hall. A computer science teacher stuck his head out of his doorway and called after them, "No running, girls!"

"We're not," Tamisin called back. "We're celebrating!"

At the next hallway, Heather waved good-bye as Tamisin turned the corner. Tamisin was still waving to her friend when she ran full tilt into a boy standing in front of his locker. They fell to the floor in a tangle of arms and legs as her backpack skidded down the polished linoleum and his books went flying. In an instant he was back on his feet, so nimbly that Tamisin wondered if *he* was a dancer.

"Sorry," she said as she scrambled to stand up. "I'm not usually this clumsy."

"Neither am I," said the boy, handing her the backpack. "I'm Jak, and you are . . ."

"Tamisin," she said.

Jak was about her height and had thick, dark hair and the deepest blue eyes she'd ever seen. The rest of his features weren't anything extraordinary—his nose was straight, his chin square, his lips full—but as a whole he was surprisingly handsome.

"Are you all right?" he asked as she stood there, speechless.

"Sure, uh . . . yes. But I should be asking you that. I ran into you, remember?"

Jak shrugged. "I was in your way."

The bell rang again, signaling the start of classes. "Darn!" said Tamisin. "I'm late!"

"I guess that means I am, too. I'm not used to the bell system yet. I just started yesterday."

"Go to class, unless you want to get into trouble," she said over her shoulder as she hurried down the hall. Reaching the door to her classroom, she glanced back. Jak was still standing where she'd left him, staring after her.

Chapter 3

"Hey, Tamisin! Over here!"

Tamisin stopped on the steps to see who was calling her. Dance practice had lasted longer than she'd expected, and she hadn't thought anyone would still be around. The other girls had rides or cars of their own, but Tamisin lived only a few blocks from the school and walked home every day.

Two boys were waiting by the curb. One was Jeremy Johnson, a friend of her brother's. He was with the new boy, Jak, which surprised her. Jeremy was into sports and usually hung around with the other jocks. Jak didn't seem to be anything like Jeremy's usual friends.

"Hi, Jeremy," Tamisin said as she reached the sidewalk in front of the school. "What's up?"

"You've met my man Jak here, haven't you?"

Tamisin nodded. "Sure. We ran into each other right after he started here."

Jak grinned, transforming his face. Where he'd looked

angry just a moment before, he now looked approachable. "You should smile more often," she said, surprising herself because she hadn't meant to say it out loud.

"All right," said Jak as if he was taking her suggestion to heart. "But why?"

Tamisin shrugged. "You'll make more friends that way."

Jeremy snorted and punched Jak in the arm. "Jak here doesn't need to worry about making friends. He's cool. Everybody likes Jak."

Jak gave Jeremy a half smile, but Tamisin thought he looked uncomfortable.

"Hi, Jeremy," cooed a voice that Tamisin knew too well. It was Kendra again with Tiffany.

"Kendra," Jeremy said, not looking too pleased. Jeremy had dated Kendra for a few weeks the year before. Tamisin didn't know exactly what had happened, but Jeremy had broken up with her.

Kendra must have noticed Jeremy's reaction because her smile became brittle and forced. "Why don't you introduce me to your friend? You're the new boy, aren't you?" she said to Jak.

Tamisin laughed. Since kindergarten Kendra had been a terrible liar. "This is Jak," Jeremy said, sounding defensive. "Jak, that's Kendra."

"Hi!" Kendra turned up the wattage of her smile until Tamisin was almost embarrassed for her, especially since Jak didn't seem the least bit interested.

"Hey," he said.

"So, Tamisin," said Jeremy. "You busy? Jak and I are headed over to—"

Jak staggered and nearly bumped into her. A gray cat from somewhere in the neighborhood had crossed the street and was forcefully rubbing against Jak's legs. "Don't do that!" said the boy, sounding more annoyed than surprised as he shoved the cat away with his foot. Only Kendra didn't seem to notice. She had turned to Tamisin the moment Jeremy spoke her name.

"So Tamisin, I didn't see you standing there. Why are you here so late? Were you getting extra help today or was it detention?"

Tamisin tried not to look as irritated as she felt. "I had dance practice and—"

"I can't imagine why you're wasting your time talking to her, Jak. You're new here, so I guess you haven't heard about Tamisin. She's a freak—everybody knows it. I bet you've never seen ears like hers. Here," Kendra said, thrusting her books at Tiffany. "Look at this!"

Tamisin was too stunned to avoid her when Kendra shoved Tamisin's hair behind her ear, exposing the one thing Tamisin never let anyone see, the pointed tip. "Have you ever seen anything like that?" Kendra asked, laughing.

Jeremy looked disgusted, but not at Tamisin. "Give it a rest, Kendra," he said. "Nobody cares what her ears look like."

"There you are!" Heather called to Tamisin as she came around the building. "I was waiting in back by the gym door."

"Sorry," said Tamisin. "I came through the building. I didn't think you'd still be here. We got out so late . . ."

"That's Heather," Jeremy told Jak.

"Hey," said Jak.

Heather smiled at Jeremy, then turned to Jak, saying, "It's nice to meet you." She sounded congested.

Tamisin peered at her friend and frowned. "Are you all right? Your eyes are getting puffy."

Heather brushed at her eyes with the back of her hand. "There must be a cat around." The gray cat appeared from behind Jak, still rubbing against his legs. "Oh!" said Heather, taking a step back. A second cat had padded across the street to join the first, and both were doing figure eights around Jak's ankles.

Jak stepped away from the cats, who ran after him, purring, with their tails straight up in the air. "I told you to stop that!" he muttered.

Heather reached into her pocket for a tissue. "I don't understand. I'm allergic to cats, but it doesn't usually bother me when I'm outside."

"I'd better get you home," Tamisin said, taking her by the arm. "See you tomorrow," she told Jak and Jeremy.

"She doesn't look so good," said Tiffany.

Kendra laughed. "Does she ever? Last year . . ."

Tamisin didn't wait for Kendra to finish before she led Heather away. Although Heather's eyelids were so puffy that she could barely see, it didn't stop her from talking. "I hate that girl," she mumbled from behind a tissue. "I remember how nasty she was in first grade when you showed me your ears. And then that boy who stole my pencil box pulled your ear to see if it was real and you punched him in the stomach."

"I remember," said Tamisin.

Heather shoved her soggy tissue into her pocket and began to look for another. "And then there was that time in sixth grade when Kendra teased you about your face. You'd gone camping with your family and when you came home you had shiny freckles. You called them spreckles and told me you got them when you danced with the fairies. I almost believed you, too. Then that awful Mrs. Pitts yelled at you for wearing glitter to school and scrubbed your face until your skin was red. Kendra thought it was so funny."

"I'd almost forgotten," said Tamisin. "Thanks for reminding me."

"You know me," said Heather. "I have a mind like a steel trap. Too bad I also have a nose like a dripping faucet. You don't have any tissues on you, do you?"

Tamisin shook her head. "No, I don't. Sorry."

"I'm sure I have some more somewhere," Heather said, searching her pockets again. "Do you remember when . . ."

But Tamisin had something else on her mind. She had seen Jak's expression when Kendra showed him her ear, expecting to find some sign that he was as put off as most people were when they saw it. Instead, he had looked pleased. His reaction confused her and left her wondering exactly what he was thinking. Aside from members of her family, he was the first person to see her ears since she was six years old. After the incident at school, she had always worn her hair down.

Tamisin touched her ear again to reassure herself that her hair was covering it. Somehow she was sure that if she turned around, Jak would still be watching her. She was fighting the urge to glance back when she heard rustling in the branches overhead. Peering through the leaves, she glimpsed a manlike creature with pointed ears and a raccoon's mask. Startled, Tamisin gasped softly. He looked just like the little man she'd seen rolling in a trash can on that long-ago Halloween.

A twig snapped and Heather looked up as leaves rained down on them. "It must be a squirrel." She rubbed her still swollen eyelids, saying, "I'm so embarrassed. I can't believe Jeremy saw me like this. Do my eyes look really bad?"

Tamisin patted her friend's shoulder. "I'm sure he understands. I think Kyle said that Jeremy's allergic to shellfish or something."

"Is he really?" Heather asked, as if allergies were more acceptable if they were shared.

While her friend looked in her purse for another clean tissue, Tamisin watched the little raccoon man. She could hear him grumbling as he struggled to hold on to a too-thin branch that bobbed up and down under his weight. "I should never have told him that I'd come," the man was saying. "One day I'm on the island, happy as a fly on dung, and the next I'm on a wild girl chase all over this goblin-forsaken town. 'All ya gots to do is find the girl,' he says. Easy for him to say. I should just go back and say no luck, couldn't do it, unh unh. I would look truthful, too, so's he gots to believe me. Or maybe not, considering it's him. . . ."

"Got one," Heather said, holding up a tissue. She glanced at Tamisin and frowned. "What's wrong? You have the funniest look on your face."

Tamisin shook her head. "Nothing's wrong. I just need to get home."

"Me, too," said Heather. "This is my last tissue."

The rustling followed them from tree to tree. When they crossed the street, Tamisin heard a small thump as if something had hit the ground. Although she didn't turn around to look, she could hear that the raccoon man was still right behind them. Her mind raced. What did the little man want? He was obviously following them, but why?

"Tamisin, did you hear what I said?" asked Heather. "I asked what you and Jeremy were talking about."

"Not much," Tamisin replied.

"He is so cute! He isn't seeing anyone now, is he? Did he mention me at all before I got there?"

"Not really," said Tamisin.

"What do you think of Jak? I saw the way he was looking at you. I think he likes you."

Tamisin glanced at her friend. "He seems nice, and he is really hot, but there's something a little odd about him. Did you see the way those cats acted?"

"That was weird." Heather scrunched her nose and made a face. "Maybe he keeps a can of sardines in his pocket."

"Maybe," Tamisin replied, only half listening to her friend because the little man was talking again.

"'Tobianthicus, ya gotta go!' he told me with that

look in his eyes that didn't give me no choice. 'Ya know what she looks like. Them other folk are too scared to go, so it's up to you.' 'But I don't wanna,' I says. 'I was scared, too!' 'Too bad,' says him. 'Ya ain't got a choice.' "

As they neared Heather's home, the trees were farther apart, and tall hedges divided one yard from the next. Now the rustling came from ground level as the raccoon goblin fought his way through the gaps in the bushes. Tamisin could hear him grumbling, "Life ain't fair" as the girls stopped in front of Heather's house.

"I'd ask you in," said Heather, "but I'd better go wash up. Maybe some of this swelling will go down. See you tomorrow."

"Bye," said Tamisin. Although she wanted to go home, she hesitated, unsure if going straight there was such a good idea. Not knowing why this little goblin had been following them made her uneasy. Of course, he might have been following Heather, but she didn't think so. Tamisin could still hear him in the shrubs behind her . . . Maybe she could lose him if she went home another way.

Turning in the opposite direction from her home, she strode quickly down the sidewalk, listening to make sure that the little man was following her. Tamisin was thinking of cutting through some backyards to lose him when the raccoon man encountered a crow. He must have gone too close to the bird's nest, because the crow began berating him in its raucous voice.

"Oh, be off with ya!" the goblin screeched. "I don't want yer lousy, rotten, stinky eggs!"

Tamisin stopped to glance up in the tree as the bird squawked, pecking at the little man. This was her chance. While the goblin fought off the crow, Tamisin circled back the way she'd come, right past the house where Rex the Great Dane lived. His owners had a big fenced-in yard that Rex guarded day and night. When he wasn't barking at passing students, Tamisin could usually see him lying in front of his doghouse in the back corner of the yard.

As Tamisin approached the fence, she saw Rex stretched out on his side, sound asleep. Checking behind her, she spotted the goblin following her once more, so she climbed the fence as quietly as she could. When the dog didn't open his eyes, she dropped down to the other side, glanced at him once again, and tiptoed across the yard. Almost as if she'd called to him, the goblin scurried over the fence. He was skulking at the base of a big maple when Tamisin scrambled back to the other side. Before the raccoon man could follow, she picked up a stone and threw it at Rex's doghouse. Rex was on his feet in an instant, barking angrily in his deep, resonant voice.

"Drat and blast it!" the goblin cried as he scurried up the tree. "Is that a dog, cur, mongrel, or mule? Get away from me, ya slobberin' hound from . . ."

But Tamisin didn't see what the little man did next. Snatching up her backpack, she ran as fast as she could away from Rex's house, around the block and toward her own home, checking every shrub and tree for little men as she ran, until she finally slipped inside her front door, exhausted and hoping that she'd never see another creature like him again.

Chapter 4

It was the night of Tamisin's first performance with the dance group, and the thought of so many people watching her made her stomach churn. Although the corridor was empty when she and her family arrived at the school, she could hear voices coming from the locker room where the girls were supposed to change.

"Your father and I will be seated with Petey in the center of the auditorium," said her mother, who had insisted on walking her to the door. "Would you like us to wave?"

Tamisin looked horrified. "Please don't! Do you know how embarrassing that would be? I've got to go. Don't forget—I'll meet you by the back door after the performance."

"We'll be there!" her mother called as Tamisin hurried down the hall.

The other girls were in the locker room, laughing nervously and talking in too-loud voices as they put on their costumes and the finishing touches to their makeup. The girls closest to the door glanced up and smiled when Tamisin came in. After a few weeks of waiting for her to mess up at the rehearsals and drop out, the other girls finally acknowledged that Tamisin was one of them.

"The costumes are on the rack by the back wall," said a tall senior named Shareena.

The girls' locker room always smelled of sweat and disinfectant, but tonight it also smelled of floral shampoo, talcum powder, hairspray, and deodorant along with the roses of the bouquets that some girls had already received. It was a good smell that only added to Tamisin's excitement.

Inhaling deeply, she smiled as she hurried to the clothes rack. She had a solo, one of several to be performed by the best dancers, and she had worked so hard on it that she'd dreamed of it while she slept.

Tamisin wasn't in any hurry to get dressed; her performance wasn't until the end of the program and she still had plenty of time. The music for the first dance was just beginning when she slipped her costume over her head and felt the cool fabric glide over her skin like water on a hot day. The dress was a confection of pink, peach, and yellow that hugged her waist and swirled around her hips in irregular not-quite-tatters that rippled when she moved.

Tamisin was inspecting her reflection in the mirror when she felt a familiar pang. The moon had risen, sending its pale light through the windows set high on the locker room walls. With all her attention focused on the show, Tamisin had nearly forgotten that this was to be the night of another full moon. She took one step, then another, and was only just able to force herself to stop before the moon's spell took hold.

She was standing in the middle of the room, shaking with the effort *not* to dance when the door opened and Shareena called, "Tamisin, you're on next!"

Tamisin nodded. It was only through strength of will that she was able to walk normally down the hallway, through the door to the back of the stage, and onto the stage behind the closed curtain. As the curtain opened and the first strains of her music began, Tamisin glanced up. The faces of the audience swam in front of her, then seemed to fade away as she took the first steps of the dance she was supposed to perform. She tried to stay with the well-rehearsed movements, but with each step and gesture the urge to dance with the full moon grew in strength until it filled her mind and body. Her dance changed from the one she had been practicing for weeks into the one that her body was aching to do. Her movements became more fluid, her leaps higher, and her gestures more graceful. When the last strains of the music drew her back to the stage itself, the auditorium was deathly silent.

Although she hadn't been able to control the dance, Tamisin was certain that the teacher would be furious—maybe even mad enough to kick her out of the dance group. But then the cheering started and she looked up from her final position, surprised.

"That was wonderful!" her friends told her as she walked behind the curtain.

"Brilliant!" said Shareena, giving her a quick hug.

But Miss Rigby wasn't smiling when she took Tamisin aside later. "You changed your dance. That wasn't anything like what you've been rehearsing."

"I know. I don't know how to explain it, but I had to dance it that way. I know I should have danced the way we planned, so I'll understand if you don't want me in the group anymore."

"I should dismiss you from the group, but how can I when you just showed everyone that you're the best dancer in the school? You danced beautifully. Even better than in rehearsals. Why didn't you show me this before? Never mind—we'll talk about it tomorrow. Run along to the dressing room. The janitorial staff is waiting to clean up."

"Thanks, Miss Rigby!" Tamisin fairly flew to the locker room, so relieved that she was still in the group that she couldn't stop smiling. Her hands were shaking as she changed her clothes, and her fumbling fingers had so much trouble with her buttons that she was one of the last to leave the building.

As she reached the door at the back of the school, she saw tiny lights darting just outside. *It was the dance,* Tamisin thought as she opened the door to greet the familiar lights. In an instant the little creatures had descended on her in a cloud so brilliant that she had to squint to see.

"Have you ever seen so many fireflies?" Heather asked from only a few feet away.

Tamisin turned to her friend and discovered that a

crowd had gathered in the parking lot. Instead of leaving, many of the dancers and their families had stopped to watch the fireflies that had arrived while everyone was inside.

"I caught one!" shouted a boy holding a paper cup. A light glowed inside the cup, banging into the side like a ball in a pinball machine, but the boy kept his hand pressed firmly over the top.

"I want to catch one," shouted another boy, but a moment later the cloud dispersed, darting off into the night sky like so many twinkling stars.

"May I see your firefly?" Tamisin asked, hurrying over to where the boy stood with his friends.

He shrugged. "Sure. Just don't let it out."

When Tamisin said, "I'll be careful," the boy moved his hand a fraction and held up the cup so she could peer inside. "I can't see anything," she said. "Here, let me have it." Snatching the cup from his hand, she held it out of the boy's reach until the little creature had escaped.

"Hey!" he shouted. "That was mine!"

"It was just a firefly," Tamisin said, handing the cup back to him.

While the boy complained to his friends, Tamisin returned to where Heather was still waiting to talk to her.

"I wanted to tell you that your dance was amazing. Here, these are for you," Heather said, thrusting a bouquet of carnations into Tamisin's hand. "You were fantastic. Everyone is saying that your dance was the best."

"I never would have tried out if it hadn't been for you," Tamisin replied.

"That's what friends are for—making you do something in spite of yourself."

Tamisin laughed. "I'll have to remember that." She glanced around the parking lot. "Have you seen my parents?" She was tired and her back itched.

"I thought I saw them over by the trees," said Heather.

"Thanks. I'd better go find them. Do you need a ride?"

Heather shook her head. "My parents are here. It looks like most of the school is, too. Did I tell you that I saw Jeremy? We even talked for a few minutes."

"That's great," said Tamisin.

"Hey, there's my dad," said Heather. "I've got to go. See you in the morning."

Tamisin worked her way through the crowd to the trees at the side of the parking lot. Suddenly she noticed that someone else had taken refuge there. The shadows were deep, and at first all she could see was a dark figure standing close to a tree.

"I can handle it!" the figure's voice said. "I don't know why he sent you."

It was Jak, and whatever the other person had said had made him angry. He had his head down and his fists clenched when he turned away from the tree and began walking back to the school.

Not wanting to be caught eavesdropping, Tamisin pretended that she had just walked up and tried to act as surprised to see him as he was to see her. "Jak, is that you?" she asked.

"Tamisin! I was hoping to catch you here. Your dance

was great! It made me think of things I miss from my old home. It was very . . . eloquent."

"Thank you," she said. "That's kind of you."

"Oh, I'm not being kind. I mean it. For the first time I think I know what it means to be homesick."

"I'm so sorry! I never intended to make anyone feel bad."

"Don't be sorry. I enjoyed your dance. You don't have any plans now, do you? I mean, if you'd like to get something to eat, we could . . ."

"Tamisin!" her father called. "Your mother and I have been looking all over for you! We have to get Petey home."

"I know, Dad. I'm coming. Thanks for the invitation," she said, turning back to Jak. "Maybe some other time."

"Yeah. About that—"

Tamisin started edging toward her parents' car. "Sorry, but I've got to go."

"Sure," he said.

Jak was still watching her as she drove away with her family, looking so lonely that she almost asked her parents to stop the car—almost, but not quite. It wasn't that she didn't like him—he was good-looking and polite and seemed very nice. It was just that there was something about him that made her uncomfortable. Even worse, she had spotted who he had been talking to when she had walked up to him. Apparently she wasn't the only person who could see the little raccoon man, which made her even more wary of Jak.

They were one block from the school when Tamisin

saw more of the not-quite-humans. A sharp-faced woman with pointed ears and a tail like a fox ran down the sidewalk in the opposite direction. A pair of owl-eyed boys clung to a branch of the old maple on the corner, using their clawed toes to keep them upright while they gestured with their feathered hands. The rest of her family couldn't see them, but Tamisin just pretended that she couldn't, turning away each time she spotted one.

While her father carried a sleeping Petey upstairs, her mother took one look at Tamisin, told her how fantastic her dance had been, and then sent her off to bed as well.

Sleep was a long time coming. When it finally did, Tamisin had one of her bad dreams. Tamisin's nightmares were always the same; she knew this because every time she had one, she remembered it the next morning.

It always began in a place so dark that she couldn't see a thing. She was wrapped tightly in something soft and warm. She was moving, too, jiggling and bouncing as if something or someone was carrying her. The moon came out from behind the clouds and Tamisin saw the old woman who was holding her. Long, frizzy hair stuck out around the woman's head like a halo. Her little eyes glittered when she looked down at Tamisin, but it was the rest of her face that was frightening. Instead of a nose and mouth, the woman had a beak, as pointed and sharp as that of a bird.

"It's awake," said the bird woman, shaking Tamisin as if to make sure it was so. Her voice was harsh, and her beak clacked each time it closed.

"Good," said another voice. Tamisin turned her head, the only part of her that she could move, and saw another woman, smaller than the first with a pointed face and hair so short it could almost be called fur. "'Tain't much time. They'll be coming for it soon. Give it to me."

Tamisin could hear herself whimpering as she was passed from one woman to the other. "Remember this," said the sharp-faced woman, holding her face so close to Tamisin's that she could feel hot breath on her cheek. Moving her head toward Tamisin's arm, the woman opened her mouth and bit down, then sprinkled the wound with a dull, gray powder. Tamisin felt a sharp pain on her wrist followed by a throbbing that wouldn't go away. She wailed at the shock of it as much as from the ache. When the woman spoke, she sounded so fierce that Tamisin would have cried out if she hadn't been crying already. "You should never have been born, not to her. She's sending you away, which is the smartest thing she's done in a tortoise's age. You stay away and don't come back, for you're not wanted here!"

"That's enough," said a new voice and a pair of hands tucked the soft covering closer. Although she couldn't see the person's face, Tamisin did see the long, slender fingers and the white fur on the back of the gentle hands.

Tamisin woke with a start and looked around the room, making sure that she really was in her own bed in her own home. She rubbed the scar on her wrist until it stopped aching, just like she always did after her nightmare. When she was younger, she thought the dream might have been real, but when she grew older and had looked in every book she could find and seen that there were no bird people or rat people, she'd convinced herself that it couldn't have been possible—at least until that hateful Halloween night. Lately, the nightmare no longer frightened her the way it once had; now it just made her angry to know that the woman was going to hurt her and there wasn't a thing she could do about it.

Chapter 5

As if her world wasn't getting weird enough, Tamisin's back itched so much the next morning that it woke her before her alarm clock went off. What had begun as a mild irritation the night before had turned into a major problem. To make matters worse, it was Wednesday, her least favorite day of the week because she had swimming class during the last period.

After enduring an increasingly itchy back all day, Tamisin couldn't wait for school to end. All she had to do now was get through swim class. For the first few minutes, the swimming teacher, Mrs. Cosgrove, stood at the edge of the pool dressed in her shorts and T-shirt, blowing her whistle and shrieking, "No running, girls!" while the students hopped around with their arms crossed in front of their chests, wishing the period was over. By the time the girls began taking turns diving in and racing across the pool, Tamisin had to pinch her arms till they were sore just so she wouldn't reach around for a good scratch.

She was trying to pay attention to the teacher's directions when Tiffany said in a loud voice, "Ooh, look at that!" Like everyone else still shivering on the slimy tiles, Tamisin turned around to see what she was talking about. To her dismay, Tiffany was pointing at her. "Mrs. Cosgrove, something's wrong with Tamisin's back. It looks like she has some kind of disease."

"Gross!" declared Kendra, wrinkling her nose in disgust. "I bet it's contagious."

"I'm not going in the water with that!" another girl said as the rest backed away.

Tamisin tried to look over her shoulder to see what they were talking about, but as far as she could tell it was just a little pink.

Heather gave the other girls an exasperated look. "Cut it out," she said as she leaned over to see Tamisin's back. "There's nothing wrong with . . . Oh, gee . . . I bet that hurts. Tam, you might want to look in a mirror."

"Step aside, ladies," said Mrs. Cosgrove. "Tamisin, let me look." Tamisin could see the teacher's face when her lips drew back and her nose crinkled. "You'd better go to the school nurse. Kendra was right; it might be contagious."

"That's so disgusting," said Tiffany. "I bet she doesn't wash properly."

"She probably doesn't wash at all," said Kendra.

"Leave her alone," Heather said. "Can't you ever take a break from being nasty?"

The other girls were still snickering when Mrs. Cosgrove sent Tamisin to the locker room to get dressed.

The nurse wasn't much help. "I'll give you a note for your mother," she said after taking Tamisin's temperature and making her uncover her back. "You need to see your doctor right away. You won't be allowed in school until your back clears up."

"What is it?" Tam asked, reaching behind her to scratch.

The nurse pushed her hand away. "Don't touch it," she said. "You might make it spread."

"It really itches!"

"I'm sure it does. I've never seen anything like it." She grimaced and scribbled something on a notepad.

The nurse made Tamisin wait until the bell rang before she could go to her locker. The halls were crowded then with students grabbing their things from their lockers and running to catch their buses. Members of the student council were taping fliers to the wall announcing their newest fund-raiser, a Halloween bake sale, to take place the following week. Jak was leaning against a locker looking bored while Jeremy talked to Heather. When Jak saw Tamisin, he stood, smiling, and followed her down the corridor.

The skin on Tamisin's back had gone from itching to burning, so she didn't feel like talking to anyone. She ran to her locker, threw it open, and dragged out her backpack. Half its contents fell out onto the floor. When she bent down to pick up everything, her hands were shaking so much that she couldn't seem to get a grip on anything.

"Let me help," said Jak, crouching down beside her.

"Thanks, but you don't need to . . ."

"It's my pleasure," he said, handing her some papers. He was smiling when he looked into her eyes, but his smile quickly melted away. "Is everything all right?" he asked, reaching out his hand to help her to her feet.

"I'm fine," she said, more sharply than she'd intended. "I can manage on my own."

His expression changed from concern to something more distant. "Sure," he said. "Don't let me keep you."

Tamisin ran the entire way home. Before she'd even opened the front door, she was ripping off her jacket and flinging it aside. Her feet thudded on the stairs as she raced to the bathroom and tore off her blouse. Turning around in front of the mirror, she saw right away what Tiffany and Kendra had meant. The skin between her shoulder blades looked red and raw. It was cracking in places, leaving a web of angry red lines. Reaching around behind her, she tried to scratch her back, but it hurt instead of making it feel better.

"I've got to do something," she said, hopping from one foot to the other in an agony of itchiness. "Maybe a shower would help."

Pulling off her clothes, she turned on the shower and climbed in. Hot water made her back hurt more, but cold water eased the itchiness a little, so she turned it to the coldest temperature she could stand. Her teeth were chattering and her nose had begun to run when she finally turned off the water. Wrapping a towel around herself, she threw open the door and dashed to her room to put on an old black T-shirt and jeans.

Once she was dressed, she hurried to the kitchen, where she took all the ice from the freezer, filled every plastic bag she could find, and carried them upstairs. She had just reached her room when she heard Kyle come home, so she locked her door before setting the bags on her bed. She tried lying on the bags, but it was too uncomfortable. Desperate, she lay on her stomach and used one hand to place as many bags as she could on her back.

Within minutes she was sound asleep and didn't wake until someone pounded on the bedroom door. She sat up with a start, groaning at the pain in her back. "Hey, Tam," Kyle shouted. "Dinner's on the table."

"Go away," she said, lying down again. "I'm not hungry."

Her mother was at the door a few minutes later. "Tamisin, are you in there?"

"I don't feel well."

"Do you need anything? If you're really sick, maybe I should call the doctor."

"I don't want to see the doctor. I just want to sleep," Tamisin said, replacing a melted bag of ice with one that still held a few solid pieces.

The next time she woke, it was dark and the house was quiet. Groaning, she sat up and swung her legs over the side of the bed. A plastic bag slid off the bed, sloshing. There was a foul smell in the air that made her crinkle her nose. Although her back no longer hurt, she felt like she was a hundred years old and nearly fell when she set her feet on the floor. Taking one slow step at a time, she shuffled down the hall to the bathroom, glad that everyone else was in bed.

Tamisin flicked on the light, tugged her T-shirt over her head, and turned her back to the mirror. At first she couldn't understand what she was seeing. Two parallel lines about five inches long ran vertically between her shoulder blades. She prodded one with her finger and a clear fluid dribbled out. A wet, blue mass oozed from the gash and hung from her back. Tamisin poked it. Whatever it was, the thing felt as warm and sticky as blood.

The other line hadn't opened as much, but she could see blue inside it as well. Since the side where the lump had already come out felt better, Tamisin decided that this one had to come out, too. She twisted and turned, working her shoulder muscles, but nothing happened. Finally she reached down to touch her toes like she did in gym class, and felt a pressure in her back suddenly give way as another smooth, wet clump slurped out to hang down like the first.

Tamisin wiggled her shoulders again and the clumps began to unfurl, growing stiffer as they dried. Although they had been dragging on the muscles of her back, they began to grow lighter and stretch out until she could see what they were. Smooth and supple, they were sapphire blue veined with violet and shimmered in the light. When fully dry, they were longer than her arm span and reached from behind her head to her thighs.

Tamisin laughed in spite of herself. "Spreckles and pointy ears were nothing compared with this," she said.

"Tamisin Warner, the strangest girl in school, has wings!"

The wings were warm when she touched them and as sensitive as her hands. They weren't lifeless like fingernails or hair, but another living part of her.

For the next hour or so, Tamisin experimented, moving her shoulder blades, bending and stretching, and eventually controlling her wings by flexing the muscles in her back. At first her wings were weak, and she could only flap them feebly, but she kept at it until the muscles ached and she could move them enough to fan the air.

After putting on a halter top that left her back bare, Tamisin was ready to run to her parents' room to show off her glorious new wings when she began to wonder how they might react. They were normal people, whereas Tamisin . . . She wasn't sure what she was, but she certainly wasn't normal. Although she'd been excited at first, the longer she looked at her wings the more she realized just what they meant. She'd always known she was different, but she'd never realized that she was *that* different. Kyle might be weird, but he wasn't any weirder than any other boy his age, and Petey and her parents were about as normal as they could be. So how could such a perfectly normal family have someone like her in it?

Tamisin hesitated, her hand on the doorknob of her parents' room. What if her parents knew something that they'd never told her? What if having wings ran in the family, skipping a generation or two? Or maybe it was all her parents' fault—maybe they'd done something that made Tamisin have wings. But how could that be? She'd never heard of a real person with actual wings.

Knocking softly on their door, Tamisin opened it and went in.

"What is it?" asked her mother's sleepy voice. "Pumpkin, is that you?"

"I need to talk to you," said Tamisin.

"Right now?" her father mumbled. "Can't this wait until morning?"

"No, it can't," Tamisin said, and she flipped the light switch on the wall.

"Why did you do that?" asked her mother, rubbing her eyes at the bright light. "What is that you're wearing? Are you going to be in a school play?"

"It's not a costume," Tamisin said. "These are real, which is why we have to talk. I need to know how this could have happened. Tell me the truth. When you were in college, did either of you do some kind of drug or participate in some weird science experiment?"

"I don't understand, sweetie," said her mother. "What are you talking about?" She patted the mattress beside her. "Your father and I were on the swim team. We told you that's how we met. The only science experiments I did were for a basic biology course. Are you having problems in science class? Do you need a tutor?"

"You aren't listening!" Exasperated, Tamisin sighed and plopped down on the bed. "Here," she said, turning her back to her parents. "Touch my wings. Don't worry, they won't come off."

Tamisin felt her mother pat one of the wings, then tug

it ever so gently. When she tugged again, harder this time, Tamisin gasped. "Hey! I told you it was attached!"

Suddenly her mother no longer sounded sleepy. She sat up, pulling the covers up with her. "Michael, look at them. I think these things are real!"

"Don't be ridiculous!" said Tamisin's father. He grunted when he sat up in bed and reached toward her wing. "Let me just..." Tears came to Tamisin's eyes when he yanked so hard that it felt as if needles were shooting into the muscles of her back.

"Ow!" she shouted, jumping to her feet. Whirling around to face her parents, she glared at them and reached behind her to rub the base of her wing. "You don't have to try to rip it off me!"

"Is this some kind of joke?" her father asked.

If Tamisin hadn't been so upset, she might have laughed at the expressions on her parents' faces: her mother looked like a guppy with her eyes wide and her mouth hanging open, and her father looked half asleep and completely befuddled.

"So how did this happen?" Tamisin demanded. "It was radiation, wasn't it? You went to a protest with Dad at some army-testing site while you were pregnant and you got a good dose of radiation. Then you had me and that's why I'm so weird! I'm a mutant, aren't I? Come on, you can tell me the truth. I'm a big girl. I can take it."

Tamisin's mother stared down at her hands. "I suppose we should have told you before. It's just that the time never seemed quite right."

48

"Tell me what? You mean I really am a mutant?" Tamisin abruptly sat on the blanket chest at the foot of the bed, shaking. She was no longer sure she was ready for the truth.

Her mother shook her head. "It's nothing like that." She glanced up at Tamisin, her eyes pleading with her to understand. "For years I've wondered how we were going to say this, and I had all sorts of speeches planned, but I'm just going to come out with it. Tamisin, you're my darling daughter and I love you. I've always loved you and I always will. However, I didn't give birth to you. Your father and I adopted you when you were just a few days old. After we had Kyle, I had three miscarriages. We wanted a little girl so much . . ."

Tamisin felt like someone had punched her in the stomach. She almost forgot how to breathe. It was the worst, most hopeless feeling in the world—everything she knew and trusted and believed in had been a lie.

"Why didn't you tell me before this?" she said when she could talk again.

Her father cleared his throat. "Your mother told you that we were waiting for the right time to—"

"And when was that going to be—my wedding day or maybe when I graduated from college? 'Congratulations, dear, we're very proud of you and just wanted to tell you that you're adopted'?"

"Please don't be angry," said her mother. "I only wanted you to be happy."

"I would have been a lot happier if you hadn't lied to

me!" No longer able to sit still, Tamisin hopped to her feet and began to pace the length of the room, unaware that while she gestured with her hands her wings were waving behind her. "And what about my wings? Are you telling me that my real parents have wings, too? Then maybe they're some kinds of mutants! Or aliens! Did you ever think of that?"

"Certainly not mutants, or aliens, for that matter, but there were times we did wonder . . . ," said her father. "Things happened to you that were a little unusual, sweetheart. Remember the fireflies when we went camping and how you got your spreckles? And the way you dance whenever there's a full moon?"

They both looked so worried that Tamisin felt the urge to comfort them—until she remembered that they had lied to her. "To think that my parents . . . But you're not, are you? Do you realize that I don't even know what to call you now? I can't call you Mom and Dad anymore. I know it always bugs you when kids call their parents by their first names, but I guess I'm going to have to call you Janice and Mike. Or should it be Mr. and Mrs. Warner?"

Her mother, or the woman she'd thought of as her mother, looked like Tamisin had slapped her. Her father frowned and shook his head. "There's no need to talk to us that way. We're still your parents. We raised you and we're still your family."

But Tamisin wasn't listening. Stopping in the middle of the room, she stared at the wall without seeing it. "I wonder what my real parents are like. Why do you think they gave me up for adoption? Do you think they might be dead?"

"I suppose it's possible," said her father.

Her mother was looking at her wings with a most peculiar expression on her face. "They're very beautiful. Do they work? What I mean is—can you fly?"

Tamisin frowned. It was an obvious question, and she didn't know why she hadn't considered it. "I don't know." She moved her wings, fanning the air slowly at first, then faster and faster, but all it did was flip the pages of the book on the nightstand and flutter the curtains on the windows. "I guess not." She didn't know who was more disappointed, her mother or herself.

"We've talked about what we would do if you wanted to try to find your birth parents," said her father. "You can if you want—it's your decision. And you know we'd help you any way we can. We love you, pumpkin, and we want whatever's best for you."

"What can you tell me about them?"

"Very little, I'm afraid," said her mother. "The only thing the lawyer who handled it told us was that your birth mother had already named you Tamisin. But we don't think your life was very good before you came to us. A doctor told us that the mark on your wrist was from a rat bite."

"What about the lawyer? Could I go talk to him?"

Her father shook his head. "We can give you all the information we have about him, but I doubt it will do you any good. He was a strange little man. He disappeared years ago. We tried to contact him when you were a few years old, but no one knew what had become of him."

"Are you going to tell Kyle about your wings?" asked her mother.

Tamisin glanced over her shoulder and watched the color on her wings ripple when she fanned them. "No, and I don't want you to either. Kyle has never been able to keep a secret. If he hears about them, it will be all over town by noon tomorrow."

"We won't tell him, but do you really think you'll be able to keep it a secret?"

"I'm sure I can," Tamisin replied. After all, the last thing she wanted to do was let all the people who already thought she was weird know that she was even odder than any of them could imagine.

Chapter 6

Tamisin slept in the next morning until everyone else had left the house and then stayed home from school. Having thought about her wings and the news of her adoption all night, she decided that she really wasn't surprised to learn that she was adopted. After all, even before her wings appeared she'd known that she wasn't anything like the rest of her family. She loved them, but there'd been too many times that she'd felt as if she didn't belong.

When Tamisin didn't get out of bed right away, her cat, Skipper, began to scratch at the door. Yawning, Tamisin sat up to stretch and was surprised when her wings twitched, trapped by the blankets. She'd forgotten about them for the moment, but as her memory of the previous night returned, her emotions were mixed. Having wings was very exciting and they were quite beautiful, but although it had been easy to say that she wanted to keep them a secret, she didn't know how that would be possible. They were so big and *obvious*.

Standing in the middle of her room, Tamisin experimented with her wings, trying over and over again to fold them close to her body so they lay flat and weren't too uncomfortable. It took some time, but when she finally had them pressed against her back so closely that she could wear clothes over them without any bumps or wrinkles, she began to feel much better about them. If she could find a way to drop out of swim class, she should be able to get by without anyone noticing anything.

Skipper meowed again on the other side of the door and Tamisin opened it to let her in. While the cat hopped onto the bed, Tamisin spread her wings wide, sighing with relief as the cramped feeling faded away. Since no one else was home, she kept them unfurled as she headed for the basement, the only room that was big enough for what she had in mind.

The room was long; it ran the length of the basement and was half as wide. For all the years Tamisin had been dancing in it, the room had seemed to be big enough for just about anything. It wasn't until she'd put on the music from her dance solo and was trying out some new steps incorporating her wings that she noticed how low the ceiling was. She'd found that beating her wings while she leaped gave her added distance, but it wasn't easy to coordinate the two kinds of movement. Although it was tiring, she did it over and over again, getting better with each try until, suddenly, she was airborne. It lasted only a second longer than her usual leap, but it was enough to make her hit her head on the ceiling and keep her feet off the ground farther than she'd ever done before. Wanting to prove that she hadn't imagined it, Tamisin stood up and tried again. This time she actually felt suspended in the air before she went too high and hit her head.

With a whoop of excitement, Tamisin tore up the basement steps to the two-floor entryway at the front of the house. She'd have gone outside, but someone was bound to see her. Although the entryway wasn't very big from front to back, it was the tallest area in the house and the only one where she wasn't likely to hit her already sore head. For the rest of the afternoon Tamisin practiced beating her wings, thrilled that she was able to go higher. It was true that she could fly, but it was her secret and hers alone. She wouldn't tell anyone about it, not her parents, not Heather, and certainly not big-mouthed Kyle. For the first time in her life, Tamisin was convinced that being different could be a truly wonderful thing, and she didn't want anything to spoil it.

⋆

Tamisin went back to school the next day with a forged doctor's note. With her wings tucked against her back and the knowledge of what she could do, she felt special and important in a way she never had before. Her wings were her overwhelming secret now, making her feel as though she no longer had to hide anything else. For the first time in years she wore her hair pulled back and her face scrubbed clean of makeup. She didn't care if everyone saw her ears or her spreckles.

Her mother had had a hard time getting Petey out of bed that morning, so she didn't look at Tamisin long

55

enough to notice the change. Heather was a different story, however. The first thing she said when they met in front of her house was how great Tamisin looked.

"I've always thought your ears were cute," said Heather as they started down the sidewalk toward school. "It's about time you stopped covering them. What made you change your mind?"

"A lot of things," said Tamisin. She felt guilty for keeping her wings a secret from her best friend, but she still remembered how Heather had laughed when she heard about the fairies. Maybe Tamisin would show Heather her wings someday, when they weren't so new. There was one thing they could talk about though. "Guess what I learned yesterday," said Tamisin. "I was adopted."

"No!" breathed Heather. "You weren't really, were you?"

Tamisin nodded. "My parents told me all about it. They thought they couldn't have any more children after Kyle was born, so they contacted a lawyer when they saw his ad in the paper and adopted me."

"Wow. That's big. Are you okay with this? I mean, it is pretty earthshaking news to find out that your parents aren't really your parents."

"Tell me about it. I don't even know what to call them."

"Petey wasn't adopted though. I remember when he was born."

"Nope," said Tamisin. "I was the only one."

"Do Kyle and Petey know?"

"Not yet," said Tamisin.

"And your parents didn't tell you until now?"

"They said they were waiting for the right time. I wish they'd told me years ago. It's like I've been living with a lie all this time."

"I know what you mean," Heather said. "I remember when I was helping my dad dig the barbecue pit and I found out my hamster hadn't really gone 'vacationing with his long-lost cousins.' So what are you going to do? Are you going to look for your real parents?"

"I don't know. After all, they did give me away. What if my mother was a drug addict? Or what if both of my parents thought I was a mistake and they split up because of me? I'd rather not know the reason they gave me away if it's something terrible."

"But they might have been great people and had a really good reason. They could have been in love, but were too young to keep you," said Heather.

"That's true," said Tamisin. "Everyone who was adopted probably wishes that their birth parents were rock stars or someone really special. But even so, I'm not sure I'm ready to meet my parents. At least not yet."

She was putting her things in her locker when Jak came up behind her. "I'm glad you're back," he said, smiling. "I heard you were sick and might be out for a few days."

"I'm fine now," she said, giving him a smile in return. She'd been thinking about Jak and the fact that he was the only other person she'd met who could see the little raccoon man. If she wanted to find out what Jak knew about the creature, and why Jak could see him, she couldn't keep shying away. Maybe if she got to know Jak better, he'd either answer her questions or let something slip while she was around. After all, if he could see the little man, wasn't it possible that Jak had wings, too?

The first bell rang for class. Tamisin shut her locker door and reached into her pocket. "I have to get this to the office," she said, brandishing the fake doctor's note.

Jak nodded. "Yeah. I've gotta go, too. But first I wanted to ask—would you like to have lunch with me on Saturday? I know a good spot for a picnic."

Tamisin thought about it for a second. They could talk during a picnic and maybe she could actually learn something about the real Jak. "That sounds like fun."

"Great!" he replied. "I'll pick you up at noon."

Tamisin wasn't thinking about the note when she dropped it off at the office. She was thinking about how pleased Jak had looked when she said she could go with him.

✦

Tamisin got up early on Saturday morning. After one glance out her bedroom window she couldn't wait to go outside. It was a beautiful day, just right for spending in the garden, so without bothering with breakfast, Tamisin headed straight for the garage to collect her gardening tools. For too many weeks she'd spent most of her time preparing for the dance performance, neglecting her garden, which was now filled with weeds.

Tamisin had always loved working in the garden. She

had learned that she had a knack for making flowers grow while she was in first grade and the class had planted bean seeds for a science class. Her seed had grown a foot tall in the time it had taken the rest of the class's to sprout. The bean plant she took home had been the beginning of her garden. She planted more plants every year until eventually her garden had taken over much of the yard. Her parents were delighted with the lush plants that flourished under her care. Even her jealous neighbors admitted that Tamisin's flowers were the best they'd ever seen and were always trying to get her to divulge her gardening secrets.

Although it was autumn and most people's gardens were past their prime, Tamisin's was still going strong, or would have been if she had been paying as much attention to it as she normally did. Feeling guilty, she used the next few hours to weed and mulch the flower beds for winter. It was easy to lose track of time when she was doing what she loved, so she didn't realize how late it was until her mother called out the window, reminding her that Jak would be arriving soon.

It took her just a few minutes to wash her face and brush her hair, pulling it back into a high, bouncy ponytail. She was partway down the stairs when the doorbell rang. Opening the door, she found three cats sitting on the porch beside Jak. "Are they yours?" she asked, bending down to pet one. The cat walked away before she could touch him.

Jak glanced down and shook his head. "I've never seen them before. Cats just sort of like me," he said as he tried to shove them away with his foot. The cats walked away a few paces, waiting until he had moved on before following him again. Two more cats joined them before they reached the end of the block.

Jak refused to tell Tamisin where they were going, so she was surprised when they walked down the street to the school and circled the building. Although she knew there were woods behind the parking lot, she'd never gone in them before, so she didn't expect to find that they were actually pretty and not just scrubby old trees. There was a little stream there as well, and she enjoyed walking beside it. Even the cats seemed to be enjoying the walk, batting at butterflies and stalking birds.

Tamisin kept expecting to stop each time they came upon another inviting spot beside the stream, but she was glad they hadn't when Jak finally led her to a miniature waterfall only a few feet high. "This is great," she said, dropping to her knees at the water's edge. "I didn't know there was anything like this around here."

Jak set the basket on the ground beside her. "I thought you'd like it. Are you hungry yet? We could eat now if you are."

Tamisin smiled up at him. "I'm famished. I didn't eat breakfast this morning. I was working in the garden, trying to get it ready for winter."

"You like to garden?" said Jak. He took an old shower curtain out of the basket and spread it on the ground. It looked odd with its neon pictures of tropical fish.

"I've always loved working with plants," she said as she set the picnic basket on the shower curtain and lifted

60

the lid. "Oh!" she said, surprised by his choice of food. She lifted out a plate of pizza slices arranged in layers. Crinkling her nose at the smell of anchovies, she gave him a quizzical look.

"Don't you like pizza?" he asked.

"Sure!" she said, glancing down at the plate. "I've just never had it on a picnic before." Tamisin was relieved when he pointed out that there were eggs in the basket as well. "Oh, good!" she said, reaching for a covered bowl. "I love hard-boiled eggs."

Jak looked puzzled. "I never would have thought of boiling them. I always eat them raw."

When he showed her how to eat a raw egg, Tamisin grimaced and had to look away. Jak must have thought her expression was funny, because he began to laugh. It was the first time she had ever heard him laugh, and he did it with such enthusiasm that she had to laugh, too. Tamisin was still laughing when Jak stopped abruptly and handed her the basket. She was about to ask if something was wrong when he suggested that she try the cookies he'd brought. He had to take care of something and would be right back.

Tamisin didn't think much of it when Jak went off into the woods. She ate some of the cookies and enjoyed watching the waterfall. When he didn't come back right away, however, she got up to see what he was doing. She hadn't been watching when he disappeared, so she didn't know which way he'd gone. Deciding that she could see more of the woods from the top of the waterfall, she followed a path that led up the little hill and stopped to look back the way she'd come. An animal howled some-where in the woods, and a moment later the sound of breaking twigs made visions of bears and mountain lions pop into her head, as preposterous as that would be in a small town. "Jak, are you all right?" she called.

"Just fine," he replied, sounding awfully far away.

She was sure there was nothing dangerous out there, but when birds squawked in the distance and something rus-tled the trees in front of her, she turned and headed back down the slope toward the shower curtain. Partway down she stopped to look around once more, and this time she spotted a brilliant red flower that stood out even amongst the yellows, oranges, and browns of the fallen leaves. "That's strange," she muttered. "That wasn't there before."

The flower was growing next to the very path that she had taken to get to the waterfall. Unable to imagine how she had missed it, Tamisin climbed down to get a better look. A bird chirruped just ahead, and Tamisin glanced up. Three flowers grew in a cluster, and beyond them a dozen more nodded on their long, straight stems.

Tamisin knew better than to pick rare flowers, but when she smelled their perfume and followed it through the forest to an open meadow filled with the blossoms, she couldn't help but pluck one. And then there was another, too tempting to resist, and before she knew it her arms were weighted down with the heady blooms and Jak was calling to ask where she was.

"I'm over here!" she shouted back. A minute later she heard the snap of twigs as he came running through the forest. "Can you believe all these flowers?" she asked as he reached the meadow. "I didn't mean to wander off, but after I saw the first one . . ."

Jak glanced around the meadow, then back at her. "I'd better get you home so you can put them in water. They won't last long if you don't."

Jak was right, of course. If she didn't take care of the flowers soon, they would all wilt and then she would have picked them for nothing. But Tamisin hadn't learned a thing about Jak, and now she had made them cut short their picnic. She glanced down at the blossoms in her arms. They were gorgeous and would have kept on growing if only she'd left them alone. It would be such a waste . . . "You're right," she said. "I didn't think of that. I'm so sorry that we never got to look around together."

"It's all right," said Jak. "We can do that another time."

Tamisin beamed at him. "I'd like that very much."

Jak hurried her through the forest, taking a different route to the street so they didn't pass near the school. Once they were out from among the trees, he walked so fast that she practically had to run to keep up, which made it nearly impossible to ask him anything. Tamisin thought it was odd that he took her home by going up one street and down another, but when she pointed out a more direct route, he took her to the library instead. They had barely stepped inside the front door before he was hustling her through the building and out the back. Tamisin would have asked what he was doing, but when she turned to face him, he was scowling and looking everywhere except at her.

It wasn't until they were standing on her front porch that Jak seemed to relax. "I'm having a party at my house on Halloween. I'd like it if you could come."

Tamisin looked dubious. "That's a school night, isn't it?"

"I guess so," he said. "Is that a problem?"

Tamisin peeked through the glass panel in the front door to see if Kyle or anyone else was inside listening. "My parents won't like it, but I'll come. Do you mind if I bring my friend Heather?"

"Not at all," said Jak. He handed her a piece of paper. "Here's my phone number and address. It starts at seven thirty."

"I'll be there," Tamisin said, but Jak already looked as if he were thinking of something else.

Chapter 7

Tamisin hadn't spoken much to her parents after the night she learned that she was adopted, partly because she was still angry with them for not having told her the truth earlier, and partly because she felt odd talking to them, knowing that their relationship wasn't what she'd always believed it to be. Every time she'd start to call them Mom or Dad, she'd stop and think, then lose her train of thought. Even so, she wasn't so upset that she couldn't be reasonable; she told them about the party at dinner on Halloween.

"It's tonight," she said. "He lives on Jefferson Street. It starts at seven thirty."

Kyle looked up from his plate. "I've heard about that party. I was thinking I might stop by."

"Will Jak's parents be there?" asked their father.

Tamisin shrugged. "I guess."

Their mother looked up from pouring another glass of milk for Petey. "Who else is going?"

"Heather . . . And probably Jeremy Johnson. He hangs out with Jak a lot."

"Good kid, Jeremy," said Kyle. "Knows how to handle a football."

"So do I!" said Petey. "Want to see?" The little boy began to push back his chair, but his brother stopped him.

"Later, sport," Kyle said, ruffling Petey's hair.

Their mother frowned and set down her napkin. "Your father and I have never met Jak or his parents. We need to know more about them and if they're going to be home."

"I have their phone number," said Tamisin. Taking the scrap of paper out of her pocket, she glanced at it again. Jak's handwriting was angled oddly, and his letters were scrunched together, making them hard to read.

"I'll be right back," her mother said, taking the note. She left the dining room shaking her head. Tamisin could hear her go into the kitchen.

"Hello, is this Mrs. Catta?" came Tamisin's mother's voice from the kitchen.

"Why didn't you go to school the other day?" Kyle asked. "You seemed fine when I got home."

"She was sick, right, Tamisin?" said Petey.

"That's right, Petey. I was sick," Tamisin said, looking directly at Kyle as if daring him to question her.

"Huh," was all he said before picking up his fork again.

Her mother was talking in the kitchen. "Perhaps I don't have the right number. Do you have a boy named

Jak? Your grandson? I see. Yes, I'm sure he's a good boy. Uh-huh. Thank you very much."

When Tamisin's mother returned to the dining room, she looked a bit bewildered. "Apparently Jak lives with his grandmother and his uncle, who I think is named Bert. His grandmother has a strange accent; it was hard to make out exactly what she said."

"Will his grandmother be there during the party?" asked Tamisin's father.

"I believe so. She said that she intends to trim her nails tonight, which struck me as an odd thing to tell someone."

Tamisin hopped to her feet and picked up her plate to carry it out to the kitchen. "So now you know that a responsible adult will be there. I'd better go get ready. Can someone give me a ride?"

"I will," said Kyle. "Don't worry, Mom. I'll check out the party for you."

Tamisin was setting her plate in the dishwasher when she heard her mother say, "I never said she could go. I'm going to call her back in here and tell her so."

"Oh, let the girl go to the party," her father said. "It will be good for her to do something fun to take her mind off . . . you know."

"What?" asked Kyle. "What does she need to take her mind off?"

"Nothing you need to worry about, son," said his father. "Just take her to the party and make sure she's all right."

"Sure," said Kyle. "But I don't know how long I'm going to stay."

Tamisin went to the party dressed as a black cat—a simple enough costume that she was able to put together with clothes she dug out of her closet. She took her purse with her, stuffing in a few extra things she thought she might need. Heather wore her grandmother's old hippie dress and a wreath of dried flowers. She made Tamisin wait while she took her allergy medicine, declaring that there were sure to be cats at Jak's house.

When Tamisin and Heather arrived, Jak met them at the door dressed the way he usually was—all in black. Tamisin was thinking about how good the color looked on him when an old woman with gray and white hair and slanted yellow eyes came to get him. "Sorry," he told the girls. "I've got to see about this. I'll be right back." And then he disappeared down the basement stairs and Tamisin and Heather were left to look around while Kyle greeted other senior jocks.

Although Jak's house was in a neighborhood of fairly modern homes, it was old and creaky with floorboards that didn't quite meet and ceilings so high that Tamisin could have practiced her dance-flying, as she had come to call it, without ever bumping her head. The first floor of the house was already crowded. Some boys were playing drums and guitars in the parlor while costumed guests danced to their music. The girls wandered from room to room, looking at the costumes and decorations and talking to the people they knew. When they came across Jeremy in the room where the band was playing, Heather dragged Tamisin through the crowd to his side.

"Hi!" Heather said, giving him her warmest smile.

"Hi yourself," Jeremy replied, his eyes brightening when he saw her.

Knowing that Heather would be occupied for a while, Tamisin peeked into the next room where Shareena was talking to the rest of the girls from the dance group. When they saw her, they crowded around Tamisin, drawing her into the room. She talked to them for a minute, then Heather and Jeremy were there. Heather was beaming when she said, "Jeremy asked me out! We're going to the movies on Saturday. Come on, let's go see the rest of the house. Jeremy said I wouldn't believe the decorations in the kitchen. He says it's at the end of the hall."

There was a pitcher of milk and a bucket of water with a dipper on a table in the hallway, but no cups or glasses. A keg of something dark and musky sat on the floor beside it. No one touched it after some boys tried the drink and announced that it was foul.

The walls of the dark-paneled kitchen had been draped with tiny skulls strung together like popcorn. When Tamisin touched one and said that it felt real, Heather grew pale and refused to go near them. An assortment of food sat on the table, surrounding a pumpkin carved with an ugly, leering face. There were hunks of cheese, but nothing to use to cut them, plates of boiled vegetables coated with salt, and a tureen of some kind of raw meat cut into small pieces. A cup of anchovies sat beside a bucket of fried pumpkin innards. A sticker on one bowl of eggs declared that they were RAW and the other was labeled HARD BOILED. No one seemed to be eating anything except for a boy in a lumberjack costume who had taken an entire hunk of cheese.

Then some new guests arrived and everything changed. Jeremy and the girls were still in the kitchen when the back door opened.

"What great costumes!" Tamisin heard people say, but she knew they weren't wearing costumes. She had seen these people before, maybe not the very same ones, but so similar that she went cold inside. Tall and short, thin and fat, every one was a cross between a person and an animal. They had ears like dogs and horses, lions and bats. She saw fangs and flippers, beaks and talons, fur and feathers and scales, and all of them, from a boy's orange bird beak to a girl's fuzzy rabbit ears and twitchy little nose, were real. The last time she had seen creatures like these, she had been the only one who could. Now everyone could see them, which she thought must mean only one thing—the half-animal creatures must want to be seen. And if Jak had invited them . . .

"I have to get out of here," Tamisin told Heather.

"What?" Heather shouted over the din of the new arrivals.

When she saw that she wouldn't be able to make herself heard without shouting, Tamisin pointed to the door and gestured for Heather to go first. Her friend nodded, and together they made their way across the room. Tamisin was about to step into the hallway when a little man with a walrus mustache and muzzle bumped into her.

"Pardon me," he said. Looking up, he saw her face. "It's her!" he squealed. "I found her!"

And then they were all around her, pushing and pulling with their hands and paws, separating her from Heather as they swept Tamisin toward the back door.

"What are you doing?" shouted Heather as she tried to fight her way to her friend. "Jeremy, help her!"

"I'm coming!" Jeremy called back, but he was on the far side of the kitchen, which was now so crowded that it was almost impossible to move.

The creatures were shoving her out the door when Tamisin began to scream, so they burst into a song in some indecipherable language to cover the sound of her voice. Lightning split the sky as they forced her into the yard. Tamisin twisted in their grip, screaming all the while even though thunder drowned out her cries.

When the next bolt of lightning sliced the night sky, some of the creatures cowered in fear, but enough held on to her that she was unable to break away. A girl with a pig's snout and bouncing golden curls shrieked and ran when lightning struck again. For the first time Tamisin could see where they were taking her. Two tall trees stood like sentinels in the rear of the yard with a path leading directly toward them. In the lightning's glare, the air shimmered between the trees like sunlight on water.

Someone behind her pushed too hard and Tamisin fell to her knees. When the creatures dragged her up, she kicked and struggled until a voice growled in her ear, and she felt the sharp prick of claws on her throat. Lightning flashed again, so close that it made the air smell acrid. A wind sprang up, carrying with it a drenching rain. Then Jak was there, fighting the creatures until only one was left, holding her with sharp claws.

It occurred to Tamisin that if Jak was trying to help her, maybe he hadn't invited the creatures after all. When she tried to call to him, the pressure on her throat was too great. She gasped at the pain, her eyes never leaving Jak's face. This time when lightning struck, she could feel the electricity in the air. Then suddenly there was another creature, bigger than all the rest, lurching toward her with its massive arm raised. After that everything seemed to happen at once: the creature struck, the pressure on her throat was gone, Jak slammed into her so that they tumbled backward through a shimmering light, and lightning zigzagged through the sky. *I've been struck by lightning,* Tamisin thought just before the world went black.

PART TWO

Chapter 8

The first time Jak stepped onto the island he thought they'd gone to the wrong one. Unlike some of the islands they'd passed, there were no beaches or sloping shorelines, and the footing was treacherous, especially for a six-year-old boy, even one who was half goblin. It wasn't until his uncle, Targin, had helped him climb the jumbled rocks that Jak knew it was the island that his nasty cousin, Nihlo, had talked about every time he came home for a visit. There were the squat, stone buildings where the elders who taught the children lived. There were the trees so bent and twisted that their branches looked like writhing tentacles frozen as they reached for young goblins. There were the stone ridges that formed the maze where goblin children practiced lurking, hiding, and ambushing. And there were the jagged outcroppings that Nihlo swore were actually monsters that came alive at night.

When his uncle tried to leave Jak in front of one of the ugly buildings that made up the main part of the school, the little boy clung to him so tightly that the cat goblin had to pry his nephew's fingers from his hand. Then Targin turned to make his way back down to the water's edge and the boat that awaited him, leaving Jak clutching his sack of belongings and blinking away the tears that only a goblin with some human ancestry could shed.

Jak knew that he wouldn't be going home for a very long time. The island was far enough from any goblin holdings that unexpected explosions or spontaneous screaming wouldn't disturb anyone's sleep and isolated enough that water-fearing monsters like the snake women couldn't eat the children. Drowned Goblin Lake was as big as a small sea, and Jak was staying on the only inhabited island.

Over the years since that day, Jak had explored the island whenever he had the chance, sometimes with friends, but often by himself. On the days that a strong wind scoured the surface, he explored the underground caves that riddled the island's core. After a few windy months he could find his way around the system of caves with his eyes shut, although even a halfling of the cat goblin clan needed only a small amount of light to see. Having decided that he wanted to map the ravines and caves, he became interested in maps in general. Learning how to read had been the next natural step, even though the other goblins made fun of him for learning something they considered useless.

When the weather was good, most classes, like Raising Battering Rams for Fun and Profit; Throwing Your Voice to Intimidate Your Enemy from a Distance;

and We Aim to Puncture—Spear Throwing, beginners through advanced, were taught out in the open. Even the more academic subjects such as Jak's newest class, Transmogrification, were taught in the shadow of the outcroppings.

On the first day of Transmogrification lessons, Jak hurried to the clearing where the students were to meet with the elder. Most of the other goblins were already seated in front of the tree stump where the elder would stand, and Jak was glad to see that his friends were there as well.

Bella, a member of the bear clan, was a halfling like Jak, and they had become friends their first day on the island. Tobi, a goblin of the raccoon clan, had befriended them during a game of capture the skull when they included him and no one else would. Small and nervous, he preferred the company of the halflings over that of the more violent goblin children.

Both Bella and Tobi looked up as Jak picked his way between the other seated goblins. "How was your holiday?" Bella asked, patting the rock beside her with a blunt-fingered hand.

"Not too bad," said Jak. He was taller than both of them, and although he had the slender build common to members of the cat goblin clan, he was already more muscular than his full-blooded relatives. "I cleaned the bone chute. Nihlo leaves me alone when I'm working so he doesn't have to help me."

Unlike Bella, whose cousins Bruno and Barth were intent on protecting her from the goblins who hated half humans, Jak had learned at an early age that the best way to get along with his goblin cousin was to avoid him.

"I can't believe yer family made ya clean that chute," said Tobi, crinkling his little masked nose in disgust. "They shoulda paid a scavenger goblin like most families."

Jak shrugged. "I don't mind. It keeps . . ."

"Shh," said Bella. "Here's Elder Squinch. Don't make him mad. I heard he pecks you if you do."

Jak turned around when he heard a soft chirruping. He could see black feathers bobbing down the path that divided the clearing; the taller students hid the rest. Whatever the elder looked like, he had to be awfully short.

There was a thunk as if someone had dropped something heavy, the scrape of claws on stone, and Elder Squinch hopped onto the rock behind the tree stump. He was a member of the bird clan, which meant he had a face like a man, but a large yellow beak instead of a nose or mouth. "Good morning, goblins!" he crowed, then cocked his head to the side as if waiting for a response.

"Good morning, Elder Squinch!" replied a few tentative voices.

"What's that?" squawked the goblin. "I couldn't hear you!"

"Good morning, Elder Squinch!" called a few more voices.

"Much better!" he replied. "Welcome to the first day of Transmogrification, the class that will change your life! Now, who can tell me what transmogrification is?"

A weasel goblin raised his hand. "It's changing one thing into another."

"Close enough . . . What's your name, boy?"

"Sneal," the goblin told him.

Elder Squinch abruptly turned to two goblin girls sitting in the front row. Both members of the rabbit clan, they had long ears that peeked out of their hair and wiggled as they whispered to each other. The girls didn't notice when the goblin hopped onto the stump and leaned down to peck them sharply on the tops of their heads.

"Ow!" the girls exclaimed.

"Listen, you two," said the old goblin, "or you won't know what's going on." His movements were quick and jerky when he hopped back onto his rock. "You there! Boy from the dog clan! We do not sniff our fellow students in class! And no lifting of legs either. That would get you an automatic detention in the Pit. Now where was I? Ah, yes . . . By the time this semester is over, I expect most of you to be adept at the art of transmogrification. However, today will be a different story. Now, to begin . . ."

Jak craned his neck to see over the students in front of him while the old goblin disappeared behind the stump. When he came back up, he was holding a lump of something dull and gray. "First, you must be in contact with the object at all times. If you break contact, you'll have to start all over again. Now, while touching the object, think about what you want it to become. Picture the new object . . . Believe in it . . . You'll feel pressure building up in your mind. That's the original shape asserting itself. When it reaches its peak—and you'll recognize this because it makes the back of your head tingle—you want to push back—hard! Gather around for the demonstration, class."

"What do ya think he's gonna make?" Tobi asked, quivering with excitement as they squeezed between other students to a place where they could see.

"As long as it isn't birdseed!" snickered Plite, a porcupine goblin. Jak, Tobi, and Bella found room to stand far from his quills on his other side.

"This," said Elder Squinch, patting the gray lump, "is lead. I want to turn it into gold, so I close my eyes to cut down on outside distractions, and think about the gold I want it to become. That's it, nice and shiny. Lovely color. It's in my mind . . . I'm feeling the pressure . . . and now!"

"Ahh!" breathed all the students at the shiny lump of gold he held in his claws.

Elder Squinch looked pleased with their reaction. "Yes, indeed. Works every time once you know what you're doing. Sneal, come up here beside me." Sneal scurried up to the old goblin, his eyes bright with interest. "Here's another piece of lead. Set your hand on it, yes, that's it. Now close your eyes and do what I told you. Imagine the gold . . . Can you feel it resisting? Wait for the tingle . . . Now push as hard as you can!"

With a mighty shove, Sneal pushed the lump of lead so that it shot off the stump, ruffled the fur on the top of a dog goblin's head, flew between Plite and Bella, and smacked into the boulder behind them.

"No, you idiot!" squawked Elder Squinch. "With your mind, not your hand! You didn't listen! Now, who else wants to try? You, raccoon clan, let's see what you can do."

Tobi gave Jak a worried glance as he went to take Sneal's place. His wrinkled forehead betrayed his intense concentration as he followed the elder's directions. When the lead actually did turn into a pallid lump of some unidentifiable kind of metal that was definitely not lead, he beamed as if he'd performed the most wonderful feat in the world.

"Not bad, but you need to focus more on what you want. You, porcupine clan, it's your turn . . ."

As Tobi returned to where he'd been standing between Jak and Bella, his excitement was obvious. "Did ya see what I just did?" he whispered. " 'Tweren't perfect, but I ne'er thought I could do that much!"

"Good job, Tobi!" said Bella. "I hope I can do as well."

The old goblin chirped and said, "That's better, Plite. You're getting closer. Any questions before the next goblin tries?"

"What if I want to turn the gold back into lead?" asked one of the rabbit goblins.

"That's a very good question. Sometimes lead is exactly what you need. If you ever want to turn anything back, just do the same thing in reverse."

"Can you turn it into anything else?" asked Plite.

"As long as you are working with natural objects you can turn anything into just about anything, as long as it is also natural. For instance, you can turn flax into gold, or a carrot into a turnip or—"

81

"Can I turn a sow's ear into a silk purse?" Sneal asked. "My mother asked me to try," he said when his friends laughed.

"No, you can't. A silk purse is a manufactured object, like my sack here." Elder Squinch held up a woven grass bag. He set it on the stump with a thunk and a lump of lead rolled out. "You see the cut ends? This grass didn't grow into the shape of a bag; someone manufactured it. The process of manufacturing takes it out of the magical loop. Goblins can change a natural object into a natural object, but not a manufactured one. You, boy with the floppy ears, it's your turn."

While the other goblins tried to change the lump of lead, Bella and Jak waited patiently. No matter what class they were in, they were always called on last. When it was Bella's turn, she told Jak and Tobi, "Watch this!" and hurried to the stump. She was still standing there a few minutes later, having tried repeatedly while students snickered at each failed attempt.

Bella looked so dejected when she came back to join him that Jak patted her on the back. "Don't worry," he said. "You'll get it tomorrow."

When Jak reached the stump, he took his time, touching the metal to get the feel of it, and comparing it to the lump of gold that sat in front of the elder. When he was sure he had an image of the gold firmly in his mind, he closed his eyes, did exactly what the elder had told them to, and . . . nothing happened. Jak tried again. He could feel the tingling, just like the elder had said, although it wasn't in the back of his mind, it was everywhere inside his head. When he felt it, he pushed as hard as he could. Again, nothing happened.

"Very good, halfling. That will do for today," said the elder.

"But I didn't do anything!" Jak said.

"Which is precisely what I wanted the others to see! I said this was easy for goblins, but there are many things that halflings are incapable of doing. Now, goblins, you're to take one of these pieces of lead and practice with it this evening. I want you to be able to turn your lead into gold and back again by tomorrow."

When Jak and Bella finally reached the stump to get their lead, the elder looked at them in surprise. "I don't know why you're here. You'll never be able to do it. As far as I'm concerned, they shouldn't even allow your kind on the island." Turning so abruptly that his head feathers snapped back and forth, Elder Squinch stalked from the clearing.

Bella turned to her friends with her mouth hanging open. "I can't believe he just said that! I know a lot of goblins feel that way, but for an elder to say it . . ."

"At least he's honest," said Jak, shrugging. "We can't let it bother us, Bella. We've both heard worse and lived through it." Even after spending years on the island, they still heard comments about how only insane goblins would breed with humans.

"Even so," Bella said through gritted teeth. "It wasn't right!"

"And someday we'll be able to do something about it, only that day isn't now. Listen, why don't you and Tobi go on," Jak suggested. "There's something I want to do while there are no other goblins around."

When he was finally alone, Jak studied the lump of lead, thinking about what the elder had said. He moved over to the stump and held the lead just as he had before. Once again he felt the tingling in his mind, but once again nothing happened. He was setting the lump down when his hand brushed the woven grass bag. On a whim, he picked it up, remembering what Elder Squinch had said about a silk purse. This time the tingling came unbidden. Not believing that anything would happen, Jak *pushed*, and when he opened his eyes, a ladies' evening bag lay draped across his fingers.

Jak laughed in disbelief. Using both hands, he felt the bag to make sure it was real, holding it up to the light and turning it inside out. It was perfect in every detail, just as if it had been made by a skilled craftsman, and was even better than he had pictured.

Closing his eyes again, Jak thought about the grass bag. A *push*, then there it was in his hands, just as if it had never been changed.

Jak was excited when he left the clearing. Who cared if he couldn't do everything a full goblin could do? He could do something that was impossible for them, something they'd never believe.

Chapter 9

"All you goblins going for the first time—you need to line up in straight rows," shouted Elder Greeble, the wombat goblin who had been leading the trip for years. "That's it. Now count off, starting with you, Thark." When they'd finished counting off, the elder rubbed his hands together, saying, "Good, good! Now you'll be divided according to your numbers."

A chorus of groans greeted his announcement as friends realized that they wouldn't be together. Bella glanced at Tobi and Jak with dismay. All their plans had been made as if they were going to be in the same group.

"Pack leaders, hold up your signs. Goblins, find the pack with your number."

"I see mine," Tobi said, waving to someone he knew in the pack. "I'll see y'all later. Just be careful out there!"

"You, too," called Bella and Jak as Tobi hurried off.

"There's your number, Bella," Jak said, pointing at a rough-looking pack. "I'm not so sure about this."

Apparently her cousins weren't either, because Bruno

and Barth, who had arranged to be in the same pack, picked up the bird goblin perched beside them and carried him to the pack where Bella was supposed to go. A growl from Bruno stopped the goblin's squawking, and then the two lumbering brothers came to get Bella. "Good luck, Jak," she called as her cousins hustled her away.

"I think I'm going to need it," Jak muttered. He'd found his pack and it was one he never would have chosen; Nihlo was the group leader. Jak wasn't surprised that his cousin was in charge of a group. One of the older students, his cousin was well liked by most of the goblins and had already visited the human world. The trip was meant to acquaint the younger students with humans; older goblins were expected to visit the human world to steal, play, or wreak havoc on their own. Having an experienced leader meant that the younger goblins were more likely to find their way back.

When Nihlo saw Jak approaching, he announced, "We got stuck with Jak-O-MAN! There goes our night on the town."

"Hey, I didn't choose to. . . . '" Jak began.

"Just keep your muzzle shut, halfling," growled Nihlo. "No one cares what you think. I'll take you with me because I have to, but you'd better pay attention and keep up." Turning abruptly, Nihlo led his pack toward the network of ravines.

There were numbers at the head of each ravine corresponding to the numbers of the groups. Beside their number, they found an X painted on the ground with the air above it already shimmering. The younger goblins lined up with Jak at the end, but Nihlo wouldn't let them start until he was ready. "Remember what you learned from old Greeble," he said. "Humans can't see us unless we want to be seen. This is Halloween, so it's okay if they see us tonight. We have four hours, our time, to do this, then we have to meet back at the Gate to come home. Their time isn't the same as ours, so I have a chronometer to keep track of it." Nihlo held it up for everyone to see. "Remember, go through the gate and move out of the way as soon as you get there."

Jak waited while the other goblins stepped on the X and disappeared with a brighter shimmer and a flash of light. Nihlo stood with his fists on his hips, scowling while the others crossed over. When it was Jak's turn, Nihlo shoved his cousin through. Although most of the others had been tentative about stepping into the shimmering light, Jak was rushed into it, which felt like the difference between slipping into the water while you check the temperature and jumping in from fifty feet up. He was staggering when he came out the other side.

"Keep moving, halfling!" shouted a rat goblin, pushing Jak out of the way.

A moment later Nihlo arrived exactly where Jak had been standing. The other goblins hurried over to hear what he would say. "Let's get out of this garden and regroup on the other side so we can get started."

It was dusk and they were in a small fenced-in garden with ordinary-looking trees and flowers. Beyond the fence the world changed abruptly; metal carts crawled past, then blared at each other and rushed to the next place where they had to crawl again. Humans, looking surprisingly boring in their sameness, strolled down cracked gray paths that ran beside the black rows that belonged to the metal carts. Buildings taller than the tallest trees loomed over it all. If this was the human world, Jak didn't like it.

The night was noisy with quick, sharp sounds and shrill, drawn-out ones. And the smells . . . Jak raised his head to sniff the air. The stench of exotic trash and the overwhelming odor of humans almost drowned out the scent of the garden's flowers.

Something nipped Jak's hand, drawing blood. "Pay attention!" said the rat goblin.

Nihlo was already standing on the other side of the black metal fence. It took Jak only a moment to hop onto the top of the fence and down to the other side. His half–cat goblin side made him stronger than a human as well as faster and more agile. It also made him more curious, so while the other goblins gathered around Nihlo, Jak watched a young human use colored sticks to create a picture on the path.

Jak glanced up; his group was still there, watching him and whispering behind their hands. When a man joined the artist and took an instrument with strings out of a long case, Jak had to stay to see what happened next.

A cat bumped against his leg, purring so hard that the halfling boy could feel the vibration. Jak looked around to see if anyone wanted to claim the animal and discovered that his group had left while he wasn't paying attention.

Knowing that if he didn't hurry he might be left behind for good, Jak began to run, knocking into people and nearly tripping over a pile of leather bags that a man was selling from the path.

Jak thought he saw the goblins up ahead. Then someone shouted and a large disc rolled down the street into the path of one of the metal carts. There was a screeching sound as the cart swerved and ran into carts going the other way. When humans began to scream, Jak vaulted over a cart that wasn't moving and dashed to one that had crashed, trapping people inside. The door was wedged shut, but he closed his eyes and pictured an open door instead. When the tingling began in his head, he *pushed* and the crushed door was exchanged for one that was intact. He opened it and went on to the next cart, making sure that everyone was all right.

After that Jak was unable to find any sign of his group, although he did see other goblins intent on mischief. He saw a group of rat goblins stealing the shoes from a man sleeping in an alley. Another group ran down children who were dressed in funny clothes, grabbing the bags they carried and leaving them crying. Jak was disgusted with what he saw and, for the first time in his life, was ashamed of his goblin half.

He was peering in the window of a building where people were eating when it occurred to him that he'd lost track of the time. He moved on, reading the words on the poles, hoping they would help him find his way back to the garden. Pausing over a difficult word, Jak was surprised when a cat stood on its hind legs and forced its head into his hand to be petted. Three other cats were sitting on the path, watching.

The cats trotted behind him as Jak hurried along the path, looking for goblins from his school, even if they weren't with his group. When he couldn't find any, he became convinced that they must all have gone back. He was trying to remember what Elder Greeble had said they should do if they were ever stranded in the human world when he saw a jackal goblin he knew chasing a horse through a grassy area. Terrified, the animal tore along the path while its rider hauled on the reins.

"Thark!" Jak shouted. "It's time to go back!"

The jackal goblin turned and ran down the path, back the way he and the horse had come. Jak followed the goblin down the street, hoping he hadn't lost yet another chance to return home. Fortunately, Thark was still trying to find a way into a fenced-in cemetery when Jak spotted him. When the jackal goblin found the hole in the fence, Jak was right behind him, shadowing him all the way to the X painted on the ground. And then the goblin was through and, a moment later, so was Jak.

The boys were leaving the ravine when Bella came running after Jak calling, "Did you hear what happened? Tobi was seen while he was using an invisibility spell!"

"Is he okay?" asked Jak. "I didn't think humans could see us unless we wanted to be seen!"

"But he didn't. A girl saw him, so he came back right away. Then Elder Greeble sent other goblins out after the girl. She saw them, too, and tried to hit them with lightning! Greeley says that if humans are going to start seeing goblins when we don't want to be seen, this might be the last time he sends a class there on Halloween!"

"After seeing how most goblins behave when they're there," said Jak, "I'm not so sure that would be a bad idea."

Chapter 10

Ever since that Halloween, Nihlo's hatred for his cousin had become even more apparent. Jak wasn't sure if it was because he'd tried to fix the damage Nihlo and his pack had done in the human world, or because Nihlo's loathing for humans was growing stronger. The cat goblin had tormented his younger cousin since the day the halfling arrived to live in his family's den. They'd fought a few times on the island, yet each time Jak's friend Bella was there to fetch her big, friendly cousins Bruno and Barth. The bear goblins were happy to separate Nihlo and Jak, and even happier to give Jak a few tips on self-defense, such as taking advantage of his agility and speed, but beyond that they weren't much help.

Then one day, just a few weeks after Halloween, Jak ran into Nihlo when no one else was around. Jak was on his way back from exploring the ravines when someone jumped him from behind, slashing a line of fire across his back. Unprepared, Jak hit the ground on his hands and knees, but he had enough sense to roll out of the way before the next blow could connect. In an instant, Nihlo was on him with ripping claws and greater strength. Jak twisted out of the way and landed a blow of his own just as his cousin went for his throat. Then the half-goblin boy was on his feet, running, with blood dripping into his eyes from a wicked gash on his forehead. He could hear Nihlo behind him, swearing under his breath as he followed Jak back into the ravines.

Having spent so much time exploring the ravines, Jak knew the terrain better than anyone. He knew which paths led to dead ends and which were the surest way out. He also knew which ravines were wide and which were so narrow that he could jump from one side to the other. Now, with Nihlo so close behind him, Jak tore between the stone walls that rose four times his own height on either side. When he couldn't lose his cousin in the twists and turns, Jak headed for a lower wall where he could scramble to the top over loose stones that slipped beneath his feet. Reaching the narrow ridge that topped the wall, Jak raced along the uneven ground and leaped, soaring over a ravine to land on the other side. When he turned around, Jak was certain that Nihlo wouldn't be able to follow, and was surprised to see the goblin put his head down and run at the gap. When Nihlo jumped, Jak backed away, preparing to run again, but his cousin's leap had fallen short and he fell, screaming as he hit the side of the ravine and tumbled to the bottom.

Jak ran to the edge to peer down. "Are you all right?" he shouted.

Nihlo's only response was to swear. He tried to sit up, then fell back, moaning. Even from above, the goblin's leg looked odd. Jak thought it was probably broken. He'd have to go get help.

Jak was on his way down from the ridge when he heard goblins in the ravine. He called to them, telling them where they could reach Nihlo while finding his own way down. When he reached the bottom of the ravine, the goblins were already there.

"What did you do to him?" a jackal goblin asked Jak.

Another was already kneeling beside Nihlo, examining his leg. "You pushed him, didn't you?" he said, turning to glare at Jak. "We saw you lead him into the maze. I bet you had this planned all along. It's a good thing we followed you. Who knows what you would have done next."

"No, I—"

"What's going on here? Why did you goblins make me come all this way just to . . . Oh, I see," Elder Squinch said as he came into view. The elder hurried to Nihlo's side, his three-toed feet clawing up the dust of the ravine.

"We saw the whole thing," said the jackal goblin. "Jak-O-MAN chased Nihlo up the ridge and pushed him off. The halfling could have killed him!"

"That wasn't how—," Jak began.

"That was exactly what happened," said Nihlo. "Jak-O-MAN has always hated me. I always said that no one with 'oman' in his name should be allowed to come to the island! Half humans don't deserve to be here."

Elder Squinch shook his head, clucking. "This is very

bad, boys. You two, help Nihlo to the witch doctor. Jakoman, it looks like you're headed to the Pit for detention."

"But I didn't do—"

"No sniveling, halfling," said the old goblin. "You'll have to take it like a goblin . . . if you can."

The Pit was little more than a deep shaft sunk into the ground near the last ravine. A wooden bucket big enough to carry one student could be lowered into it much like a well, though the Pit was dry. Carved from stone, it had curved walls and a flat floor that had gained a deep layer of wind-deposited soil over the years. A colony of brown beetles had fallen in and couldn't get out. When they moved, the floor almost looked as if it was alive. The hole was so deep and dark that anyone standing up above could not see whoever was down below, but as Jak learned, if you stood in just the right spot, you could look up and see the person standing above outlined in sunlight. He discovered this when Tobi came to visit him after the last class of the day.

"Hey, buddy! How ya doin?" the raccoon goblin shouted from the edge of the Pit.

"Is that you, Tobi?" Jak called back. He was seated on the floor resting his head on his knees, but he stood when he heard his friend.

"I brought ya somethin'!" shouted Tobi, and before Jak could stop him, the little goblin had tossed a stoppered jug filled with water down into the shaft. Jak jumped back as the jug hit the ground and exploded into a thousand shards, some stinging his cheek as he turned his head away. The water soaked the soil, turning it into mud.

"Don't do that!" Jak shouted at his friend just as Tobi dropped a hunk of meat into the Pit. The meat hit the ground so hard that most of it sank into the mud. Insects swarmed over the rest until it disappeared as well.

"That's all for now!" shouted Tobi. "I'll bring ya more in the mornin'. I hear ya got detention for breakin' old sourpuss's leg. Good for you!"

"But I didn't," Jak replied. "I just—"

"I've gotta go," shouted Tobi. "Someone's comin'. No one's supposed to feed ya when you're down there, so don't tell nobody that I did this. See ya tomorrow!"

Only a few minutes after Tobi left, someone else stood at the edge of the Pit. Jak didn't know that anyone was there until the first stone hit the ground hard enough to send up a plume of mud. He jumped up and moved so that his back was pressed against the wall. The next stone hit the ground on the other side of the Pit.

"Did we get you yet, Jak-O-MAN?" yelled Nihlo. "I brought some of my friends with me. We don't think being in the Pit is enough for a halfling like you. We think you need a little entertainment while you're down there. Let us know if this helps."

Suddenly the pit was deluged with stones as if someone had upended a dozen buckets filled with them over the opening. Jak crouched and tried to cover his head with his arms while staying as close to the wall as he could get. Only a few hit him, but one struck his head a glancing blow that stunned him momentarily.

"The dinner bell just rang," shouted Nihlo. "We have to go now, but we'll be back in the morning with bigger rocks. Sleep well, Jak-O-MAN!"

Jak stayed where he was for a few more minutes, just in case they had some stones left. When he stood up, his head was pounding and he had to set his hand on the wall to support himself. The stone was rough there, and crumbly, almost as if it wasn't stone at all. He didn't think much of it until he took his hand away and felt a powdery substance on his fingers. It felt like the old mortar the goblins who had made his uncle's den had used to fill in cracks and openings, but that didn't make sense unless . . .

Jak set both of his hands on the wall, running them over the surface until he found the rough patch again. It wasn't just a patch though, because it was threaded between a fairly good swath of stones that ran up as high as he could reach and at least a body's width over. In some places the mortar was very narrow and in others it stopped, then started again as if part of it had fallen away. From the shape of it, Jak thought it might be a doorway, or at least an opening that had been sealed off when the Pit was made.

Turning away from the wall, Jak felt in the mud for the shards of Tobi's water jug. When he found one that was more than just a sliver, he held it in his hand and thought about a sturdy knife. Then there it was, a knife, stout and strong and just what he needed.

Jak didn't think he should stick around for any more torture. The knife did a good job of digging out the mortar, and before the night was half over, Jak had removed all of it. The stones came out easily after that, and he was soon out of the Pit and into one of the caves that he had known had to be close by.

Jak recognized the cave, having explored it just a few weeks before. It was damp and draftier than most, however, so he moved on until he found the one where he and his friends had left their stash of food. There was an old blanket there as well, and in moments, Jak was warm, fed, and sound asleep.

※

Jak felt at home in caves and had ever since he was four years old and his grandmother Gammi had gone to visit an ailing relative, leaving Nihlo's mother, Karest, to watch over the halfling child. Although she never let on when Gammi was around, Karest seemed to dislike Jak as much as Nihlo did and saw to it that the lowliest chores became Jak's responsibility. Before Jak learned his alphabet or how to tie his shoes, he became adept at cleaning the fur out of the drains in the washroom and scrubbing the floors after the monthly spitting contest. He didn't mind too much because he learned to make games out of the work. And on the days when Nihlo was home from the island and had nothing better to do than torment him, the older goblin usually left him alone until Jak had finished working. It was when Jak wasn't busy that his cousin liked to taunt him. Nihlo especially liked telling him about the monsters that roamed the land of the fey at night, the very reason that all goblins lived underground.

"They're snake women," said Nihlo. "They have the head and body of a woman, but the rest is all snake. They slither around at night catching anyone who is still outside, and when they catch them, they eat them alive!"

"That isn't true," Jak said the first time he heard the story.

"Yes, it is," Nihlo said, nodding vigorously. "Gammi's here. Go ask her."

Jak couldn't wait to ask his grandmother. When she confirmed that the story was true, he was so frightened that she had to cradle him in her arms until he stopped shivering.

One evening, while Jak was cleaning up the still-twitching remains of a family meal, he could hear Nihlo lurking in the next room. Gammi had left that afternoon to visit her sister and wouldn't be back for several days. Jak had no one else to turn to if anything bad happened. Knowing that Nihlo would have something obnoxious planned, Jak took his time, cleaning up the blood and bits of bone with extra care. When he couldn't put it off any longer, he carried the trash to the chute in the kitchen.

"Are you finished, human?" Nihlo asked from the door to the next room.

"Don't call me that! I'm part goblin, too."

"But it's the human part that taints your blood. Why do you think your name is Jak-O-MAN? It's so people know that you're part human and can't be trusted. All humans are liars and cheaters who hurt each other for fun."

"Just like you, you mean?" said Jak.

Nihlo's ears went back and he snarled, showing his fangs. "Did you know that you can hear when a snake woman is about to strike because she shakes the rattles in her tail? I know you don't believe me since you think I'm such a *liar*, so I think you should find out the truth for yourself."

"What do you mean?" Jak asked, not liking the look on Nihlo's face.

Nihlo took a step closer. "I mean that you are going outside tonight!"

"But it's dark out!" said Jak.

"Exactly!" said Nihlo, pouncing on his little cousin.

The two boys struggled; Jak kicked and hit with his fists like a human while Nihlo bit and scratched like any good member of the Cattawampus clan. Unfortunately for Jak, Nihlo was bigger and stronger and soon held the little boy in a tight grip with his arms pinned to his sides. When Jak started to shout for help, Nihlo shook him, saying, "I'd be quiet if I were you. Loud noises attract the snake women. They'll be on you before you've taken three steps if you keep hollering like that."

"You can't do this!" Jak said as Nihlo carried him to the door.

"Who's going to stop me? Gammi isn't here and no one else cares. It's about time you saw how great you have it here, safe from all the creepy crawlies! One night outside will do you a lot of good, if you make it until morning, that is!"

Jak kicked and flailed his legs the entire way down the

corridor. And then they were in the entranceway facing the door to the outside. Heavier than any other door in the den, it was made of six layers of wood and was impenetrable to any weapon an enemy of the Cattawampus clan might wield. Buried deep in the wood, the lock was an intricate mechanism that would open only with a special key. Both lock and key were made by gnomes, the sole members of the fey capable of manipulating metal, and imbued with gnomish magic. Although left open during the day, the door was always locked at sundown and opened after dark only under special circumstances.

"You'll get into trouble if you open the door!" said Jak.

"No, I won't," replied Nihlo. "I'll tell everyone that you did it. Now hold still while I get the key."

"Let . . . go . . . of . . . me!" Jak said and, using all his strength, he flung his head back just as Nihlo leaned forward. Jak's head hit his cousin's chin with a *crack*! slamming the older boy's jaw shut. Nihlo howled as Jak wriggled free and ran back down the corridor. A moment later Nihlo was after him, spitting blood from his bitten tongue.

They were in the main corridor of the den, a warren of rooms that made up the living quarters for the head of the Cattawampus clan. With rooms and smaller hallways leading off on either side, the corridor was longer than most, ending at a door that was always kept locked. In the two years that he had been living there, Jak had never known the door to be open and had no idea what might lie beyond it.

Fearing what his cousin would do, Jak ran as fast as his legs could carry him. With Gammi gone, there really wasn't anywhere safe he could hide. His heart was racing when he dashed to the end of the corridor and turned to face his tormentor. Nihlo slowed when he saw that his cousin was trapped. With his tail twitching, he transfixed Jak with his gaze, and stalked the little boy.

Jak was whimpering as he set his hand on the latch. When the door swung open behind him, he staggered backward through the doorway and nearly fell. Seeing that his prey was about to get away, Nihlo shouted and began to run. Jak turned and slammed the door behind him, then took off into the dimly lit corridor that lay beyond. His breath rasped in his throat as he ran, too frightened to consider what might lie ahead; whatever it was, it had to be better than facing Nihlo.

Then the door opened and Nihlo shouted, "Come back here, halfling!"

There was nothing that Nihlo could say or do to make Jak return to him, but the little boy did stop running to press his hand against a cramp in his side and look back the way he'd come. He saw Nihlo outlined in the brighter light of the corridor behind him, and could hear his cousin swear and shout incoherent threats. And then the light shrank until it disappeared, the door clicked, the bolt was shot home, and Jak knew that Nihlo had locked him in.

Jak was trapped in a place he knew nothing about, yet with Nihlo on the other side of the door, he felt safer than he had in a long time. No longer worried about being thrown out into the night to be dinner for some horrid snake women, the little boy felt such relief that he laughed out loud. With a light step and a lighter heart, Jak started down the corridor again, intent on exploring.

The corridor wasn't completely dark. Splotches of a sickly greenish white glowed on the walls, giving his half-goblin eyes more than enough light with which to see. As he walked, the floor began to slope downward, taking him deeper underground than he'd ever been before. The air was colder now and the little boy began to shiver. He was tired, too; it was past the time he normally would have gone to bed. Then suddenly he felt the faintest hint of a warm breeze coming from somewhere up ahead. It smelled musky, a not-unpleasant odor that reminded him of his travels with his mother before she'd left him at his uncle's home.

Enticed by the promise of warmth, Jak hurried down the corridor until it opened out into a large chamber. With the greenish glow banished to the widely set walls, the light in the chamber was dimmer than the corridor had been. A low wall divided the chamber in two; a pool of water lapped at Jak's side of the wall. Stumbling from fatigue, he followed a path to the wall and crawled over the top. The floor on the other side was warmer as if heated from beneath. The little boy was yawning when he lay down, and soon he was sound asleep.

Jak woke to something soft and moist snuffling his cheek. Before he could open his eyes, his face was wet from chin to ear. Startled, he sat up, lurching away from whatever was touching him, and bumped into something hard. When it nudged him, Jak scrambled to his feet. He was surrounded by animals taller than he was, with hindquarters that came up to his shoulder. The light was so dim that Jak could barely see them, but as they jostled each other trying to sniff him, one of them growled at another and Jak decided that they must be very big dogs.

He was frightened, but not terribly so, and when one of the animals nipped him, he reacted without thinking and swatted it across the nose. The big animal squealed and jumped back. Pleased by his success, Jak turned to the dogs pushing him from behind and pushed them in turn. They backed away and he was able to climb over the low wall, away from the milling animals.

He was thirsty now, so he cupped his hands and drank from the pool at the base of the wall. The water was cool and fresh; after he drank he washed his face just as Gammi always made him do when he got out of bed. He soon realized that the light wasn't as dim inside the chamber, and when he looked up, he saw that a hole in the ceiling directly above the pool let in a shaft of light. Although he leaned out over the water, he couldn't see up the shaft, but a leaf drifting down through the light told him that it was open high above. There was bird-song, too, faint and far away.

He could see the animals better now, and suddenly he wasn't quite so sure that they were dogs. Although they had sharp, pointy teeth and blunt faces, they had long necks and longer legs and almost looked like young horses.

When Jak stood, he noticed that the animals were

watching him and decided that they were thirsty, too. At first he tried to carry water to them in his cupped hands, but he needed his hands to climb the wall. Some of the animals were panting, so he climbed back down to the pool and used his shoe to carry water to them, pouring it into a depression that ran, trough-like, in front of the wall. Back and forth he climbed, over and over again, until the animals were no longer thirsty.

Then he walked among them, scratching their necks under their manes and giving them names. A black one was Night, a spotted one was Spot, a more delicate-looking one was Primrose, named after Gammi's favorite flower. One of the horse creatures, stocky and bigger than the rest, liked to have his rump scratched. Jak named him Putterby for the sound he made when he was happy.

The animals crowded close to Jak, liking the attention. They were rough at first, but after he'd swatted the more aggressive ones, they quickly learned that they had to be gentle around him if they wanted to be scratched. Jak was using one hand to scratch Spot's neck and the other Putterby's rump when he heard voices coming from the corridor that led into the chamber. The animals heard them as well, and became agitated. With their ears laid flat and ridges of fur rising along their backs, Jak thought that they looked quite ferocious. They were pawing the ground and growling when the little boy slipped away to hide in the deepest shadow of the uneven wall.

Jak watched as his uncle, Targin, and two of his assistant goblins came into the chamber. The horse creatures rushed at the other side of the wall, snarling and snapping.

"Look at how stupid they are—running into each other like that," said a goblin. "No wonder the fairy queen outlawed breeding them."

"These are weanlings," Targin said. "You'll see why Titania's so afraid of them when they grow up. Hipporines are as fierce as the wolverines and as fast as the horses that spawned them. Nothing can best them in battle, including fairy warriors."

The goblins began to toss hunks of meat to the hipporines. While they were occupied tearing the meat apart, Targin and his goblins hopped over the wall and bent down beside the trench Jak had filled with water. There was a grating sound as they moved a large stone, and water rushed from the pool into the trough.

While the goblins were moving the stone back into place, Jak crawled over the wall and ran up the corridor as quietly as he could. It wouldn't do to have his uncle find him there, but Jak was glad to have found this place. For the first time since he'd moved in with his relatives, the little boy felt as if he had made some friends.

Chapter 11

Asearch party found Jak the day after he escaped from the Pit. He was sent home that very morning, accompanied by a silent mole goblin, disgraced for not serving out his confinement.

It took most of the day to reach his uncle's den. The entire way Jak wondered how he would break the news. When he arrived, his aunt Karest announced that his uncle had important guests and was too busy to see him. Gammi wasn't there so Karest was shorthanded and had too much to do seeing to the needs of the guests to worry about him.

Relieved that his announcement had been delayed, Jak ate some leftovers in the kitchen, then went to bed with a book Gammi had given him. He could hear muffled voices talking in the room down the corridor from his, although he couldn't make out who was talking or what they were saying.

Jak had fallen asleep with his book still in his hand when Karest opened his door. "Your uncle wants to see you now. Get up and get dressed. You can't go in like that."

Bleary-eyed, Jak stumbled out of bed and pulled on his pants and shirt. He was still putting on his shoes when Karest came back to get him. "Be polite," she said. "Don't speak unless you're spoken to and then tell them only what they want to know. Answer their questions, but don't volunteer anything else. You don't want to bore them with your chatter."

"Who's in there?" he asked as they approached the door.

"The head of the wolf clan," she whispered, "and your great-aunt, Lurinda. She was with the fairy queen's court for many years. Behave yourself. It's an honor to be called before them!"

Jak didn't feel honored when his uncle, Targin, introduced him to his guests. Wulfrin, the leader of the wolf clan, was lean and grizzled, but he looked like an intelligent goblin and seemed very interested in Jak. The lady goblin seated beside him looked older than Gammi, with long white hair and pale, nearly translucent skin. Her eyes were the youngest thing about her; their emerald green color was as vivid as if she were Jak's age. Jak stood silently watching her stroke her neck with the retractable claws of her long, thin fingers, the single ring she wore glinting in the candlelight. He decided that she was the most beautiful goblin he had ever seen.

"Now, Jak, tell me and my guests why you're home from school in the middle of the week," his uncle said.

"It isn't a special holiday that I've forgotten, is it?" asked his great-aunt, Lurinda.

"No ma'am," said Jak. "I was sent home because I got in a fight with Nihlo. I'm sorry, Uncle. He has a broken leg."

Targin frowned and grunted, but all he said was, "Go on."

Jak nodded. "They gave me detention, but I got out of the Pit before my time was up and—"

"You got out of the Pit!" said Wulfrin. "How the blazes did you manage that?"

"I found some loose stones and dug my way into a neighboring cave," said Jak, remembering his aunt's admonishment to answer their questions and nothing more.

Wulfrin smiled. "Most resourceful."

"Indeed," said Lurinda in a voice that was almost a purr. "Thank you for coming to meet us, Jak. I think you'll do very well."

Jak returned to his room, but it was a long time before he fell asleep again.

Early the next morning he was in bed when his uncle came to see him.

"Are your guests still here?" Jak asked.

"Lurinda is. She's gone to bed. Wulfrin left a short time ago. We've made a decision about you, but I wanted to talk to you about it before discussing it with anyone else. You won't be going back to the island, Jak."

Jak sat bolt upright. "Why?" he asked. "The elders never said anything about—"

"It has nothing to do with them. Lurinda brought me some news yesterday. I need someone who looks more human than most to carry out a task. I've talked to Lurinda and Wulfrin about giving you the responsibility, and they both agree that you are the best candidate. You're smart, resourceful, brave . . ."

"And I look like a human," said Jak.

"Precisely," said Targin. "Do you think you could stand being in the human world for an extended period of time?"

"What would I have to do?" Jak asked.

"There's a girl we want you to get to know. She came to our attention recently. Unlike most humans, she can see us."

"I think I heard about her," said Jak. "Is she the one who can throw lightning bolts?"

"We're not sure what she can do, but yes, there is a rumor going around that she can. You're to meet the girl, get to know her, then bring her back with you once you've earned her trust. Do you think you can handle that?"

"It sounds simple enough," said Jak.

"You'll have a private tutor who can teach you every-thing you need to know before you go. I want you to study humans and learn how to act like one."

"If it would help you," Jak said.

"Remember, it's important that she feel safe with you. We don't know what she's capable of doing, but on the chance that she can control lightning, you won't want to upset her."

"Why do you want her here, Uncle, if she's so dangerous?"

"It's been nearly four years in the human world since the Halloween when the girl saw our goblins. Everything indicates that all the Gates will open during the next Halloween and the human world will be flooded with the fey. We can't have that girl seeing them, Jak. Who knows what kind of trouble she could stir up if she were to tell someone?"

"Wouldn't they think she was crazy?"

"Maybe, maybe not. Believe me when I say that we can't take the chance."

It occurred to Jak that his uncle wasn't telling him everything. Instead of looking worried, he looked eager, as if he'd gotten the scent of a particularly tempting prey. Even so, Targin was right when he said that the girl would have to be handled with care if she actually could call up lightning. As far as Jak knew, the only person who could control the weather was Titania, the queen of the fairies, and no one wanted to cross *her*. If his uncle wanted the girl, perhaps it was *because* she could control the weather. Befriending someone like that would only help Targin in his position as a leader of the goblins.

Whatever the reason might be, Jak would do his best to get the girl. Since the day Jak's mother had abandoned him at his uncle's cave, the halfling boy had been in awe of the goblin who had taken him in. His uncle had given him everything and asked for nothing in return. Now Jak felt honored to be given such an important assignment.

At last he might be able to do something to make his uncle proud of him.

Even as a small child Jak had known that his uncle was an important goblin in the land of the fey, not only as head of the Cattywampus clan, but also as a leader among all the goblins. He was often called away on goblin matters, but when he was home a steady flow of visitors came to see him. Sometimes they came on clan business, wanting to discuss land rights or trading agreements or to have Targin settle a dispute. There were times, however, when goblins arrived claiming to want to play dice and drink a few ales, only Jak knew better. He would get very little sleep on those nights, because his room was only a few doors down from the one where they met, and he often heard them talking in louder and louder voices as the night wore on and they drank more and more ale. The pattern became predictable. What started out in friendly tones became tirades against the fairies' repressive laws and how good life was before the fairies conquered all of goblin-kind.

"Remember how the trolls put up signs for a hotel one day, then served dinner the next? Everyone knew they were serving roast travelers for dinner; you couldn't get a table at all, the place was that popular!"

"Why, I remember when a goblin could terrorize an entire human village for a month, then go on to the next town and no one was around to stop him!"

"If it wasn't for the blasted fairies we'd still be at it! The stories my grandfather told could make your skin crawl and your heart proud."

"Ah, the old bedtime stories! Those were the days."

"It's all Titania's fault. If she and Oberon hadn't made their peace, none of this would have happened. They never would have gotten such a strong army, nor so many magic users on their side."

"We were a proud, free folk until Titania and Oberon led their armies to defeat us in battle," Targin would say. "It's been many years now, but there isn't a goblin alive who wouldn't like to see us free again. The day is coming when that chance will present itself, and there are those of us who will be ready to take it. And that, my goblin friends, is why I invited you here." It was what Jak was waiting for, because after that their voices would get quiet and he could finally go to sleep.

*

Wulfrin, the leader of the wolf clan, had been one of the more frequent visitors to stay late into the night. Lurinda, however, was another story. Jak had learned about her from Gammi, who had Lurinda's picture on the wall of her room. Now, having finally met his great-aunt, Jak tried to remember everything he'd heard about her.

Gammi had looked up to her older sister, who had been smart, beautiful, and the most likely of all her siblings to get into trouble. Shortly after Lurinda finished her studies on the island, the fairy queen's guards had come to get her. Like all the fey under fairy rule, each goblin clan had to send representatives to serve the queen.

"Hostages," Uncle Targin called them.

"Honored," his grandmother said.

Every few months Gammi had received a letter from Lurinda and they always said the same things—she was happy, she loved her job, and the queen was wonderful.

"She's content," Gammi always said. "She's living the life most goblin girls would envy."

"She's lying," Targin always replied. "She knows that the queen's guards read all the mail before it leaves the Old Forest."

Even when she wasn't around, Lurinda had stirred up controversy in the family den. Jak wondered what would happen now that she was actually there.

Chapter 12

Over the next few months, Jak didn't have one tutor, he had several. They had all lived in the human world for extended periods of time and knew more about humans than most goblins. The first one was a member of the rat clan who had lived in the sewer across from a library in the human world. He told Jak about the library and how it was filled with books.

"Did you read them all?" asked Jak.

"Read? *Fft!* I not read! Heard you do. Here," he said, dumping a pile of shiny, colorful books on the table in front of Jak. "Learn more about human world from these than from musty, dusty books."

As Jak flipped through the books, he saw that they were actually catalogs and were filled with pictures of clothes, gardening supplies, and kitchen tools. Jak liked the catalogs because they made him look at humans in a new way, but he found a lot of the items confusing. When Jak finished reading, he had more questions than answers, but the tutor replied, "I not know" until he got tired of saying it. Jak never saw him again.

The next tutor was a ferret goblin who showed Jak pictures of everyday objects that he would see in the human world. Although the tutor could name them and say what he saw humans using them for, he had no idea how they worked.

The last tutor came the day after Jak's fifteenth birthday and just a few days before he was to leave for the human world. His name was Bert, and he was Bruno and Barth's older brother. Like the twins, he had bearlike features, small ears perched on top of his head, and ferocious-looking teeth, but his features weren't as pronounced, his bushy hair covered his ears, and a mustache and beard covered his mouth and chin. As a result, he looked more human than his brothers.

The goblin was there to teach Jak how to behave more like a human and less like a goblin. "You move like a cat," said Bert. "Humans aren't that graceful. Watch me."

Jak tried to imitate his tutor's lumbering gait. Although Bert didn't walk exactly like a human, copying him did make Jak look less goblinlike. Bert also showed him how to sit with one leg crossed with his ankle resting on his knee like a man, how to clap his hands when he was pleased, and to hold up one finger when he wasn't. He showed him how to wave good-bye and hello, to snap his fingers when he wanted something, and to hold his nose when he didn't.

Over the days they were working together, Jak and Bert became good friends. Only hours before Jak was supposed to leave he learned that Bert would be going with him. Gammi had volunteered to go as well, saying that Jak wasn't ready to go out into the big world all by himself, whether fey or human. It would help that she had spent some time in the human world.

✦

The house looked neglected with the grass growing knee-high in the yard, the shutters falling off the windows, and the uneven floorboards on the porch. Gammi and Bert thought the house looked perfect. Gammi swore that she felt as if she'd come home. Bert was the first one inside, saying that he had to make sure it was safe for the others. The bear goblin immediately claimed the basement for himself, leaving the top two floors for Jak and Gammi.

While Bert thumped around downstairs, Jak and Gammi investigated the kitchen. Gammi was opening kitchen cupboards when Bert came up the steps to see what they were doing. He and Jak went into the living room and sat on the dilapidated furniture that had been left behind. They flicked the light switch in the dining room, making the lights hanging from the ceiling go on and off until one of the lights went out with a pop! When they reached the bathroom, they learned how to turn on the faucet. After they flooded the room, they also learned how to turn it off. Jak used the couch cushions from the living room to soak up the water.

Gammi was inspecting the still-wet bathroom and Jak was wondering what he should do with the cushions when Bert returned to the basement. He came back a short time later carrying an armload of cans and dumped them on the kitchen table. "See what I found," he said, looking proud of himself. "They were on a shelf in a little room. I think they have food in them."

Jak selected one of the cans and studied the picture of fresh tomatoes. "How do we open it?" he asked.

"That's easy." Bert picked up another can and squeezed it until his face turned red. The can got smaller in the middle, but it didn't open. "Maybe if I do this," he said, and hit it against the table. The can got dented, but it didn't open. Bert growled at the can as if it were purposely defying him. Holding it up to his mouth, the bear goblin bit the top of the can. When liquid spurted out, he got a funny look on his face. "My tooth ith thtuck," he said, trying to tug the can free.

"Pull harder," said Gammi, who had just come into the room.

"I don't want to pull out my tooth!" mumbled the bear.

"Then I'll do it," said the old goblin woman. Grabbing the can, she pulled on it until it came free. She raised the can to her mouth and sucked noisily, then smacked her lips and said, "Rotting cabbage!"

"It's called sauerkraut," said Jak, reading the label on the can.

❦

When they had finished inspecting the first floor, Jak helped his grandmother up the stairs and encouraged her to choose a room. The old goblin woman examined every one before making her choice; she wanted the room that overlooked the backyard, where she could see the two trees that defined the local Gate to the land of the fey, the real reason the house had been selected.

Although it was night in the human world, they were still on goblin time, so neither Jak nor his grandmother was ready for bed. When Jak discovered the ladder to the attic, Gammi insisted on going with him, so she was there when he found the cartons. The old couple who had lived in the house had been unable to throw away anything. Jak found a treasure trove of human life and a better education than he'd received from any of his tutors.

While Gammi sat on the floor, Jak brought out one carton at a time, opening them in front of her so they could exclaim over them together. They found old clothes, tattered magazines, ice skates, roller skates, shoes, umbrellas, broken toasters, broken Crock-Pots, broken lamps, used hardware, rusty tools, and children's toys, most of which were missing parts. They found the old mattresses and springs from six beds and enough blankets for a dozen. Gammi seemed to think that all the boxes were equally important, but Jak was most interested in the heaviest boxes that contained the books. There were books of every size and shape, books for children and adults, books with pictures and without. To Jak every book was a wonder. While Gammi sorted the clothes to find something she could wear, Jak thumbed through the books, reading bits and pieces. After looking at the pages, he examined the bindings, sniffing the musty smell of stored knowledge. He had such a look of reverent awe on his face that Gammi finally said, "If you want them, take them, boy. You're the only one who can read in this house."

It took Jak most of the rest of the night to lug the cartons of books down the stairs to his bedroom. When he was finished, he began going through them again and was mesmerized until his grandmother came to him saying, "Now, that's enough of that! We have work to do, so no more playing. Didn't you notice the sun's up? Come downstairs for breakfast; then you should be on your way. I just hope there's something left to eat," she grumbled as she started down the stairs. "Bert can tuck away enough for five goblins."

When Jak arrived downstairs, it was obvious that Gammi had been busy. She'd taken a load of the clothes from the attic and washed them in the kitchen sink. They were already hanging on the curtain rods in the living room, dripping onto the hardwood floor. She'd found a way to open the cans and had emptied them into a pot while Bert, who could smell food from two miles away, had come back upstairs and been talked into figuring out how to work the stove. After burning his fingers and singeing his beard, Bert got the stove turned on, which pleased both him and Gammi immensely.

The new "family" sat around the linoleum-covered kitchen table, eating directly from the pot. Gammi's soup had an odd flavor, having been made from cans of sauerkraut, peas, pears, cranberries, tuna, and cocktail franks in barbecue sauce, but they were hungry and enjoyed it anyway.

"Are you ready for school, Jak?" asked Gammi, "They'll probably ask you all sorts of questions when you go sign up."

"I can handle anything they throw at me. Don't forget, I took a lot of extra classes on the island. I doubt they teach anything in this school that I haven't heard before."

Bert wiped his mouth on his sleeve. "When I lived on the island, I studied The Fine Arts of Coercion and Trickery, and Throwing Your Voice to Intimidate Your Enemy from a Distance. Do the elders still teach those?"

"Yeah, but I didn't take either of them," Jak said.

Bert picked up a bowl of water and slurped it loudly while a strangled voice shouted in the next room, "Put up your hands and throw down your arms!"

"Very good!" said Gammi. "I thought someone was there for a moment. I'm confused though. Why would you want your enemy to put his hands up and his arms down?"

"By arms he means weapons," Jak explained to his grandmother. Then he turned back to Bert saying, "But wouldn't you want him to throw down his arms first?"

"Could be," said Bert. "I never did well in strategy lessons."

When he'd finished eating, Jak went upstairs to change his clothes. He'd studied the catalogs that his tutor had brought, and he'd seen humans when he went to Halloween with his class, so he thought he had a pretty good idea of what humans wore. He'd found some clothes in the attic and put on the ones he thought would be the best for school and set off down the street.

Unfortunately, when he walked through the front door of the school, he saw just how much the blue satin athletic shorts, gray pinstriped jacket, and green plaid shirt *didn't* belong.

The first student who saw him stood gaping in disbelief. When the next two did the same, Jak knew he had to do something. He disappeared into the janitor's closet and with a little of his own personal magic, he was wearing khakis and a shirt much like theirs when he came out.

Headmaster Serling's office was the most luxurious room Jak had ever seen. He had a deep red carpet with golden swirls on his floor and long velvet drapes on his windows. Portraits of old humans decorated the walls along with photographs of the headmaster and a lot of smug-looking human men and women. When his secretary showed Jak into the room, the headmaster was looking out the window with his hands clasped behind his back.

"I understand that you want to attend our school," he said without turning around. "You realize, of course, that Worthington is a highly respected institution and we require much of our students. Because we provide the finest of educations, we are inundated with applications."

While Jak listened to the man prattle, he let his gaze wander around the room. The two high-backed chairs facing the headmaster's desk looked inviting, and when he raised his head and sniffed, he could smell them from where he stood. Approaching the closest chair, he ran his fingers along the arm. It was made from the hide of an animal.

"Therefore, we must be highly selective in our acceptance procedures," said Headmaster Serling. "In order to be accepted, you must pass a stringent exam, provided that we have an opening in the class for which you are applying. What grade are you in, Mr. . . . I don't believe I heard your last name."

"Catta . . ." Jak flinched. He'd almost given himself away by telling the human his clan affiliation. "I'm Jak Catta."

Headmaster Serling took the seat behind the desk and gestured for Jak to take the one across from him.

"I'm as tall as any elder," said Jak as he curled up on the chair. "I'm in the class for taller-than-averages."

"I see," said Headmaster Serling, although he looked as if he didn't like what he saw. He was watching Jak with a most curious expression when he set his hands on his desk and leaned forward. "I'm sorry to tell you, Mr. Catta, that we have no openings in the 'taller-than-average class.'"

"But I need to start school today," Jak said.

"That won't be possible," said the headmaster. "You may see my secretary on the way out. She'll be happy to give you an application. However, in all honesty I must say that chances are slim that there will be any openings in the foreseeable future. Even if there were, you wouldn't be able to start until the beginning of the next semester."

"You don't understand," Jak said. "I have to start

today. I'm a very good student. I study hard and learn quickly."

"I'm sure you do," said the headmaster as he slid his hand across his desk and tapped a silvery box. "Miss Throckmorton, please see this young man out. He would like an application for admission." Taking his hand off the box, Headmaster Serling pointed at the door. "Good day, Mr. Catta."

"They won't let me go to school there," Jak said, throwing himself onto one of the kitchen chairs. "Headmaster Serling said that I had to fill out an application and wait until the next semester starts, and even then they probably won't have room for me."

"What? I never heard of such a thing!" Gammi said.

"Here's the application," said Jak. He dropped a wadded-up paper on the table. It rolled across and stopped in front of Gammi. She swatted it back and Jak pounced on it without thinking.

Gammi set down the tooth necklace she'd been stringing and turned to Bert. "We'll have to do something about this."

Bert rolled his shoulders until they made a cracking sound. "Leave it to me."

Jak was lying in bed reading when his door creaked open later that night. Bert stuck his head in the room and smiled at Jak. "Put that book down and go to sleep," he said. "You have to get up early tomorrow for school."

"You mean you saw him?" Jak said, dropping the

book on the floor. "How did you get the headmaster to change his mind?"

"Let's just say I used a little something that I learned when I lived on the island," the bear goblin said, smiling a truly frightening smile.

Chapter 13

When Jak reached the school the next morning, he was still wondering how he'd find his classes, but he needn't have worried. Headmaster Serling met him at the door with a class list and the directions and combination for a locker. "Welcome to Worthington Academy, Jak," he said with a hesitant smile. While the headmaster told him about his classes and what would be expected of him, Jak noticed that the man kept looking behind him and seemed awfully skittish.

"Are you all right, sir?" Jak finally asked.

Even the question made the headmaster jump. "Don't I look all right? Because I assure you, I am. Everything is all right and you can tell your uncle Bert that I said so. Everything is great, in fact. Here," he said, thrusting the list into Jak's hand. "Have a wonderful day. Don't hesitate to come see me if you have any questions or concerns."

"Thank you, sir!" Jak called after the headmaster as the man scurried down the hall.

"Hey, kid! Who are you?" called one of the boys who had watched the whole exchange.

"I'm Jak," he replied. "I'm new here."

Jak was already walking down the hall in search of his locker when he heard the boys talking behind him. "Did you see the way Serling was looking at that kid?" said the boy who had spoken to Jak. "His old man must be *really* loaded. My dad owns a string of banks and Serling doesn't even say hello to me."

"Yeah," said a girl who had joined them. "It's only the superrich who can afford to be as eccentric as that. Did you see what he was wearing?"

Jak blanched. True, he hadn't taken as much time making over his clothes as he could have, but he'd thought they were pretty good. Reading the words on the doors, Jak slipped into the first one marked BOYS and locked the door behind him. His clothes were the same style as the khaki pants and blue shirt he'd worn for the meeting the day before—only the colors were different. As someone banged on the locked boys' room door, Jak thought about what he wanted his clothes to look like. A moment later both the electric blue shirt and metallic green pants became the matte black that he had favored in the goblin world. He even turned a loose thread into a shiny white string, tucking one end in his ear and the other in his pocket, just like the other students he'd seen.

A bell rang, startling Jak and making him look around in dismay. He saw that the other students were going into the classrooms, so he headed for algebra, the first class on his list. The day went by quickly as Jak discovered just how much of the subjects he already knew. French class was the easiest because no one had to *teach* goblins new languages. Goblins had to hear them only once in order to pick them up. The teacher thought she was being kind when she lent Jak the CD that went with the textbook and told him to listen to the first three chapters. She said that if he needed any help she'd see about getting him a tutor, but he had already learned most of what she had to teach.

As Jak went from class to class, it occurred to him that any of the blond girls might be the one he had been sent to find. Although he had been given a picture of the girl, drawn by a nymph who had spoken with the goblins who had followed the girl on Halloween, the picture was vague with nothing really distinguishing the girl aside from her blond hair. He tried to picture the girls in his class aiming lightning bolts, but none of them seemed fierce enough to handle it.

Jak went home that night wondering how he'd ever find the girl. It wasn't going to be as easy as when the headmaster handed him his list of classes; no one was going to give him her name and address. Jak knew he'd just have to watch for something unusual.

The next morning Jak walked in the front door of the academy and noticed a group of girls clustered around a paper attached to the wall. Some were excited and some were crying, so he stuck around, listening for the rumble of thunder in case the girl he was looking for got upset enough to throw lightning bolts. When nothing happened and the girls looked as if they were about to leave, he hurried down the hall to his locker. He was still there when a girl came running around the corner and slammed into him, sending them both sprawling on the floor.

Jak jumped to his feet. When he reached for her backpack, the girl got up without taking her eyes off him. "Sorry," she said. "I'm not usually this clumsy."

"Neither am I," he replied. "I'm Jak, and you are . . ."

"Tamisin," she said, gazing at him with eyes that were an amazing shade of turquoise. Hair the color of sunlight and gold framed her heart-shaped face, which he thought was covered with far too much makeup. Although she was about the same height as Jak, she looked fragile enough that a strong wind could carry her away.

"Are you all right?" Jak asked when she just stood there, staring at him.

She looked flustered as if she suddenly realized what she'd been doing. "Sure, uh . . . yes. But I should be asking you that. I ran into you, remember?"

Jak suddenly felt the need to protect this delicate creature, even if it was only from taking the blame. "I was in your way," he said.

A bell rang, and Tamisin glanced at the clock. "Darn!" she said. "I'm late!"

Jak turned to look both ways at the now-empty halls. "I guess that means I am, too. I'm not used to the bell system yet. I just started yesterday."

Tamisin turned away and started down the hall, but she slowed long enough to look back at him and say, "Go to class, unless you want to get into trouble."

"Too late," murmured Jak, wishing he had an excuse to stay with her as he watched her disappear into a room.

Chapter 14

Jak wasn't really sure how he and Jeremy got to be friends. It had happened in gym class when Jak had decided to help the struggling students through the obstacle course. Jeremy had ended up helping, too, even though the gym teacher had been angry at both of them. Suddenly Jak felt comfortable with Jeremy, almost as if they had known each other for years.

They'd gotten in the habit of meeting after Jeremy's football practice to hang out or go to Mama Mia's for pizza. Jak had discovered that he loved human food and ate there as often as he could to avoid Gammi's cooking. She meant well, but even for a goblin her cooking was awful.

The two boys were walking down the street in front of the school late one afternoon when Jak saw Tamisin on the front steps. "Do you know her?" he asked.

Jeremy followed his friend's gaze and nodded. "Sure. That's Tamisin. She's an underclassman like us. Her brother's a senior. He's on the football team. Good guy. I'll introduce you to him some time."

"Yeah, okay," said Jak, still watching Tamisin.

"Oh, I get it! Tam is the one you want to meet. Hold on just a second and I'll call her over. Hey, Tamisin! Over here!"

Tamisin looked up and waved. She was smiling when she reached the curb and said, "Hi, Jeremy. What's up?"

Just like the first time he saw her, Tamisin wore her hair loose so that it framed her face. Her hair looked like spun silk that caught the sunlight and seemed to hold it. Jak's fingers itched to touch it to see if it was as soft and warm as it looked. He missed what Jeremy said, but caught Tamisin saying, ". . . ran into each other right after he started here."

Jak smiled, unaccountably pleased that she remembered.

"You should smile more often," Tamisin said, smiling in return.

Sure that she knew something he didn't, he nodded and said, "All right. But why?"

He liked the way her hair rippled when she shrugged. "You'll make more friends that way," she replied.

A cat meowed and Jak glanced across the street. Cats had been following him everywhere he went, just like they had that Halloween. He liked cats, of course. He couldn't help but like them; everyone in the Cattawampus clan did. It was just that they tended to get underfoot at the most inopportune times.

Jak turned away from the cat when he heard Jeremy talking to someone else. Two girls had arrived while he'd been distracted. One of them was looking at Jeremy, but the other was staring at Jak as if he were a piece of pizza and she hadn't eaten for three days. "You're the new boy, aren't you?" she asked.

"Yeah," he said and turned back to Jeremy. Catching his friend's eye, he jerked his head at Tamisin.

"So, Tamisin," Jeremy began. "You busy? Jak and I are headed over to—"

The cat Jak had seen across the street had crossed over to his side. Purring loudly, it rammed its head into the back of Jak's knee, almost knocking him off balance. "Don't do that!" Jak said, trying to push the cat away with his foot.

He forgot all about the animal when he heard the new girl say Tamisin's name. ". . . Why are you here so late?" the girl asked, smirking. "Were you getting extra help today or was it detention?"

Startled, Jak turned to Tamisin. If they had detention here, did they have a pit as well? He couldn't imagine someone as frail looking as the girl with hair like sunshine at the bottom of a hole that sunlight never reached.

"I had dance practice and—," said Tamisin, but then the girl interrupted her.

"I can't imagine why you're wasting your time talking to her, Jak. You're new here, so I guess you haven't heard about Tamisin. She's a freak—everybody knows it. I bet you've never seen ears like hers. Here," the girl said as she handed her books to her friend. "Look at this!"

Jak was surprised when the girl reached out and pushed Tamisin's hair behind her ear. "Have you ever seen anything like that?" the girl said, looking pleased with herself.

Jak didn't know what to say. Tamisin's ears were narrow and pointed, just like those of certain fey back home. From the way the other girl was talking, ears like that couldn't be normal in the human world. Instead of thinking Tamisin looked freakish, however, Jak thought her ears were beautiful.

"Give it a rest, Kendra," Jeremy told the girl. "Nobody cares what her ears look like."

A second cat had joined the first, and now both animals were rubbing against Jak's ankles. He was trying to shoo them off when another girl joined them.

"That's Heather," Jeremy told Jak.

"Hey," said Jak.

"It's nice to meet you," she said, her voice sounding odd. Jak wondered if she was sick.

Tamisin must have thought so, too, because she took a close look at the girl and asked her if she was all right.

Heather rubbed her eyes and mentioned something about a cat. When she noticed the two cats rubbing against Jak's legs, she backed away as if he had the goblin plague or something. Self-conscious now, Jak tried to get away from the cats, but they followed him, still purring. "I told you to stop that!" he said.

Heather sneezed and a moment later Tamisin was hustling her away, talking about taking her home.

R

The next few weeks were confusing for Jak. He suspected that Tamisin was the girl he was meant to take back with him, but that was based solely on her ears; she never did

133

or said anything unusual, and the weather seemed to be normal when she was around. If she was the girl, being able to control lightning meant that she was a creature of power, human or not, and as such he couldn't treat her like a normal person.

On the weekends Jak explored the end of town where the school was located. He found the lightning-blasted tree the goblins had told him about and the street where they had first seen the girl. Then, one day he came across a forest. It was tiny compared with anything in the land of the fey, but it was pretty and there was a stream leading to a small waterfall.

As time passed, Gammi became more insistent that Jak do something and do it soon. "Time's a-wasting and Targin won't take kindly to a delay. The Gate has already opened once since we've been here. Who knows when it'll open again? If you're sure Tamisin is the one we're looking for, invite her over the next time the Gate opens. We'll find a way to get her through."

"That's just it," said Jak. "I'm not sure Tamisin is the one. I don't want to rush things and scare her. If she really can control lightning, she'd be harder to get through if she was frightened."

"Frightened . . . Ha!" Gammi said, pulling a live mouse out of a cage by its tail. "I'll frighten her myself if it means we can get her through the Gate."

Jak looked away as his grandmother popped the squirming mouse in her mouth and bit down. "I'll take care of it," he said.

Although Jak saw Tamisin in the halls at school, it was

always from a distance and she usually had a group of friends around her. He listened for any news of her, however, and asked Jeremy about her while trying not to seem too anxious. According to Jeremy, her brother said that all she did lately was dance and that he was sick of hearing the same music over and over again. Then Jak heard that the dance group she was in was going to perform, and he was the first one in line at the school box office.

The night of the performance Jak told Gammi and Bert where he was going.

"Good," said Gammi. "I have my jewelry-making group coming over tonight. Bert's going to get me more teeth for necklaces, aren't you, Bert?"

Gammi had met some old ladies in the park and offered to teach them her favorite crafts. Most of them were too nearsighted to see that she looked a little different, and the others didn't seem to care.

When the first of Gammi's friends came to the door, Jak slipped out the back and walked the eleven blocks to school. Since he'd gotten his ticket early, he'd been able to get a good seat up front and center. At first he watched the dances without much interest, disappointed each time Tamisin failed to appear. But when she finally stepped onto the stage, he didn't recognize her right away. She looked like something from another world—his.

Her beginning steps were tentative, but when the music quickened, her movements became stronger and bolder. As she leaped and twirled, Jak held his breath.

She seemed to float across the stage like the dandelion puffs he had chased when he was young.

Jak wasn't the only one caught up in her dancing. All around him people gasped when a leap carried her farther than they'd expected or when she twirled longer than they thought possible. Her dancing made Jak think of a breeze cooling his face after a good run, or rustling the leaves in the forest around his uncle's den. It was a calming dance, it was a ferocious dance, and through it all Jak felt closer to home than he had since the day he'd left.

The only sound in the auditorium was Tamisin's music. No one spoke, or coughed or shuffled their feet or got up to get a drink of water, and when it was over and the last note faded away, the room remained silent until it seemed everyone was frozen in place. Then the cheering began as one person after another broke free of the reverie Tamisin's dancing had created. She looked up from her last position, smiling, then rose to her feet and bowed as gracefully as if she were still performing.

As soon as Tamisin left the stage, Jak got up from his seat. He thought about waiting inside for her, but decided not to when he saw the people milling around, so he went to the parking lot in the back, hoping she would come out that door. He was surprised to see lights twinkling around the school, knowing exactly what they were. "What are fairies doing here?" he wondered. "There must be a Gate open nearby." Most fey wouldn't travel to the human side without good cause; those who did never went far from an open Gate since the magic that escaped diminished the farther they traveled from it. Those who went too far were unable to do even the most basic magic, like disguising themselves from curious eyes. To have so many fairies come through at once meant either that multiple Gates had opened, or something truly extraordinary had happened to summon them.

The crowd that had filled the auditorium began streaming into the parking lot. People began pointing at the fairies, calling them "fireflies" and "amazing," and then something rustled in the branches of the tree behind him, saying, "*Psst*! Hey, Jak, is that you?"

"Who is that?" Jak asked, peering into the shadows.

There was the scrape of claws on bark and a masked face emerged right above him. "It's me, Tobi! How ya doin', Jak? Yer friends were all worried about ya."

"I was sent home. Didn't you hear?"

"Yeah, but we thought ya were comin' back. Then Nihlo told everybody that ya were in big trouble and that his father was real mad at ya and was sendin' ya away. We knew it couldn't be over breakin' Nihlo's leg. He deserved it. Anyway, when ya didn't come back, I thought Nihlo might be tellin' the truth for once, until I talked to yer uncle, that is."

"*You* talked to my uncle?" said Jak.

"He sent for me," said Tobi. "Somebody told him I'd seen the girl who threw the lightnin'. She didn't throw it at me, of course, but I seen her face when she saw me."

"What did Targin want from you?" asked Jak.

"To help ya find the girl. Yer uncle said that he gave ya a picture, but it was lousy, so he sent me 'cause I'd gotten a good look at her. I've been livin' in the trees near here fer weeks now. I saw her once, but she got away. I think she lives in a big building with stone statues out front and a lot of other humans goin' in and out, 'cause that's where she goes every day after school."

"A big building? Maybe she lives in an apartment."

"All I know is lots of people come out of it with books, but she's the only one I seen goin' into it every day."

"It sounds more like the library than an apartment. Why would she go there every day, unless . . . Are you sure she didn't see you?"

"What, me? I'm so good at sneakin' around that nobody could see me! Even my own mother wouldn't . . . Wait . . . There she is, over there by that other girl."

"Your mother?"

"No, the girl who saw me! There she is right there!"

"Do you mean the girl with the blond hair that looks like sunshine and—"

"Yeah, that's her. The one with yella hair. She's the one who looked right at me with her eyes all big and scary."

Jak smiled to himself. He'd been right all along. "Thanks, Tobi. I guess you did what you came for, so you can go back now." Jak didn't want him around when he was about to talk to Tamisin.

"Actually," said Tobi, "I'm supposed to stay here. Yer uncle thought ya'd need some help bringin' her back."

"So now he thinks I can't handle it? I already have two goblins here to help me. How many more does he think he has to send? You go back and tell my uncle that I can take care of this myself, and I don't need any more help!"

"He ain't gonna like that and I don't want to be the one to tell him anythin' he ain't gonna like. He's already irked that ya haven't brought her back yet."

"Just blame it all on me. Tell him that I made you go back."

"But ya wouldn't! Yer too nice to . . . Okay, okay, I'm going!"

Jak had bared his teeth and growled the way he'd seen Nihlo do, making the little goblin scoot backward up the branch. Since his own teeth were just teeth and not fangs, Jak doubted that he looked very frightening, but it appeared to be enough to convince Tobi that he was serious. "Tell him that I said I can handle it!" Jak shouted after the fleeing goblin. "Tell him that I don't know why he sent you!"

Jak was so angry when he turned away from the tree that he forgot why he was there until he saw Tamisin coming toward him across the parking lot.

"Jak, is that you?"

"Tamisin! I was hoping to catch you here. Your dance was great! It made me think of things I miss from my old home. It was very . . . eloquent." Jak felt stupid after he said it. There were a thousand things he should have said instead, but the only thing that came to mind sounded flat.

Even so, Tamisin smiled at him as if he'd said the most wonderful thing. "Thank you," she said. "That's very kind of you."

Jak didn't want her to get the wrong idea. He hadn't said it just to be nice. "Oh, I'm not being kind. I mean it. For the first time I think I know what it means to be homesick."

Tamisin's smile faded. "I'm sorry! I never intended to make anyone feel bad."

Jak could have kicked himself, certain that he'd finally said the worst thing he could have. "Don't be sorry," he said in a rush. "I enjoyed your dance. You don't have any plans now, do you? I mean, if you'd like to get something to eat, we could . . ."

And then her father was calling to her, telling her that they had to go.

"I know, Dad. I'm coming," she shouted, then turned back to Jak saying, "Thanks for the invitation. Maybe some other time."

This was all wrong. Jak had to talk to her and it had to be soon. "Yeah. About that . . ."

But Tamisin was already moving toward her parents' car, saying, "I've got to go."

"Sure," he said, so disappointed that he felt like kicking something. He watched as the car drove away, taking with it the girl he'd come so far to find.

❦

Jak hung around Tamisin's locker on Monday morning, but she got to school late and didn't have time to talk. He didn't see her that afternoon. When the same thing happened on Tuesday, he began to think that she was avoiding him. Even so, he was watching for her on Wednesday morning. He could see right away that Tamisin wasn't feeling well. Her cheeks were flushed and she didn't seem to notice him when he called to her in the hall. That afternoon he was hanging out while Jeremy talked to Heather when Tamisin ran past them to her locker. Jak was already walking over when she pulled out her backpack, letting a flood of books and papers cascade onto the floor. Her hands were shaking when he bent down to help her.

Although Tamisin turned down his offer, Jak insisted on picking up the papers. He was smiling as he handed them to her until he saw a look of pain in her eyes. "Is everything all right?" he asked. When he tried to help her get up, she shook off his hand.

"I'm fine," she said through gritted teeth. "I can manage on my own."

I've been so stupid, thought Jak, suddenly convinced that she didn't want to have anything to do with him. "Don't let me keep you," he said.

When he got home that afternoon he called to Gammi as he walked in the door. "We're going to have a party on Halloween. The Gate will be open then and it will be the perfect time to take Tamisin through. I'll drag her here if I have to. She made it clear today that she doesn't like me, which is going to make it that much harder to persuade her to go through the Gate with me. I doubt she's going to change her mind between now and Halloween."

"I'll talk to Bert," said Gammi. "He'll take care of the decorations and I'll see to the food."

Even though Jak had made his plans, he hated the idea

of forcing anyone through a Gate, and was still hoping to get Tamisin to trust him. When she didn't come to school the next day, Jak learned from Jeremy that her brother Kyle had said that she had been sick the night before and had locked herself in her room. He didn't know what was wrong with her.

It was Friday when Tamisin finally returned to school. She looked different that morning, and it took Jak a moment to understand why. Her long hair was pulled back and secured with a ribbon, leaving her ears uncovered. She wasn't wearing any makeup either, and when she walked in front of one of the big floor-to-ceiling windows in the hall, her cheeks and the bridge of her nose sparkled in the sunlight. Jak pushed his way through the crowded hallway and reached her locker when she was putting her things inside. When she glanced up, he smiled and said, "I'm glad you're back. I heard you were sick."

"I'm fine now," she replied, flashing him a brief smile of her own.

The first bell rang and she took a note from her pocket. "I have to get this to the office," she said.

Jak nodded. "Yeah. I've gotta go, too. But first I wanted to ask—would you like to have lunch with me on Saturday? I know a good spot for a picnic."

Tamisin paused, then surprised him when she said, "That sounds like fun."

"Great!" he replied. "I'll pick you up at noon."

Jak watched her walk away. She seemed different somehow, and it wasn't just her hair and skin. She seemed more vibrant, as if she'd changed from the inside as well. He wondered what could have happened to make such a change in just a few days.

Jak got directions to Tamisin's house from Jeremy. When he mentioned that he was taking her on a picnic, Jeremy told him to put the food in a basket and to take a blanket to sit on. All the blankets in the house had been mouse-chewed, but Jak had found an old plastic shower curtain decorated with neon tropical fish that he thought would work.

When he arrived at Tamisin's house, she looked happy to see him. Three cats had followed him to her door, but she didn't say anything when the animals joined them on their walk. It was a glorious day with a clear blue sky and only a slight chill to the air. As they headed back toward the school property and into the woods beyond, Jak took a deep breath and relaxed. The school was her territory. The woods were his.

They didn't have to go far into the woods before they reached Jak's stream, which they followed until they could no longer hear traffic from the road. Jak led Tamisin to the waterfall and a pretty spot under the trees. Her eyes lit up when she saw the tumbling water. "This is great," she said. "I didn't know there was anything like this around here."

"I thought you'd like it," Jak said as he set the basket on the ground. It wasn't anything special—he knew of much prettier places near his uncle's den—but it would do. "Are you hungry yet?" he asked. "We could eat now if you are."

"I'm famished," said Tamisin. "I didn't eat breakfast this morning. I was working in the garden, trying to get it ready for winter."

"You like to garden?" he said, taking the shower curtain out of the basket and shaking it so that it billowed out before settling onto the ground.

"I've always loved working with plants," she said.

Jak glanced at her ears and nodded. That made sense, considering. He'd been wondering ever since he first saw Tamisin's ears that day in front of the school, but it wasn't until he'd seen her without makeup that Jak had been certain. Tamisin had fairy ancestry; the sparkles on her cheeks, the translucent skin, and the slender-tipped ears were all a giveaway. Jak wondered if she knew the truth herself. More than likely she was a halfling like him, although he had seen both of her parents the night Tamisin performed and he could have sworn that neither of them had a drop of fey in them. Being a halfling would explain why she could see the fey, but it didn't explain the weather.

While Jak straightened the shower curtain, Tamisin set the basket in the middle and opened the lid. "Oh!" she said, taking out the plate piled high with slices of cold pizza. Jak had made a special trip to Mama Mia's that morning and had bought the biggest pizza they had—with anchovies, of course, which he considered the best part.

"Don't you like pizza?" he asked.

"Sure!" she said. "I've just never had it on a picnic before."

144

"There are eggs, too," he said, pointing at the basket.

"Oh, good! I love hard-boiled eggs."

"I never would have thought of boiling them," Jak said. "I always eat them raw. Here, you're supposed to eat them like this." Using one hand, he cracked the shell, broke it apart, and poured it into his mouth. When he glanced at Tamisin, she was grimacing, an expression he thought looked awfully funny on her sweet, delicate face.

Jak couldn't help himself and began to laugh. His laughter must have been contagious, because soon Tamisin was laughing with him. Then something moved on the other side of the stream, catching Jak's eye, and he no longer felt like laughing. The cats had noticed it as well. One by one they stood and stalked toward the stream, ears flattened to their heads and tails lashing. They were growling deep in their throats so softly that only someone with cat-goblin hearing could hear them.

"Here," Jak said, handing Tamisin the basket. "Why don't you try the cookies? My grandmother's friend sent them over. I have to take care of something."

"Sure," Tamisin said, setting the basket on her lap.

Trying to act nonchalant, Jak strolled to the stream. Although he couldn't be sure, he'd thought he'd seen a goblin face peering at him through the leaves. He wouldn't have noticed it at all if it hadn't been autumn with half the leaves already on the forest floor. The face had been there for just a moment, and had gone just as quickly. It occurred to Jak that his uncle might have gotten tired of waiting and had sent someone else to get the girl. He resented that his uncle didn't trust him to do it;

145

he also felt more than a little angry. After all, he was the one who had found the girl and gotten to know her.

Noting where he thought the face had appeared, Jak crossed the stream in one bound. The cats dashed across a fallen branch, following him to the other side. An orange tabby ran under his feet, making Jak stumble into the underbrush. A goblin who had been hiding under the fallen leaves squawked in surprise and jumped up, scattering leaves and twigs as he ran off, clacking his sharp little beak. Jak followed the goblin as far as a sycamore tree, where a shower of broken twigs and pieces of old bird's nest pelted him from above. Protecting his head with his arms, Jak dodged out of the way and peered up into the tree where two bird goblins were crouched amid the branches. "I just want to talk to you," he said.

"Jak, are you all right?" Tamisin called to him.

He paused long enough to call back, "Just fine" before grabbing one of the lowest branches and swinging up into the tree. The bird goblins chattered at each other and climbed higher. Jak was halfway up when the goblins jumped out of the tree and disappeared into a tulip poplar.

Lowering himself from branch to branch, Jak tried to decide what to do. While he wanted to run the goblins down and make them tell him what they were up to, he was eager to get back to Tamisin so the date wouldn't be completely ruined. When a rock clipped his ear, Jak nearly fell the last few yards. He slipped and caught himself, but now he was really mad. Silently seething, he returned to the stream long enough to collect a fistful of stones and check to make sure that Tamisin was still all right.

"I'll be right back!" he shouted, not wanting her to think he'd deserted her. She was sitting with her back to him, but instead of turning around she just waved.

Certain that she was still eating, Jak returned to the woods and waited for a goblin to show itself. The moment he saw movement in a tree, he took careful aim and hurled a rock, hitting something with an audible *thunk*!

"Ow!" yelled a voice and Tobi peeked out, the orange and yellow leaves framing his small, masked face. "Why'd ya do that?" he shouted, rubbing his chest.

Jak was frowning when he stalked to the base of the tree. "What are you doing here?" he asked. "Are you with the bird goblins? Did my uncle send them?"

"Do I look like I've sprouted feathers?" asked Tobi. The cats pressed themselves against Jak's legs as if to protect him, glaring at the raccoon goblin. When the big tomcat took a step toward Tobi, the little goblin raised his cudgel and shook it. "Call off yer cats, Jak. Ya know I'm on yer side."

"Then tell me why you're here," ordered Jak.

"I came to warn ya that there are other goblins who want the girl now, and ya gotta be extra careful. Word got out that Targin wants her, so they're comin' over every time they find an open Gate, tryin' to get her for themselves. They figure if Targin wants her, she must be worth wantin'. Some are stayin' too, spendin' all their time lookin', though they don't know what she looks like. They shouldn't be able to get their claws on her unless ya show her to 'em."

Jak turned and started running back toward the stream. Branches whipped his face while gnarled roots tried to trip his feet, making his pace frustratingly slow. Like a fool, he had left Tamisin alone in the woods, easy prey for a goblin. No matter what anyone said about her, he doubted that she could defend herself, with or without lightning. When he saw that Tobi was scurrying alongside the cats, trying to keep up with him, he asked, "Why didn't you tell me this sooner?"

"I came . . . soon as I heard about it!" panted Tobi.

Jak paused to look across the stream. From where he stood he could see Tamisin sitting where he had left her, yet even from a distance he could tell that something wasn't right. Her hair no longer looked like sunlight and gold, but was dull and limp. The way she sat was different, too; she normally had a graceful quality that came out even when she wasn't in motion. It was apparent in the way she held her head and positioned her body, an unconscious thing that was as much a part of her as the way she breathed. Only now her body looked stiff and she held her head angled to the side like a . . .

Jak fairly flew across the stream and was at her side before he could draw another breath. And then he knew why she looked so different—it wasn't Tamisin at all. A girl of the bird-goblin clan sat holding the picnic basket on her lap. Cookie crumbs dotted her beak when she glanced up at Jak, and she cackled with laughter when she saw how mad he looked. "We've got her now!" she said, just before she threw the picnic basket at him.

Jak caught the basket and tossed it aside, but the girl had already fled into the forest, the cats on her heels.

"Who was that?" asked Tobi.

"Not Tamisin, obviously," growled Jak.

"Did ya think it was?" When Jak didn't reply, Tobi gasped. "Ya did, didn't ya? Ya don't mean to say that ya brought her here? What were ya thinkin'?"

Jak glared at his friend. "Not what I would have been if someone had warned me in time." Turning away from Tobi, Jak cupped his hands around his mouth and shouted, "Tamisin, where are you?"

"I'm over here!" she shouted back, as if there was nothing wrong.

Jak began to run in the direction of her voice. He found her in a meadow surrounded by out-of-season wildflowers with her arms already loaded with an enormous bouquet. The relief he felt when he saw her was enough to make him stagger.

"Can you believe all these flowers?" she asked. "I didn't mean to wander off, but after I saw the first one . . ."

"I'd better get you home so you can put them in water," Jak said, wanting to hurry her out of the forest as quickly as he could. "They won't last long if you don't."

Tamisin looked stricken. "You're right," she said. "I didn't think of that. I'm so sorry that we never got to look around."

"It's all right," said Jak. "We can do that another time." He had no intention of looking around anymore. He'd already seen enough. Flowers blooming out of season usually meant that fairies had been there, and with so many in one spot it probably meant that there was a Gate to the land of the fey somewhere in the meadow. The bird goblins must have moved a few flowers, luring Tamisin there so they could take advantage of the Gate and make her walk through. If he hadn't found her when he had, she might very well have gone through the Gate without knowing it. True, he could take her through himself, but he had no idea where they might end up and who might be waiting for them. The Gate in his backyard led to somewhere familiar and safe, where the other goblins wouldn't be ready for her. It was the only Gate he intended to use.

Since he had unknowingly shown Tamisin to the bird clan, he wasn't about to compound his mistake by showing them where she lived, so he copied what he suspected Tamisin had done to Tobi and took her home the long way, stopping at the library long enough to walk through and out a back door. They were standing on her front porch when he finally asked her what he'd wanted to all along.

"I'm having a party at my house on Halloween. I'd like it if you could come."

"That's a school night, isn't it?"

"I guess so," said Jak. "Is that a problem?"

Tamisin glanced at the door to her house, then back at him. "My parents won't like it, but I'll come. Do you mind if I bring my friend Heather?"

"Not at all," said Jak, wondering who else he should

put on the guest list. He was about to leave when he remembered a paper in his pocket. "Here's my phone number and address. It starts at seven-thirty."

"I'll be there," she replied before slipping through her front door.

Jak spent the entire walk home puzzling over some things that were bothering him. There was too much about what his uncle wanted him to do that just didn't make sense. He was convinced that Tamisin's ability to see goblins wasn't the reason Targin wanted her, despite what he'd said. Humans probably wouldn't believe her if she told them what she'd seen, and even if they did, what could they do? And that story about the lightning . . . Jak hadn't seen any sign that Tamisin was capable of controlling it. If Targin wanted her because of the lightning, he was going to be awfully disappointed. And if it wasn't the reason, Jak couldn't imagine what it might be.

And then there were the bird goblins. Tobi had said that they wanted her because they'd heard that Targin did. That goblin girl had acted as if it was a competition and whoever took Tamisin back had won something. But they might not even know about Tamisin's supposed skill with the weather. Goblins were known for being vicious, especially when they were angry. If Tamisin couldn't call lightning and the bird goblins found out that they'd gone to so much trouble to fetch a human whose only special talent was that she could see the fey, they were bound to take it out on her.

Although it hadn't mattered to Jak before he met Tamisin, he was getting to know her now and didn't like the idea of tricking her into going with him. Then again, if she couldn't control the weather, there was no real reason to take her back. But he couldn't leave her behind, knowing that the bird goblins were after her.

Chapter 15

After years of watching his uncle, Jak found he was good at delegating tasks. Gammi and Bert were already taking care of the food and decorations, so he asked Jeremy to arrange for the music and help him invite the guests.

The day before the party, Jeremy told Jak that a band led by a friend of his from another school would play at the party for free; it would be their first performance in front of a real audience and they liked the idea of working out the kinks before taking their act public. Jeremy assured Jak that he'd invited plenty of people and that his party was sure to be a success, but Jak didn't care who was there as long as Tamisin was one of the guests.

Jak had made his decision—he'd have to take her back even if it was just so they could straighten out the mess with the other goblins. As the time for the party drew near, he became increasingly restless. It wasn't the party itself that worried him, it was finally taking Tamisin on the long-awaited trip through the Gate.

On Halloween night, Jak put on his traveling clothes. He packed a knapsack with a few essentials, hoping that he could make whatever else they needed. Gammi and Bert would be going with him, just as they'd planned all along, and together the three of them would keep Tamisin safe should the bird goblins—or anyone else—come after her. By the time the first guests arrived, Jak felt better about the plan. He would take Tamisin to his uncle, convince Targin that she couldn't control lightning, and get the bird clan to leave her alone.

Jeremy was the first to show up along with half a dozen of his football-playing buddies. Then the band arrived and everything was in turmoil as they set up their equipment in the living room. More guests came to the door and then, before Jak knew how it had happened, the house was full of people—yet Tamisin still wasn't there.

Feeling crowded and uncomfortable, Jak went outside to get some fresh air. He was watching the neighborhood cats cross into his yard when a car pulled up beside the curb and Tamisin got out. Jak was so pleased to see her that he almost didn't notice her friend or the boy who had been driving.

"Do you know my brother Kyle?" Tamisin asked.

"Hey, man," said Kyle, extending his hand to Jak. "Great house."

"Thanks," said Jak. And then a boy came out the front door, saw Kyle, and clapped him on the shoulder, and the two disappeared inside.

Jak glanced at the girls' costumes as he escorted them

154

into the house. Tamisin's black cat costume almost made her look like a cat goblin. "I like what you're wearing," he told Tamisin. "You, too," he told Heather.

They were standing in the entrance hall when Gammi threw open the basement door and scurried up to Jak. Standing on tiptoe, she whispered in his ear, "We need to talk." She'd already told him of her intention to stay in the basement with Bert while the party was going on, so he knew that whatever she had to say must be important.

Jak maneuvered Tamisin and Heather around so they were facing the other way. There was no telling what they would see through the open basement door, and the last thing he wanted to do was try to explain Bert. "Sorry," he said, edging toward Gammi and the basement door. "I've got to look into this. I'll be right back."

Jak took the steps two at a time. It was dark in the basement; they could all see well without lights. Gammi and Bert were sitting in two reclining chairs. To his surprise Tobi was there as well. "There's somethin' goin' on that I thought ya should know about," said the little raccoon goblin. "There's a rumor goin' 'round 'bout a reward for a human girl with special talents. Now mind, they ain't sayin' her name, but I know as sure as nuts fall from a tree that they're talkin' 'bout Tamisin. I wanted to warn ya that ya might have yerselves some visitors—the kind no sane body wants to have. Give ya time to get prepared to do what-some-ever."

"They're coming here? How would they know—"

"Because they're goblins, that's how. They've been watching ya ever since ya got here. And most goblins are bad at keeping secrets 'cause they're just too much fun to tell. Pretty soon what one knows, they all know. Say," said the little goblin, perking his ears toward the ceiling. "What's that I hear?"

Jak tilted his head to listen. At first all he could hear was the not-very-good music that Jeremy's friends were playing. It was loud and repetitive and . . . Between one beat and the next there was a pause, and in that semi-silence Jak heard a sound that made the hair on the back of his neck rise and his fingers flex as if he had claws like Gammi's. A strange goblin was cackling right here in Jak's own house.

Jak was up the stairs in two bounds with Bert shoving him from behind. They burst through the door into a scene straight from a nightmare. Goblins that he had never seen before were pouring from every room into the hall that led to the kitchen. A scream cut through their excited voices and they began to sing, covering the sound with their own. Jak knew beyond any question that Tamisin had been the one who screamed.

While the human partygoers watched as if the whole thing was being staged for their entertainment, Jak shoved past the last of the goblins into the kitchen, where they were streaming out the back door. There was no sign of Tamisin, but Heather's pale face and look of horror told him all that he needed to know. "Oh, no you don't!" he shouted. Whatever their reason for wanting her, Jak wasn't going to let them get Tamisin.

One leap and Jak was on the kitchen table. Another leap and he landed on the back of a goblin with the body of a human and the eyes and snout of a hyena. The goblin went down as Jak ran out the door and into the dark beyond.

Lightning split the sky as thunder shook the ground. Some of the goblins shrieked and ran, but enough stayed clustered together that he couldn't see the still-screaming Tamisin. They were halfway to the towering trees when they paused, and then they were moving again as lightning struck the ground nearby. The wind began to blow as a heavy rain pelted him, but Jak was close enough now that he could see her in the outline of the shimmering Gate.

The goblins were trying to push and drag her toward the trees when Jak pounced on the first one, knocking him out with a single blow. Frantic that they might be hurting her, Jak used everything he had learned from fighting Nihlo, and took on one goblin after another. Then Bert was there, adding his astounding strength to Jak's until only one last goblin held Tamisin. Jak paused, confused. It was Nihlo with a sneer on his lips and a cast on his leg. Could his uncle have sent his son, thinking his nephew was a failure? Jak clenched his jaw when he saw that his cousin had his hand around Tamisin's slender neck. Watching Jak's face, Nihlo squeezed the girl's throat until ruby droplets of blood beaded the tip of each claw.

Tamisin gasped and lightning struck, much closer now, deafening everyone who stood near. Jak could feel its power make his hair stand on end and his nostrils burn with the biting stench. Glancing at Tamisin's face, he saw the plea for help in her eyes. He couldn't let Nihlo have her, even if his cousin was just taking her to Targin.

Jak's muscles tensed as he prepared to spring, but Nihlo saw and forced Tamisin's head back as he dug his claws in deeper. Once again Bert arrived, and with a swipe of his meaty hand he knocked the cat goblin aside just as Jak leaped to snatch Tamisin away. The wet ground was slippery, and Jak skidded as he landed, catching part of the blow so that it spun him around. Instead of pulling Tamisin out of the way, he fell into her. As a bolt of lightning cracked the sky in two, they tumbled toward the trees and through the shimmering Gate to the land of the fey.

PART THREE

Chapter 16

Tamisin groaned and shut her eyes. She had to be dreaming; there was no way that she could be lying on the ground with the sun warming her back. The last thing she remembered was that creature ... and Jak ... and a storm that came out of nowhere.

A faint breeze carried the scent of pine, mingling it with the smell of damp soil. The sunlight glowed red beyond her closed eyelids. "Jak?" she said, and turned her head toward an answering groan. A figure dressed in black lay sprawled beside her. "Jak," she said again. "Are you all right?"

Jak rolled over onto his back, moaning. "Fine," he croaked. "How are you?"

"Okay, I guess," Tamisin said, sitting up so she could look around. They were on a path of pine needles with towering pine trees growing on either side. A shimmering light danced between two of the trees only yards away. "If this is a dream, it's so realistic! I can smell those pine trees. I can't usually smell things in my dreams."

"I'm afraid this isn't a dream," Jak said, wincing when he touched a fresh bruise on his cheek. "We must have crossed through the Gate during the fight, but something went wrong. This isn't at all where we're supposed to be."

Tamisin drew her knees up to her chin and hugged them. "What Gate?" she asked. "Where were we supposed to be other than your backyard?"

Jak sighed and sat up to face her. "The Gate to the fey side that opened in my backyard. It's my fault. If I hadn't tripped we wouldn't have come . . . here," he said, looking around. "Maybe it was the lightning . . ."

"I don't understand," said Tamisin, her voice sounding thin and wavery. "What do you mean when you say 'fey'?"

"The fey are fairies, goblins, nymphs, trolls . . . Beings who have magic. The land of the fey is where I'm from," said Jak, getting to his feet and reaching down to help her up. "Don't worry—it really isn't that different from what you're used to. The same laws of physics apply and everything. The only real difference is that magic still exists here, whereas it's been a long time since it flourished in the human world."

Tamisin let him take her hand in his and pull her to her feet, but when he began to walk she let go of him and said, "There's never been magic . . ."

"Of course there has," said Jak. "Back before the spell was cast, it was all one place. You don't think the people in the old days were crazy, do you, making up stories about unicorns and dragons? Creatures like that were real. In fact, they are real, they just aren't on your side anymore."

"My side of what?" demanded Tamisin.

"Maybe I'm not explaining myself very well," Jak said. "Let's just say that once upon a time, the human world and the fey world were still one big happy place, only it wasn't really happy. Humans were at a disadvantage, not having magic of their own. The most powerful magician had some of their blood in his veins, so he decided to protect humans by separating them from the magic users. He cast a spell that put up a wall, only it wasn't really a wall, more of a divider that was thinner in some spots and thicker in others. Anyway, his spell was very strong, but it wasn't perfect, and when he died, the thin spots began to fray. Those frayed places are what we call Gates. Humans and fey from either side can cross over when a Gate is open, only no one can really predict when that'll be. Except for certain Halloweens, of course, when the magic on our side builds up so much that the Gates can't help but open. But Gates never stay open for long. The spell is still strong enough that they heal themselves and close up again, usually after just a few hours."

Tamisin asked, "How do you know all this?"

"I'm half goblin," said Jak. "I meant to tell you, just not like this."

"And on those Halloweens, do a lot of your people come through the Gates?" Tamisin asked, her voice barely louder than a whisper.

Jak nodded. "More then than at any other time. With so many Gates open, more magic comes through, so the fey can travel in your world for greater distances. The fey who visit through an ordinary Gate have to stay near that Gate or their magic fades. And there's always the chance that the Gate will shut suddenly, leaving them stranded. A lot of humans have thought they've seen ghosts when it's really just a fairy or a goblin who's using weakened invisibility magic."

Something howled in the woods nearby, making Jak reach for her hand again. "We need to go. There are creatures in these woods that we don't want to meet."

Tamisin stepped aside, avoiding his grasp. "Why should I believe you?"

"Because you saw the goblins, and I know you've seen fairies. That night after you danced at the school . . . They came because of you, didn't they?"

"Those *things* at your house were goblins?"

Jak scowled, making his handsome face look fearsome. "I'm one of those *things*, as you put it. Or at least half of me is. I'm a halfling—half human, half goblin. You shouldn't scoff at something you don't understand. Back before the spell was cast, ancient Egyptians revered goblins. They even considered some of them to be gods. Hawk goblins, jackal goblins . . ."

The sound of singing came from deeper in the woods. It grew louder until they could make out the words.

> *Gore and guts and blood and bile*
> *Served up on a platter,*
> *Anything you think is vile,*
> *That's what makes us fatter.*

We are hungry all the time
And looking for our meals.
We'll think any food's sublime
That talks or barks or squeals.

"We've got to go," Jak said, taking Tamisin's hand.

"These Gates . . . You said they go either way."

"That's right," said Jak. "When a Gate is open, it works from either direction."

"Then I want to go home," Tamisin said, planting her feet.

Jak glanced back into the forest. "Didn't you hear that? It was a troll-eating song. From the different voices singing it I'd say the troll has at least three heads. We need to go before it learns we're here. I'll take you home as soon as we clear up a few things."

"Like what?" asked Tamisin.

Jak sighed. "I have to take you to my uncle. There are goblins after you and he's the only one I know who can make them leave you alone. If I take you back before that, who knows what they'll do to you. Listen, if you come with me now, I'll answer all of your questions the first chance I get."

"Fine," said Tamisin. "But I consider this a promise."

"You do that," said Jak. "I'll just add it to the long list of promises I've come to regret." Trees at the edge of the path behind them began to shake, and a hairy creature with two long arms and four heads crashed through the underbrush. "Run!" Jak shouted, but Tamisin was already sprinting up the hill.

Tamisin could hear the troll running behind them,

shouting with the voices of four men. The heads seemed to be arguing and the footsteps stopped after the second curve in the path. Even so, Tamisin kept going with Jak keeping pace at her side until the pine trees ended. They slowed to a walk then, but Jak kept them on the path as it wound between jagged boulders until they arrived at a large, flat-topped rock. Four paths converged at the rock, leading away in four different directions. Three of the paths led into various parts of the forest. The fourth ran along an exposed ridge, rising and falling like a dragon's spine. As the day had grown uncomfortably hot, that path was the least appealing. "I've seen that ridge on a map before," he said. "That's the way we should go."

Tamisin's stomach growled.

"What was that?" asked Jak.

"I'm hungry. I didn't eat much at dinner last night, and I didn't eat anything at your party." Tamisin opened her purse, pleased that she'd been able to keep it with her through everything that had happened to them. She rummaged around, taking out a hair clip and a bandanna before showing him a pack of mints, saying, "You wouldn't happen to have food on you, would you? All I have are these breath mints and frankly, I don't care what my breath smells like now."

"Let me see those," said Jak. Taking the mints, he slipped behind a rock. When he came back, the mints had become a handful of lemon cookies.

Tamisin gasped. "How'd you do that?" she asked.

"I have my ways," Jak said, handing the cookies to her.

"So why are goblins after me?" Tamisin asked.

Jak looked away for a moment, then turned back to her and said, "They want you because you're special. You can do things that most other people can't."

"Is it because I'm fey, too? I don't know what I am, but you've seen my ears, and my spreckles," she said, touching the sparkles on her cheek. "I am, aren't I?"

"Yeah," said Jak. "I think you're part fairy."

"A fairy!" she breathed. "That explains a lot! My ears and my wings . . ."

"You have wings?"

Tamisin frowned and turned away, making it clear that she didn't want to talk about it. She hadn't meant to tell him about her wings, at least not until she knew if she could trust him. His revelation that he was half goblin had made her even more reluctant to give him her trust, although it hadn't been as much of a surprise as it might have been. She had known that he was different since the day they met, she just hadn't known *how* different.

They were rounding a boulder when she glanced down the length of the ridge and sighed. "I don't suppose your uncle lives close enough that we'll reach him sometime today?"

"We're nowhere near his den," said Jak. "It'll be a few days before we get there."

"I hope you're about to tell me that there's a hotel on the way."

"There is an inn, but I don't know if it would be a good idea to stay there. No one knows where we are now, but somebody is bound to notice us at an inn. All we need is for the goblins to hear about it and . . ."

"You mean we can't attract attention. I can do that. We just won't talk to anyone. I don't want to sleep out in the open if there are things like trolls around."

"I suppose you're right," said Jak. "I just wish we had another choice."

Soon they were walking above the tops of the tallest trees, but it wasn't long before the forests receded on either side and the ridge descended into a cultivated land of pastures and hedgerows. Although they didn't see any people, they eventually came across a sign that showed a squat building and the words GREEN BEETLE INN with an arrow pointing in the direction they were headed.

"I want to stay there," Tamisin declared.

Chapter 17

Having learned at his Halloween party that Tamisin actually could control lightning, or at least summon it, Jak was even more nervous about escorting her through the fey countryside. As a person who'd proven to have real power, not only was she dangerous to be around, but she was valuable to all kinds of fey. And since those goblins at the party had seen what she could do, word was bound to have spread.

They were passing between two farmers' fields when the first cat streaked through the hay to fall in step just behind them. Another arrived the moment they entered the forest, dropping down from a branch to land lightly on its feet and start off down the path in front of them.

It was nearly dark by then, but at the first curve in the forest Jak saw lights shining through the windows of a squat stone building with an oddly peaked roof. A picture of a large, emerald green beetle decorated a swinging sign above the door.

"Thank goodness," said Tamisin. "I was afraid we wouldn't reach it before nightfall."

"I'm not so sure this is a good idea," said Jak, but he wasn't looking at Tamisin or the inn when he said it. The cats had stopped on the path directly in front of the inn and had turned to face him. With the fur on the arched spines of both cats bristling, their ears pinned back, and their tails lashing, Jak was sure they were trying to tell him something. "Maybe we should just . . ."

The door to the inn flew open behind the cats, revealing a manlike figure in the doorway. Wielding a broom, he darted out of the inn and swatted at the cats, chasing them off into the night. "Won't you come in?" he asked, hustling Jak and Tamisin inside.

It took a moment for Jak's eyes to adjust to the dim light filtering through the smoke from the fireplace, and so he was startled when a goblin appeared out of the shadows to greet them. His mottled scalp was hairless, and he had neither lashes nor eyebrows to soften the appearance of his bulging eyes. He wore dark moleskin pants and an apron over a brown shirt that was rolled up at the elbows, exposing big, muscular arms and little, short-fingered hands. Even before he spoke, the goblin flicked his tongue at each of them, tasting their scent.

"Bob, of the lizard clan, at your service," he said, wiping his hands on his apron. "Welcome to the Green Beetle Inn. I'm the proprietor. How many people in your party?"

"Just two," said Jak.

The innkeeper grunted and turned to survey the room. Although it was early in the evening, it was already crowded. The only unoccupied table was near that of three old women dressed in gray who sat hunched in the corner by the fireplace. Jak could tell why no one had sat at the empty table when he saw that the smoke from the fireplace always blew in its direction. "Come along, sir," said Bob as he threaded his way between the tables.

Jak was starting to follow when Tamisin grabbed his hand and pulled him back. "Is he a goblin?" she whispered into his ear. When Jak nodded, she said, "Maybe you were right and we shouldn't be here. If those other goblins were after me—"

Jak squeezed her hand. "We're here and everyone in this room has already seen us. It wouldn't do any good if we left now. Just let me do the talking and don't let them see that you're afraid. Don't worry, I'll take care of you."

"If you're sure . . ."

With Tamisin still holding his hand, Jak led the way to the table. They had no sooner taken their seats facing the hearth than she began to cough. "Did you want a smoking or nonsmoking table?" asked Bob.

"Nonsmoking, please," Jak said, glancing at Tamisin.

"Ah," Bob said. Taking a pinch of something from his pocket, he sprinkled it on the table. The smoke swirled and changed direction, heading into a six-inch hole in the center of the tabletop. Apparently the smoke had been coming from the table, not from the chimney. "Sorry about that. A fire elemental sat here last, and we all know how much they like smoke. Now, what will it be—a bite of supper or a good stout drink? We're known for our bug juice. I make it fresh myself every day. Our most popular is the green beetle juice, though we also have cricket and wasp."

"Just the supper, please," said Jak.

Tamisin leaned toward the innkeeper. "Could we have a menu?"

Bob looked surprised. "What would we be doing with menus, I'd like to know? I can tell you what I'm serving, seeing as I cooked it. We have vegetable soup and some rattlesnake stew," he said in a singsong voice.

Watercress salad with dressing of dew,
Fricasseed slugs with a green pepper slime,
A nice fresh puree of turtle and lime,
Skunk-cabbage rolls and some Mayapple pie,
Roasted pig snout and rhinoceros thigh,
Hair of the dog and the cat it dragged in,
Fresh rodent custard, with artichoke skin.

Tamisin was looking a little green, so Jak gave his order first. "I'll have the rodent custard."

"Vegetable soup, please," said Tamisin.

The innkeeper smiled, revealing sharply pointed teeth. "Very good. I made a vat of it yesterday. And what would you like to drink? If you don't care for bug juice, we have ale—pale, dark, or sludge. We also have cow's milk, rabbit's milk, and mouse's milk."

"Water, please," Jak said. "For both of us."

"Spring, river, or rain? Clean or dirty?"

"We'd prefer the clean spring water."

"There will be a five percent surcharge for that."

As Bob left to fetch the order, Jak turned to see who else was there. Two other lizard goblins wearing aprons bustled about, serving food and taking orders. A group of leprechauns sat at a long table in the back of the room. Jak was watching them when a voice at the next table said, "It's my turn!"

After glancing at the three women beside them, Jak found it difficult not to stare. With their gray hair, grayish complexions, and long, sad faces, they looked alike enough to be sisters. Two of the women had empty eye sockets, and the tallest had one red-rimmed eye through which she was warily watching the thinnest woman reach toward her face. "Oh, all right!" she said finally. "You can have the eye, but I get the tooth now."

"You can't have the tooth yet. I just got it!" declared the shortest of the three, exposing an old, yellowed tooth in her otherwise empty mouth.

"Then hurry up and finish eating," said the old woman as she plucked the eye out of her socket.

The woman with the tooth grumbled, then took one more bite of the bread she clutched. When she'd swallowed it, she brushed her hand across the table, pushing the crumbs into the hole in the middle. Jak expected the bread to fall through the hole and land on the floor, but it seemed to have disappeared.

Glancing at the tables behind him, he saw that there were holes in all of them. A young man wearing travel-worn clothes and mud-splattered boots dropped a crust into the hole at his table and it too disappeared.

"Here you go, miss," said Bob, setting the soup in front of Tamisin. "And for you, sir . . ."

Jak sniffed the bowl set before him. It smelled deliciously mousy with a touch of rat, just the way he liked it. Picking up his spoon, he poked the green artichoke skin covering the custard, but before he took a taste, he glanced at Tamisin. "How's your soup?" he asked.

Tamisin dipped her spoon in the soup and tasted it. "Really good, actually." She gave his bowl a sideways glance. "A lot of things are different here from what I'm used to back home. I'm just going to have to try to get used to it."

"I know how that goes," said Jak, remembering how hard it had been to adjust to his uncle's household when he'd moved in as a young kit. He'd lived with his parents before that and had never seen either one eat something that was still alive.

They were almost finished when one of the goblin waiters set two enormous glasses filled to the brim with a green liquid on their table. The waiter resembled the innkeeper so much that he might have been a younger version of the goblin. The only thing that wasn't the same was the way he looked at Jak and Tamisin. It made Jak uneasy, and when the waiter said, "Green beetle juice, compliments of the house," curling his lip in the imitation of a smile, Jak became more than a little suspicious.

"No, thank you," said Jak. "The water is fine."

"I insist," said the goblin, his smile broadening until his face looked like it might split in two. "You won't know what you're missing unless you try it."

"We really don't want—," Tamisin began.

The goblin's vertical pupils narrowed and the false smile disappeared. "Around here, it's considered rude to turn down a fine drink like this."

Jak felt the hair on the back of his neck go up. "We weren't trying to be rude—"

"Good. Then drink it," said the waiter. Although he wasn't very tall, he looked threatening as he hovered beside their chairs. He was still standing there when Jak picked up the glass and sniffed. It smelled like mud and rotting straw, although there was a hint of something acidic, too. There was no way either Jak or Tamisin was about to swallow *that*.

"Thank you," Jak said, forcing himself to smile.

The goblin nodded, but he didn't leave until a leprechaun shouted from across the room, "Waiter, another round of drinks for my friends!" Tucking his tray under his arm, the goblin sneered at Jak before leaving.

"We can't drink this," Jak told Tamisin as soon as the waiter was gone.

"Thank goodness!" said Tamisin, looking visibly relieved. "I thought you were going to say that I had to."

"There's something in it besides freshly squeezed beetles," Jak said. "Watch what I do, then do the same. Just make sure that none of the goblins see you doing this."

Moving his bowl so his body blocked it from the goblins' view, Jak poured half the beetle juice into the bowl, then emptied the bowl into the hole in the middle of the table, hoping any goblins who saw would think it was the last of the custard. He kept his eyes on the goblins while Tamisin copied him, and whispered, "Don't pour it all out at once. He'll never believe that you drank the whole thing that fast."

Tamisin did what he'd said and had already set her bowl back down before the waiter returned. "Do you like it?" he asked, pointing at Jak's glass.

"It's very good," he said, trying to look sincere.

The waiter grinned at them again, and was about to say something else when one of the gray women called, "Over here, young goblin." Scowling, the waiter went to her side, looking impatient while she peered into a small gray bag with her one eye. When she'd found what she was looking for, she smiled toothlessly and handed him a piece of amber containing a beetle. "That should cover the room as well," she said.

"Yes, indeed," said the waiter. "With change left over."

"Are you ready, ladies?" she asked her companions. After a great deal of fuss during which they knocked over their chairs and bumped into one another, they held hands as they tromped across the room single file, the one with the eye leading the others to the staircase.

Jak yawned until his jaw made a cracking sound. When Bob stopped at their table and asked if they wanted a room to spend the night, Jak was ready to accept. After a long walk and nearly two days without sleep, he couldn't face going out into the dark and trying to find somewhere to sleep that would be safe.

Jak and Tamisin were following the innkeeper up the stairs when Jak glanced back at the dining room. The goblin waiter stood by the stairs, watching them almost as if he expected something to happen. Whatever it was, Jak was certain that it wasn't anything good.

‹R›

Tamisin was so tired that she had to struggle to keep her eyes open, and she knew Jak was just as tired. When the innkeeper opened the door to a room, she kicked off her shoes, collapsed on the board-hard mattress, and flung her arm across her eyes to block out the light. She heard the goblin leave, but it wasn't until she heard another bed creaking that she realized Jak was still there. He was sitting on a narrow bed on the other side of the tiny room. A wavering candle was the only source of light.

"They said this is all they had," Jak said in response to Tamisin's questioning look. "Do you have any money with you?"

"Yeah," she replied. "But I doubt American money is going to do us any good."

Jak held out his hand. "All I need is one coin."

Tamisin shrugged and reached into her purse. "You can have it, but they aren't going to take it. You saw as well as I did what kind of money they want, and believe me, I don't have any green beetles in amber."

"No," said Jak, "but I do." Where he'd been holding a quarter in his hand just a moment before, he now had a piece of yellow amber and the same kind of beetle that Tamisin had seen in the gray woman's hand.

"That's amazing!" she said, reaching for it. "How did you manage that?"

177

"It's just something I can do," he said.

"Can all goblins do that?"

Jak shrugged. "Goblins can change natural things, but as far as I know I'm the only one who can change stuff like this. You know, things that have already been made into something else."

"What are you doing now?" Tamisin asked when Jak dropped onto his knees beside his bed.

"Looking at these beds. You were right when you said that we couldn't stay outside at night, but we're not a whole lot safer in here. We're going to have to take a few precautions. Most goblins won't give anything away unless it benefits them. There was something in that beetle juice the waiter gave us, either a poison or some kind of drug. If I'm right, we should be having a visitor later tonight, and I'm not going to let us become victims. Yeah, just as I thought . . . These beds are bolted to the floor so we can't move them to block the door. If you look, you'll see that there are no locks on the doors either. This is all laid out to make it easy for them."

"So what do you suggest?" Tamisin asked.

Jak stood up and brushed off his hands, then went to place his palms on the door. "I can change the door like I did that coin, to start with," he said. "I'll make it so no one can open it." He closed his eyes and a moment later there was a shiny metal lock on the door.

"That should be enough, shouldn't it?" asked Tamisin.

"I don't know," Jak said. "Those goblins could have a dozen ways into this room and that was just the most obvious. I think we should sleep under the beds, just in case. It would be harder for them to find us there, and it might give me enough time to do something. It's dirty, but a little bit of dirt is better than a whole lot of dead."

"You mean he wants to kill us?" Tamisin asked, her voice rising to a near squeak.

"That's one of the possibilities," said Jak. "But we're not going to give him the chance. Take that blanket off the bed. You can roll yourself up in it. I want you to crawl under the bed and make yourself comfortable. There's no telling how long we'll have to stay there. And whatever you do, don't come out until I tell you to. I don't know much about lizard goblins, but if we're lucky, they don't see well in the dark."

The cobwebs and layer of dust under the bed made Tamisin glad that she had taken Jak's advice and brought the blanket with her. Using her purse as a pillow, she curled up in the musty-smelling blanket and stared at the underside of the bed above her. She tried not to fall asleep, but after Jak blew out the candle and crawled under the other bed, the darkness was absolute and her eyes kept closing.

"When do you think that goblin will come?" she whispered to Jak.

"Probably as soon as he thinks we're asleep."

"Pretty soon then, huh?"

"As long as we're quiet."

"So what if we stay up all night talking? Do you think they'd leave us alone?"

"I don't think I could," Jak murmured. "I'm practically asleep as it is."

"Yeah," said Tamisin, "me, too."

"Jak," she whispered a minute later. "What will happen to us if we both fall asleep? Jak?" When he didn't answer, she knew he had already drifted off. It was up to her to stay awake, so as long as she could manage it . . . Tamisin yawned and rubbed her eyes. A moment later, she, too, was asleep.

"Snake snot!"

Tamisin's eyes shot open when someone swore only a few inches away. She recognized the voice of the goblin waiter even though he hadn't said much. He couldn't have found her already, could he? Thunder rumbled in the distance. Tamisin held her breath as the goblin scrambled to his feet. Apparently, he couldn't see in the dark, because he still acted as if she was in the bed, not under it.

"What is it, Gob?" whispered a scratchier voice.

"I tripped over somebody's shoes! It's so dark in here I can't see my hand in front of my face! First the door wouldn't open, and now this. I'm glad I oiled the hinges on the trapdoor last week."

"Shut up, Gob. You'll wake them!"

"I put the potion in the juice. We can't wake them. They're sleeping like the dead."

"Or will be soon enough," Gob snickered. "Got your knife?"

"In my hand. Where's the bed?"

"Ow! You jabbed my belly, you brainless flea! Stop waving that knife around and get over here. Take my hand, Hob . . . that's it. The bed's right there. I'll go to this one . . . Ready? Now!"

Tamisin cowered under the bed as the two goblins hacked and slashed at the mattresses. She wondered if Jak was awake or if he was sleeping through it all. Even if the goblins didn't wake him, surely the thunder would. It had gotten closer and a whole lot louder. The two goblins didn't seem to hear it though, because they kept stabbing the beds as if nothing else in the world mattered. When they finally stopped, they were both panting from exertion. Tamisin was afraid to think about what would come next.

"That should do it," said Gob. "They'll have more holes in them now than Granny Nutshell's cheese. We'll have the money come morning. Let me see if this one . . . wait! Nobody's here!"

"Of course somebody's there. We just stabbed them, didn't we? Wait a minute! This one's empty, too!"

Tamisin could hear the goblin beside her fumbling with the bedding, trying to find her blood-soaked body. It wouldn't be long before they started looking somewhere else—like under the bed.

Suddenly the goblin on the other side of the room crashed to the floor. "Hey!" he shouted. "Why did you trip me?"

"What are you talking about?" said the one standing over Tamisin's bed. "I didn't . . . Ow! My nose! What's the big idea!"

"I didn't touch you, you big baby! What makes you think . . ."

Tamisin heard the thud of a blow landing. "That hurt!" squealed a goblin. "Don't think you're getting away with that, you slippery-tongued . . ."

"Why you—!"

Tamisin lay under the bed, not sure what to think. It sounded as if the two goblins were fighting, but she couldn't imagine why they would be unless . . . It occurred to her that Jak might have done something. He'd talked about luck and whether or not the goblins could see in the dark. If he got the two of them fighting with each other . . .

Voices outside the room were shouting, "What's going on in there?" "We're trying to get some sleep!" "Quit making that racket!"

The door flew open and candlelight from the hall lit the room. Tamisin saw Jak step behind the now-open door.

The hallway was full of the inn's patrons, but it was one of the gray ladies who stomped into the room. She was still poking her eye in place when she shouted, "Stop it this instant, you two!" in a voice that reminded Tamisin of a gym teacher she'd once hated. The goblins drew apart, scowling furiously at each other. Neither one seemed to notice Jak.

"Bob!" the gray woman shouted into the hallway. "Come see what your nephews have done."

"Is it safe to come out now?" Tamisin asked from under the bed.

"Sure," said Jak. Seeing him standing there for the first time, the two goblins looked confused.

"What's going on in here?" asked Bob, forcing his way into the room. When he spotted the ruined mattresses, he looked almost expectant, but then disappointment set in and finally anger. It struck Tamisin that he had known about the attack and had thought to find them dead in their beds. If so many of his other guests hadn't been standing there, she thought he might still have done something awful to her and Jak. As it was he didn't dare touch them now, so he began shouting at the two younger lizard goblins.

"Gobbledygook, Hobnob, what do you two think you're doing?" roared Bob.

The waiters turned with a start, their mouths gaping in surprise.

"Uncle Thingamabob! We were just—"

"We didn't mean—"

The innkeeper's face was bright red. "Were you trying to kill a guest?" he said. "How will we get repeat customers if you kill them on their first stay? And what about the mattresses? I paid good money for them! The cost of replacing those is coming out of your wages."

"We're sorry, Uncle Bob!" croaked his nephews.

Bob was still scolding the two younger goblins when the gray woman turned to Tamisin and said, "Are you all right, my dear? From the look of things, I'd say you've had a dreadful experience. Why don't you come with me so you can freshen up?"

"That's very kind of you," said Tamisin, trying not to

look at the woman's gaping eye socket. "Can my friend Jak come, too?"

"That's okay, Tam. You go ahead. I want to make sure that we get another room." He gave the innkeeper a look. The goblin opened his mouth to protest until he saw the faces of the other guests.

"I'll take care of it," Bob said.

The three gray women were very gracious to Tamisin. They let her use the pitcher of water they'd paid to have brought to their room, claiming that she needed it more than they did. While Tamisin washed the grime from her face and hands and combed the cobwebs from her hair, the old ladies sat on their beds facing her as if all three could see what she was doing. When Tamisin turned to thank them, the woman with the eye said, "You're quite welcome, my dear. If there's ever anything else we can do to help . . ."

"Tamisin, are you ready?" Jak said from the open doorway. "Bob found us another room."

"I thought they didn't have any others," said Tamisin, following him into the hall. She was closing the door when she saw that the three women were sitting with their heads together, whispering. When she thanked them and waved good-bye, the one with the eye waved back, giving her a wide, empty-mouthed smile.

Jak took her hand in his. "It's amazing how much a story can change when you have witnesses."

Their new room couldn't have been more different from the first. A shiny lantern glowed on a table between two comfortable beds. There was a window with curtains and, just as Jak had been promised, a real lock on the door that worked from the inside. Tamisin groaned as she lay down on the soft mattress. "This is so much better," she said. "Don't you think so, Jak? Jak?" She turned her head to look at her companion, but he was already asleep.

Tamisin pulled the blanket up to her chin and snuggled down under the covers. She'd been wary of Jak almost since she met him, but he had always been nice to her and had gone out of his way to protect her from the nastier goblins, first at his party and then that very night at the inn. It was foolish to distrust him just because he was half goblin. Having seen how well he could fight and how protective he was of her, Tamisin realized that she felt safe when she was around him. It was a nice thought, especially when she was drifting off to sleep.

When they went downstairs to pay their bill the next morning, some of the guests who had been there the night before still lingered in the taproom. The three gray women were seated at the table closest to the door. Everyone grew quiet when Tamisin walked into the room, but when she turned to stand beside Jak she could hear them start talking again in not-quite-whispers.

"She looks just like her."

"I told you so!"

"I seen her once when I was a girl. It can't be her, though. What would she be doin' in a place like this?"

Tamisin was wondering who they were talking about when a familiar masked figure walked through the door.

"Tobi, what are you doing here?" Jak asked.

The little goblin looked relieved to see them, but all he said was, "I thought ya might like some company on the road, seein' ya've got a long way to travel."

"We need to go." Jak cast a nervous glance at the people seated at the tables, who had all stopped talking and were obviously trying to listen in on his conversation. "Come on, Tamisin," Jak said, hustling her past Tobi.

The cats were outside, waiting under an old oak. They stood and stretched, then fell into line behind Jak and Tamisin as they set off down the path. "We don't want everyone knowing where we are, remember?" Jak said, keeping his voice low. "We were trying to avoid attracting attention, not wave a flag and say, 'Look at us!' After last night everyone who was at the inn will be talking about what happened. Soon everyone will know that we stayed at the Green Beetle. And now, with Tobi showing up and announcing where we were headed . . ."

"But he didn't," Tamisin began.

"He was about to," Jak said, scowling.

"Hey, you two! Wait for me!" Tobi was running down the path, waving his tail behind him. "Ya left so fast," Tobi panted, "that I couldn't keep up. Ya always were faster than a griffin late fer dinner, Jak. Back at school when we was runnin' races . . . Lookie there! Ya got cats followin' ya. I know they liked ya on the other side, but I didn't expect to see 'em here."

"You were in school together?" asked Tamisin.

Tobi nodded. "Sure. Jak and me been best buds since we was young 'uns. Ya mean ta say he never told ya bout good ole Tobi?"

"No, he never did." Tamisin gave Jak a curious look, then smiled at the raccoon goblin. "But then, I never told him about you either. Like how you followed me every day for weeks."

Tobi grimaced. "Ya knew 'bout that? I could-a sworn . . ."

Tamisin's smile grew. "And how much you like big dogs in fenced-in yards. Now, Jak," she said, turning to face him, "I want to know: who is this 'she' those people were talking about back there?"

Chapter 18

Jak shook his head. "I heard them talking, too, but I have no idea who 'she' is."

Tamisin turned to the little masked goblin. "The people back at the inn said that I looked like someone. Do you have any idea who it might be?"

Tobi looked away as if he couldn't meet her eyes. "Me? I ain't got no idea, thought, opinion. Maybe it was a friend of theirs?"

"Tobi," said Jak. "What do you know that you're not telling us? You're talking in threes, and you do that only when you're agitated."

"I don't know anything, less than nothing, no idea!" said Tobi.

"Really?" said Jak. "Why do I find that so hard to believe? Well then, tell us something you do know. Have you heard anything more about that reward?"

"I still don't know who offered it, if that's what ya mean," said Tobi. "The reward itself is the usual—twelve pieces of fairy gold for delivering the girl, dead or alive. Did I forget to mention that last part?"

"Yeah, you did," Jak said. "But it explains what happened last night. The innkeeper's nephews tried to kill us."

"And I heard them mention money," Tamisin added.

"What?" squeaked Tobi. "They can't . . . They shouldn't . . . No one can . . ." The little goblin's tail twitched and his ears flicked back and forth. "I knew there were goblins lookin' for her, but I never thought . . ." Squaring his shoulders, he looked up at his friend. "Ya can't go to yer uncle's, Jak. It wouldn't be safe, secure, out of harm's way. Ya gotta take her to the fairy queen. She's the only one who could protect the girl."

"Titania? Why her?" asked Jak.

"Because no one will try to hurt a fairy while she's under the queen's protection."

"My uncle . . ."

"Doesn't command all the goblins or any of the rest of the fey. It has to be Titania! Look at it this way, Jak. If ya take her to yer uncle, ya'll be drawin' a whole lot of trouble straight to his doorstep. The fairy queen can handle it. Can yer family?"

"I don't want to cause your family any problems," said Tamisin.

Jak glanced from one earnest face to the other. He had promised his uncle that he'd bring her and had been hoping to make him proud. If he didn't take her now, his uncle would think he was a failure, or even worse, a traitor.

However, if he did take her to Targin, he could be endangering the very person he was trying to help. Somehow Tamisin's safety had become a lot more important than his pride, so Jak straightened his shoulders and nodded. "To Titania, then. It makes more sense that we'd go there anyway. Nihlo's up to something and he already knows we were going to his father's den. He'd probably be waiting for us when we got there."

"Good thinkin', Jak!" exclaimed Tobi. "This time of year Titania'll be in the Old Forest, gettin' ready for the midsummer's dance."

"Which way is that?" asked Tamisin.

"Through the woods," Jak said. "We'll have to go around the Sograssy Sea. But before we go any farther, I want to make sure no one's following us. I wouldn't put it past Bob and his nephews to want to finish what they started."

"I'll go with you," Tamisin said.

"No," said Jak. "You won't. I want you and Tobi to hide somewhere off the path where no one could see you. Over here looks good." Jak began following a deer trail back into the woods, then left the trail and picked his way through the underbrush, circling around so their tracks wouldn't be easy to find. He stopped when he found a small clearing, and gestured to the ground. "Have a seat right here. I'll be back for you as soon as I can. Tobi, you keep an eye on her. I'm counting on you."

"If you're gone too long, I'm going to come looking for you," Tamisin warned.

"Me, too," piped up Tobi.

"Fair enough," said Jak and he disappeared into the underbrush along with one of the cats.

⚓

Tamisin could still hear Jak making his way back to the path when Tobi started eyeing the closest tree. "Ya'll have ta 'scuse me fer a coupla minutes. I got some business ta see to."

"But Jak said you should stay here with me," said Tamisin.

"I won't be long," he replied. "Ya just hunker down and don't move. I'll be back before ya know it."

"All right, just . . . ," Tamisin began, but he was gone.

Tamisin's stomach rumbled. Jak had made them skip breakfast in his hurry to leave the inn, so after finding a mossy patch without too many anthills, she sat cross-legged on the ground and opened her purse to take out a lemon cookie that had once been a breath mint. She was wondering how much longer Jak would be gone when the leaves of the undergrowth rustled. The cat that had stayed with her stood up and sniffed the air. Whatever the cat smelled didn't leave her too concerned, because she lay down and rested her head on her paws. Tamisin decided that Jak must be coming back already and was about to call out to him when a huge white horselike head bearing a long silver horn parted the leaves and a unicorn stepped into the clearing.

Tamisin had seen pictures of unicorns, of course, but most of the artists who had drawn them had made them

191

look delicate. This unicorn was sleek and beautiful, but there wasn't anything delicate about him. Except for the horn, he looked like a white racehorse, but was bigger than any horse she'd ever seen. He snorted when he saw her, and his brown eyes flashed almost crimson. His mane was silver streaked with gold, and it shed sparks when he shook it. He took a step toward Tamisin, then pawed the ground as if not sure what to do.

Tamisin tried to remember the magazine articles she'd read about how to act when encountering wild animals. Should she run to the closest tree and climb it? Should she jump up and shout, trying to make herself look big and fierce? Maybe she should lie down and play dead, hoping the unicorn would sniff her and walk away. She sat motionless, unable to make up her mind.

The unicorn lowered his head and approached Tamisin, one slow step at a time, until he stood towering above her. She was about to jump to her feet when he knelt so that his brown eyes became almost liquid gazing into hers. Sighing, he lay down and rested his heavy head on her lap.

Tamisin wasn't sure if she should be honored or frightened. She decided not to move. The creature's horn was sharp and could easily swing around to skewer her. The last thing she wanted to do was make him angry. Maybe Tobi would know what to do when he came back. And where was he anyway? He'd already been gone longer than a few minutes.

The unicorn looked up at Tamisin's face and snuffled. He was magnificent with his gleaming mane, his velvet hide, and his glittering silver horn that spiraled from his well-formed brow. She couldn't resist touching his neck ever so gently. He snorted, his nostrils flaring, but his head stayed on her lap. When she brushed his mane from his eyes, he sighed and blinked. Her fingers wandered to the base of his horn. He closed his eyes and she could feel him relax, his head becoming even heavier than before. Tamisin idly scratched his brow, and he seemed to enjoy it, shifting his head so her fingers stayed by his silver horn. It reminded her of the way her cat, Skipper, liked to have her head scratched in a certain way.

Tamisin could have sat there for hours if her legs hadn't started to go numb. Trying to shift her weight didn't work since the unicorn was too heavy to budge. She was wondering how long she'd have to sit like that when Jak stepped out of the underbrush with the cat on his heels.

He scowled at the unicorn. "Who the heck is that?"

"Shh!" said Tamisin. "He's a unicorn. Be quiet or you'll startle him."

"We'll see about that." Jak crossed the clearing in three steps and bent down so his mouth was near the animal's twitching ear. "Hey, buddy!" he shouted. "What do you think you're doing?"

The unicorn opened his eyes and looked up at Jak. "Go away," he said in a deep voice. "This is my maiden. You have to find your own."

Tamisin was startled. "You can talk! Why didn't you say anything before?"

The unicorn gazed up at her with adoration in his

193

eyes. "Words aren't important when you have an under-standing like ours."

"Understanding? I don't even know you," she said.

Jak looked disgusted. "Unicorns spout the worst kind of drivel. Get up, you old fool," he said to the creature, whose head still rested on Tamisin's lap. "She's not like most maidens. She's . . . Oh, forget it. We don't have time for this. Where's Tobi? I told him to stay here with you."

"I don't know," said Tamisin. "He said he'd be gone for just a few minutes, but he hasn't come back yet. I was beginning to get worried."

The unicorn raised his head and opened his other eye. "Of course she's not like most maidens. I wouldn't be here if she were. Do you know how hard it is to find a maiden who's pure of heart? I'm keeping her, no matter what you say."

"You can't. She's in danger here and I have to take her away. Now get your head off her lap so we can go."

"Oh, all right." The unicorn shook his head, then heaved himself to his feet. Tamisin brushed the sparks from his mane off her shirt, surprised that they were cool to the touch. "It isn't fair," said the unicorn. "All the pure maidens are already taken! I just wanted her to be my friend."

Jak gave Tamisin a hand up. "I know about you uni-corns and your *friends*. You'll want to monopolize all her time so she'll forget about everyone else. Forget it. You're just going to have to keep looking for a new friend. And so is Tobi," Jak said, glancing at the trees. "We're not waiting."

Although they started walking, the unicorn wasn't ready to give up. Every time Tamisin glanced back, he was there, trailing behind them like a dog hoping for scraps. The cats ignored him, more interested in the path ahead, but finally Jak had had enough. Turning on his heel, he fixed the unicorn with an angry glare and said, "Stop following us. Tamisin and I don't want to draw attention to ourselves and you're making that impossible."

The unicorn stopped. "Tamisin," he breathed softly. "What a beautiful name. If anyone is interested, my name is Silver Dancer, but everyone calls me Herbert. Call me if you ever need me, Tamisin, and I'll come running."

Tamisin glanced back once more, just before the path curved again. The poor beast was standing where they'd left him, watching her with mournful eyes. "In the stories I read, unicorns wouldn't approach anyone except a maiden, but I never did learn why."

"It's because of their horns. They say that the base of their horns is particularly itchy. If they try to scratch it themselves, they get their horns caught in branches or wedged somewhere they can't escape. Unicorns are suspicious creatures. The only ones they trust near their horns are maidens who are pure of heart. Once they find one they like, they never stop pestering her. If I hadn't come along, he'd have had you scratching his head for the rest of the day."

"Aren't their horns supposed to have some magical properties? Aside from being so beautiful, I mean."

Jak snorted. "Don't ever let a unicorn hear you say

that. They're vain enough as it is. As to the magic, yes, it's true. A unicorn can purify poisoned water by dipping his horn in it. A cup made from the horn will also nullify any poison in a drink, which is why the beasts are hunted every fall."

"Do you suppose he'd let me ride him?" she said, looking back over her shoulder. "If we really have that far to walk . . ."

"He might, but only if he could claim you as his maiden, and we don't have time to argue with him again."

The cats looked up, staring into the branches overhead.

"Speakin' of huntin'," said Tobi as he dropped from the tree directly into their path. "Did ya see any sign that we're bein' followed? 'Cuz I sure didn't."

Jak glared at the little raccoon goblin. "Where have you been? I told you to stay with Tamisin."

Tobi shrugged. "I was hungry. Ya can't be too mad at me. I got ya these." Holding out his hand, the little goblin opened it to reveal a few slightly smushed berries, the same color as the stains smearing his fur.

"No thanks," Tamisin said, grimacing.

It was obvious that Jak was furious. "You're so irresponsible, Tobi! Why are you even with us if we can't count on you?"

"Ya can count on me, Jak. Ya know I've always been there fer ya. Why are ya so bloomin' mad? I just . . . Oh, I get it. Yer riled because-a her, ain't ya? I think ya got a thing fer Tamisin. Ya ain't in love with her, are ya, Jak?"

"You talk too much, Tobi. Next time I tell you to do something, just do it."

"Maybe if ya ask me instead-a tellin' me Jak, I'd be more inclined ta listen. Here's the berries I brought ya. Try 'em. They'll make ya feel better."

Jak took the berries from Tobi's hand, but he still looked angry.

"So was anyone following us?" Tamisin asked.

"Not so far," said Jak, "which doesn't mean that they won't be coming after us soon. How did you find us in the first place, Tobi? The lightning must have messed up the Gate in my backyard, because we didn't end up anywhere near where I thought we would. How did you know where to look?"

Tobi glanced up from licking berry juice off his fingers. "I waited till Bert chased Nihlo and his buddies off and all the ruckus died down. Then I came through the Gate, same as you. Course it was a while later, seein' as how time passes a whole lot faster there than it does here. Say, did ya eat all those berries yet?"

Chapter 19

Jak and Tobi agreed to avoid the path, so they started downhill, passing a rocky outcropping and thick stands of oaks, poplars, and maples. Ferns dusted their legs as they walked and fairies peeped at them from the hoods of jack-in-the-pulpits.

"This is lovely," said Tamisin, turning to look around.

Jak glanced back, half expecting to see someone behind them, but the only creatures following in their trail were the cats, their ears swiveling as they listened to the sounds of the forest. "That all depends on how you look at it," he grumbled. "There are too many trees for goblins to hide behind."

Tamisin gave him a quizzical look. "Will it be better by the sea?"

"No, we'll be out in the open there," Jak said, sounding surly even to himself.

It was midafternoon when they reached the Sograssy Sea. Instead of water it was a sea of waving grass, knee-high at the edge, but higher than their heads farther out.

Although Jak had known about the grass, and that the sea was big, he didn't know how enormous it really was or that it was impossible to see from one side to the other.

Tamisin stepped to the very edge, which was closer than Jak cared to go. "Is the water on the other side of the grass? How long will it take to get across?"

The cats darted to where Tamisin stood and began to circle her, pushing against her legs so that she staggered away from the grass. Jak reached out and pulled her back, too.

"That grass is the sea," said Tobi. "Contrary-like to yer misconception, nobody crosses the Sograssy Sea. You gotta go 'round it."

Tamisin shaded her eyes with her hand and gazed out across the sea. "But wouldn't it be faster to go across? I mean a straight line is . . ."

". . . the shortest distance between two points," Jak replied. "Yeah, I went to school, too. It would be, but grass isn't the only thing in the Sograssy Sea. That's where—"

"Well, well, well! Look what we have here! If it isn't a couple of humans and a runty little goblin all alone in this big, bad world."

The two cats turned and hissed, their eyes narrowed and glaring.

Nihlo had found them. Jak spun around at his cousin's first word, hiding Tamisin behind him. He'd recognized Nihlo's voice, but he was surprised to see his cousin wielding a knife as other goblins emerged from the woods. The cats had moved closer together and now stood between Tamisin and Nihlo.

"I see ya brought yer buddies, Nihlo," Tobi said. "I didn't know ya *had* any friends. Whaddya do when yer together, see who's better at pullin' legs off bugs?"

"Tobi!" Jak reached out and clamped a hand over his little friend's mouth.

Nihlo made a show of licking his lips when he looked at Tobi. "Keep your pet quiet, Jak, or I'll carve him up and eat him for dinner."

The other goblins had gathered behind Nihlo, who seemed even more sure of himself with them there. "Where are you going, Jak? This isn't the way to my father's den. Or have you decided to betray his trust and get the reward for yourself?"

"I would never turn on my family for money," said Jak.

Nihlo smiled. "Don't sound so self-righteous. Have you told the girl the real reason you wanted to meet her? He was sent to kidnap you," he said, turning to Tamisin, "and bring you back to my father."

Jak could hear Tamisin's sudden indrawn breath behind him. He wanted to explain it all to her, but he didn't dare take his eyes off Nihlo.

"Is that true, Jak?" she asked with a catch in her voice. "I thought we were friends. I thought you were trying to help me." Lightning streaked the sky in the distance, and the goblins behind Nihlo glanced up.

"We were," said Jak. "I mean, we are. It's a long story and—"

"Just give me the girl, Jak, and I'll let you go. You know you can't beat me in a fair fight."

Jak narrowed his eyes at his cousin. "When have you ever fought in a fair fight?"

"I can't trust either of you, can I, Jak?" Tamisin asked. "You wanted to kidnap me and he wants to take me from you."

"He isn't taking you anywhere," Jak whispered back. Even if his cousin did intend to take her to Targin, Jak wasn't about to let him get near her.

Nihlo waved the knife in Jak's direction. "Get out of the way, Jak-O-MAN. Give the girl to me and I'll let you go."

Jak was surprised by how angry the thought of seeing Tamisin in Nihlo's hands made him feel. He was about to reassure her when he turned his head and saw her edging toward the grass. "Tamisin, no!" he shouted.

"I have to, Jak. I can't trust either of you." And she bolted into the sea.

Tails twitching, the cats yowled in protest as she ran farther into the grass, but neither of them followed her. Jak took his hand off Tobi's mouth and for a moment considered going after Tamisin.

"She shouldn't have run off like that," said Nihlo. "Call her back."

Tobi spat at the ground and rubbed his mouth with the back of his hand. "Now that'd be plumb stupid," he said. "He ain't about ta call her back just so's ya can wave yer knife in her face! Jak's a whole lot smarter'n that. Heck, he's a whole lot smarter than all of ya put together!"

"Shut up, Tobi," grunted Nihlo. "Go after her, you!" he told a boar goblin who had come with him. "She's getting away."

The goblin shook his head. "I'm not going in there, and there's nothing you can do to make me."

"You're going," said Nihlo, "unless one of your friends would like to volunteer."

The other goblins that had come with him glanced at each other and melted into the forest.

"Uh, uh," said the remaining goblin. "She's not paying me enough to—"

"Either you go in after the girl, or I'll take care of you right now. And if you run off like your cockroach friends, I'll hunt you down and serve you at the next clan feast."

The boar goblin looked frightened, but he clenched his jaw and took a step toward the sea. "You owe me for this," he said. "And my whole clan will come after you if anything happens to me!"

"Why don't you go in yourself, Nihlo?" asked Jak.

"Why don't you shut up, Jak?" the goblin said, glaring at his cousin.

"I think I see her!" shouted the boar goblin as he took off running.

While Nihlo argued with the boar goblin, Jak had taken off his watch behind his back and was changing it into a knife, longer and sharper than Nihlo's. Jak had never used a knife in a fight before, but he was sure he could do some damage with it if he had to. He would have felt more confident if he hadn't caught sight of the film of blue liquid tinting Nihlo's blade. Whatever it was, it couldn't be good.

The knife was forming in his hands when he asked Nihlo a question that had been bothering him. "Who are you and your friend working for, Nihlo? Who is this 'she' who's paying you? *She* must be giving you a lot of money for you to turn against your father like this."

"She's giving me respect, Jak-O-MAN, something you wouldn't understand. Unlike my father, who doesn't mind lowering himself by dealing with people like you, she knows the value of a true goblin. When she has the girl, she'll see that some real changes are made, not the half measures that my father's working toward."

"Who is this wonderful person, Nihlo? Is it anyone I know?"

"I'm not wasting any more of my breath talking to you. Halflings are too stupid to understand what's going on."

Tobi had scuttled behind Jak the moment he'd let him go. He must have just noticed what Jak held in his hands, because he suddenly exclaimed, "There's my boy, Jak! Ya got a knife! It's bigger than yers, ya foul-breathed slime licker," he shouted at Nihlo.

"I'm glad to hear it," growled the cat goblin. "I'd hate to kill an unarmed halfling."

"I don't know why," said Jak. "You've tried often enough."

Sneering, Nihlo feinted with his knife. "If I had wanted to kill you, Jak, I would have. I was just waiting until the timing was better—like now!"

Jak jumped out of his cousin's reach and tightened his

grip on his knife. He'd known for a long while that he was going to have to face Nihlo again, only this time he didn't intend to run.

⚘

Tamisin was afraid to run into the tallest grass until she heard one of the goblins shout, "I think I see her!" Glancing back, she saw the boar goblin enter the sea, so she turned and ran into the taller, more concealing growth, parting the blades with her outstretched arms. Her heart thudding in her chest, she kept expecting the goblin to grab her from behind. The grass flew by in a blur, then suddenly she was stumbling over an enormous bronze- and copper-colored tube that twitched beneath her feet.

A woman's head rose above the grass so that Tamisin had to look up to see her. She was beautiful, with flowing dark hair that gleamed blue-black in the sunlight. Her neck was long and slender; her skin was pale with just a hint of pink on her cheeks. The grass that brushed her bare shoulders hid her from the collarbone down.

The woman looked startled, as if Tamisin was the apparition. "What are you doing here?" she said in a whispery kind of voice.

"Running from goblins. I was told that no one comes into the sea, but at least one of them is following me. Why are you here? Are you running from something, too?"

"I wath taking a nap," said the woman, patting her mouth delicately with well-manicured fingertips. "And

204

jutht what do you mean, nobody cometh into the thea? Who told you that? Hath thomeone been thpreading rumorth about me again?" A soft shushing sound came from the depths of the grass.

"I'm sorry I woke you. It's just, well, do you have somewhere I can hide?"

"You want me to hide you? That'th very funny. Nobody exthept my relativeth ever athked for my help before. Let me thee if anyone ith thtill chathing you. No, no one ith there. But if thomeone chathed you here on purpothe to dithturb my nap, I'll thee that that foul . . ." The woman rose up until her head towered over Tamisin's. Her upper body was wrapped in a silky fabric that didn't cover much. She didn't need clothes below her waist, because the rest of her body thickened into that of a snake.

Tamisin gasped and started to back away, but the woman was too busy working herself into a rage to notice. "Jutht wait until I get my fangth in . . ."

Tamisin might have escaped if she hadn't tripped and landed on something cushiony. Putting her hands on the ground, she tried to push herself up, then snatched them back when she felt smooth, dry scales. She was sitting on the snake woman's enormous bronze and copper coils with her legs draped over their sides. The end of the woman's tail vibrated above Tamisin's head, shaking a cluster of bead-shaped rattles that made the shushing sound she'd heard.

The woman swung her head around and glanced down at Tamisin. "What *are* you doing?" she asked.

"I'm sorry! I . . ."

Three bright lights no bigger than Tamisin's little finger darted past. She cringed when the snake woman opened her mouth and hissed. Long white fangs curved from her upper jaw, and Tamisin could have sworn she saw drops of venom on their tips. In a flash, the snake woman lunged at the lights, dumping Tamisin out of her coils onto the ground. The little lights bumped into one another, then fled over the undulating grass.

"Thtupid fairieth," said the woman, turning back to Tamisin. "They're thuch a nuithance. They probably think I'm going to eat you."

"You wouldn't, would you?" Tamisin said with a mouth so dry that the words came out in a whisper.

"Of courthe not!" said the snake woman, her eyes flaring with indignation. "I don't do that kind of thing anymore. I admit that I uthed to enjoy frightening people and I relithed the occathional thpirited thnack, but a girl geth lonely after a couple of centurieth. Now I jutht want to have thomeone to talk to, thomeone who won't run off when he theeth me. I've been lonely for motht of my life and I'm tired of it." The snake woman glided toward Tamisin, lowering her head until they were the same height. "You aren't afraid of me, are you?"

"You are a little scary," Tamisin admitted as she struggled to her feet.

The woman's eyes filled with tears. "I don't mean to be," she said. "I can't help being different. I wath born thith way."

Tamisin couldn't help but feel sorry for her. While

206

tears trickled down the snake woman's cheeks, Tamisin reached into her purse for a tissue, but all she could find was a pink bandanna. "Here," she said, offering it to the woman. "You can dry your eyes with this."

"You're giving thith to me?" she asked, appearing incredulous.

Tamisin nodded since she didn't really want it back.

The woman sniffed and patted her eyes. "No one'th ever given me a gift of her own free will before! Thank you."

Tamisin stepped back when the woman looked as if she wanted to give her a hug. "You know, you wouldn't be so scary if you didn't hiss at people or show your fangs."

"Oh," the woman said, looking surprised. "I hadn't thought of that." Pulling her lips over her teeth, she leaned toward Tamisin and said, "Ith thith better?"

The tips of her fangs still showed. Tamisin shook her head. "Not really," she said, and she began to back away.

The woman followed, her head only a few feet above Tamisin's. "Pleathe help me," she said as a big tear trickled down the side of her nose. "I really want to know what to do."

"You're still hissing," Tamisin replied. "Maybe a good speech therapist could help." The rattle vibrated again, making her jump. "And don't shake your rattle. That's really scary."

"Oh, right," said the woman, but her rattle continued to shake. Muttering to herself, she grabbed the end of her tail with both hands. "It'th a nervouth habit."

"Habits are made to be broken," said Tamisin. "I'm sure you can if you try."

Peering into the grass around her, Tamisin tried to decide what to do. In a world where everything was strange and often threatening, she was beginning to think that Jak wasn't so bad. He was familiar and had never hurt her, even if he had been sent to kidnap her. She knew that she didn't want to go anywhere with the goblin that Tobi had called Nihlo, nor could she stay in the sea with the snake woman. And Jak had promised to take Tamisin to the fairy queen, even though it meant going against his uncle's wishes.

"I'm sorry, but I have to go now," she told the snake woman. "I need to find my friend."

"I can go with you, if you'd like." The snake woman sounded as eager as a small child who's offered a special treat. "No goblinth will bother you if I'm around."

"I'm not sure which way to go from here," Tamisin said.

"No problem," said the woman, rising up on her tail. "I can thee your trail. And look, that mutht be your friend at the edge of the grath. He'th lying down. Maybe he'th taking a nap."

The woman slithered beside Tamisin as they forced their way through the grass. Butterflies fluttered past and a swallow skimmed the rustling sea, but suddenly Tamisin was too worried about Jak to notice them. Jak wouldn't be taking a nap; if he was lying down, something must be terribly wrong.

Chapter 20

Jak lay with his feet in the grass, his head pillowed on the root of an old maple. The fight had been brief. He and Nihlo had been parrying with their knives, and his cousin had nicked Jak's arm just above the elbow. A moment later, Jak was sprawled on the ground, as weak as a newborn kitten. The fast-acting poison on Nihlo's blade had left Jak fully conscious, yet feeling as detached as if his emotions belonged to someone else. It also left him unable to do more than blink while Nihlo wondered aloud how long he'd have to wait for the boar goblin to bring Tamisin back. And then the goblin was back, tearing through the grass, whimpering that he'd seen a lamia. A moment later they had fled into the forest, leaving Jak to the mercy of the denizens of the sea.

Then the cats returned, licking his face and brushing against him. He couldn't move when one rubbed his mouth, leaving him with loose fur on his lips and in his nose. And then the cats ran off, too.

The grass swooshed in the sea just past his feet. Someone

was coming. Jak immediately recognized the sound for what it was, having spent many sleepless nights as a child imagining what the lamia's approach would be like. When he heard Tamisin talking as well, he decided that the poison was making him hallucinate. He was sure that if his mind had been clearer, he would have felt guilty for not having told Tamisin about any number of things—the lamias, his mission to get her, and how he had never meant her any harm. He would have felt sad, too, for she was most likely dead by now.

"Jak!" cried his hallucination, sounding exactly like Tamisin.

A few seconds passed while he went cross-eyed, staring at the praying mantis that had come to investigate his nose. Then a strong hand gripped his shoulder and flipped him onto his back. "He'th thtill alive," said a beautiful woman with long dark hair, who, strangely enough, had her lips pulled over her teeth so at first he thought she didn't have any.

"Oh, Jak, I was so frightened. I thought you were dead!" exclaimed Tamisin's voice, and he felt two warm hands cradle his cheeks and turn his head to the side, where, to Jak's great joy, he could actually see her face. He thought she was the loveliest sight he had ever seen, and he would have told her so if only he could get his mouth to work. Somehow, even blinking was getting difficult. In a halfhearted way, Jak wondered how long it would take his eyeballs to dry out if he could no longer blink.

Some not-too-gentle fingers poked Jak's arm. "He'th

been poithoned," said the dark-haired woman. "Thee that blue thtuff? He'll be dead in a few minuteth if we don't do thomething."

Jak watched as Tamisin turned to look at the woman. *She is so beautiful,* he thought and wondered why she was starting to cry.

"Do you have any ideas?" Tamisin asked the woman.

"Don't look at me," the woman replied. "I know how to put poithon in, not take it out."

"You're being so brave, Jak," Tamisin said, turning back to gaze into his eyes and brush the ants from his face. "I was furious when I thought you'd tricked me, but I see now that you would give your life for me. You never meant to hurt me, I'm sure of it. I have to do something to help you. Maybe I can draw the poison out with my lips."

"That'th a terrible idea!" said the woman. "Then you'll both be dead and I won't have any new friendth."

Tamisin's face lit up as she looked at the woman, making Jak happy in a distant sort of way that she no longer looked so sad. "New friends? That's it! I know what we should do! I don't mean to be rude, but would you mind waiting in the sea? I'm going to call someone and I don't want to scare him off."

"Thure," said the woman. "But I'll be right here if you need me."

Tamisin frowned as she waited for the woman to leave. "What was his name?" she murmured. "Oh, yes." Raising her head, she turned to face the forest and called out in a loud, clear voice, "Herbert! I need you!"

"It's about time," said a voice from somewhere behind Jak.

A twig snapped in the forest and Jak thought that Tamisin looked surprised. "You're already here?" she said. "How did you know that I needed you?"

Jak couldn't see the newcomer, but he heard him snort and say, "I've been waiting here for you ever since you left the forest. I knew you'd come back sooner or later. The attraction between us is too strong for you to stay away."

It occurred to Jak that he knew who it was; only a unicorn would talk like that, and they had met one that very day. If he could have moved, Jak would have stood up and put the overdressed horse in its place.

"There's no attraction," Tamisin said. "I need you to—"

"You couldn't get along without me, could you? I must admit, I am a fine specimen of unicorn flesh. My mother always told me, 'Lester'—that's my brother's name, but she never could tell us apart—'Lester,' she'd say, 'you're a fine—'"

"Would you please just listen to me?" said Tamisin. "I need you to help my friend, please. He has poison in him and we have to get it out."

Jak could hear the unicorn coming toward him and suddenly he was there, breathing into his face. "Say, isn't this the goblin boy who was so rude to me?" said Herbert. "I don't want to touch him. Look at his eyes. I think he wants to hurt me."

Tamisin frowned at the unicorn. "Don't be ridiculous.

He can't even move. He's not going to do anything to you. Please, just bend down and touch him with your horn or whatever it is you do. And hurry. He doesn't have much time."

There was a swooshing sound in the sea. "Ith he better yet?" called the woman.

The unicorn gasped and his eyes seemed to glaze over. "Who is that enchanting creature?" he whispered out of the corner of his mouth. "Is she a friend of yours?"

"I guess you could say that," Tamisin said. "I'll introduce you if you'll tap Jak with your horn."

"Yeah, yeah, a light tap," said the unicorn. Sparing Jak only the briefest of glances, he bopped him on the head with his horn before turning back to the woman.

There was a tingling sensation in Jak's arms and legs. His hands and feet felt as if they were on fire. He wondered if this was another part of the hallucination or if he was about to die.

The unicorn was making soulful eyes at the woman when Tamisin asked him, "Are you afraid of snakes?"

"No," he said. "Why do you ask?"

Tamisin grinned. "It doesn't matter. Herbert, I'd like you to meet my friend . . . I'm sorry, I never did get your name."

"Lamia Lou," said the woman, and Jak could hear her slithering out of the grass. Herbert's only reaction was to wuffle his lips and take a step closer.

"Hello, Herbert," Lamia Lou said.

"Hello, gorgeous!" said the unicorn, his brown eyes flashing.

Just before he passed out, Jak decided that he had been hallucinating after all.

*

Jak had come to while Tamisin was telling the lamia that they were trying to reach the fairies' forest by circling the sea. The snake woman had insisted that she would take them across it herself. They'd waited while she bid Herbert, the unicorn, a heartfelt farewell. Jak could barely stand when the lamia offered to let them ride on her snaky tail and Tamisin had to help him climb on, but he felt a lot better when Tamisin climbed on behind him and wrapped her arms around him. She'd told him that she was still mad at him, but he was too fuzzy-headed to worry about it. Nor did he worry about Tobi, who had disappeared during Jak's fight with Nihlo. No matter what happened, Tobi always seemed to reappear, unhurt.

If Jak had felt stronger, he would have found the beginning of their trip across the sea exciting as the grass flashed past and birds shot into the sky at their approach. By the time his strength returned enough that he was able to sit up on his own, he realized that he couldn't see above the grass, and so had no way to judge time or distance. He grew bored even though the snake woman was very good-natured, telling them about the birds flying above them, the creatures that lived in the grass, and, eventually, what she could see of the forest ahead. She didn't stop to let them off until she was within easy walking distance of the Old Forest, but she left as soon as Jak and Tamisin slid off her back.

Now that they'd reached the forest where the fairies lived, Tamisin began to look nervous. "Maybe this isn't such a good idea," she said. "What am I supposed to do—walk in and say, 'Hi, I'm part fairy. I need the queen's protection because I have goblins chasing me'?"

"Something like that," said Jak. "We don't have much choice."

Tamisin shrugged. "I suppose. It's getting late though. It'll be dark in a few hours. Why don't we come back and see her tomorrow?"

"We've come all this way to see her and we're not turning away now. Besides," Jak said, glancing back the way they'd come, "our ride just left."

Although the forest fronted the rippling grass for as far as they could see, there weren't very many places where someone could enter the fairies' domain. The trees grew so close together that they resembled a solid wall of bark and leaves. From where Jak and Tamisin stood, it looked as if there was only one opening.

They waded through the shorter grass that lapped at the shoreline. As they drew closer, they could see that a path led into the forest. They had scarcely set foot on the path when a hideous bearlike monster jumped out from behind a tree and roared at them. It was big and burly and half covered with a dense coat of fur. Its face was so contorted that its eyes were nearly shut. Tamisin screamed and jumped back when the monster gnashed its fangs and flailed at her with its horrible claws, but Jak wasn't as easily intimidated.

"Bruno, is that you?" he asked, peering at the monster.

The monster unscrunched its terrifying face and opened one eye wider, revealing a warm brown color. "Jak?" it said, opening the other eye. Suddenly it looked a lot friendlier. "Hey there! Good to see you're back."

"What *are* you doing here?" asked Jak.

Bruno rubbed one of his bearlike ears and grunted. "I'm a guard now. They offered me the job right after I left the island. Who's your friend?"

"What *are* you doing?" grated a gnome with a white beard and red cheeks as he stepped out from behind a tree. The pair of spectacles dangling from a string tied around his neck bounced against his chest as he walked. Crossing his arms over his potbelly, he planted his feet and glared at Bruno. "You're supposed to scare away intruders, not start a conversation!"

"Sorry, Mr. Leadless," grumbled Bruno. "I'll do better next time."

The little man's face flamed red and a vein bulged in his forehead. "There will be no next time if you don't do better this time! Now try again."

"But Jak here is an old friend of mine and . . ."

"I don't care if he's your great-aunt Peachbottom. Do your job and scare him off!"

"Actually," said Jak, "we're here to see the queen."

"Well, why didn't you say so?" the gnome said. "That makes you *just like everybody else!* Bruno?"

"Sorry, guys. Gotta do my job." The bear goblin drew

himself up to his full height so that he towered over them. Taking a deep breath, he waved his paws in the air, scrunched his face to make it look hideous again, and roared so loudly that Jak's ears hurt.

✿

"What's the meaning of this?" A shirtless man wearing shaggy white pants popped out from behind a tree. Tamisin found herself staring when she realized that he wasn't really a man, but a satyr, just like she'd seen in books. Small horns protruded through his curly hair, and his legs resembled a goat's, angled backward and ending in the same kind of split hooves. A set of pan pipes dangled from a strip of leather tied around his neck.

"It's the goblin's fault," grumbled Leadless. "He wasn't doing his job."

"That may be so, but it's your responsibility to keep out . . ." The satyr's voice trailed off when a swarm of twinkling lights darted out of the forest to flutter around him. They must have said something, because he stopped to listen, then glanced at Tamisin. "Well, I'll be . . . ," he said. Reaching for his pan pipes, he played a short melody. A moment later another tune answered his from somewhere in the forest. "You may pass," the satyr told Tamisin. "But the goblin has to stay here."

"You mean me?" Bruno asked, scratching his head.

"No," said Jak. "He means me."

"Why are you letting her go?" said the gnome. "You know the rules. No unexpected guests without official business may pass unless—"

217

"The girl is expected," said the satyr. "If you'd wear your spectacles, you'd understand why."

"What do my spectacles have to do with anything?" the gnome asked even as he set them on his nose. "The girl is just . . . Oh, my!" he said, and his ruddy cheeks turned even redder.

"But I don't want to go without Jak," protested Tamisin.

"Go ahead," Jak said. "I'll wait right here."

The satyr gestured to Tamisin. "The fairies will take you where you need to go."

"Where is that?" Tamisin asked as the twinkling lights surrounded her.

"To talk to Titania, of course," said the satyr. "Isn't that who you came to see? Now go! Go! We'll watch your goblin!"

Although Tamisin didn't like going into the fairy forest without Jak, the fairies didn't give her time to think about it. Darting from tree to tree, they moved so quickly that she had to run to keep up. At first all she could see of them were bright lights the size of fireflies, but the deeper they led her into the forest, the darker it became and the better she could see the tiny beings. Soon she was able to discern individual clothes and faces. Their wings were still a blur, however, and it hurt her eyes to look at them because they seemed to be the source of the fairies' light.

At first they didn't encounter anyone, but after many twists and turns they saw a water nymph rearranging pond lilies in a small lake. Another turn in the path and

Tamisin saw a woman with brown skin and hair like willow leaves conversing with a birch tree. Then a pale nymph with leafy hair leaned out of the tree and turned to watch her.

Still following the fairies, Tamisin saw one amazing creature after another. She saw goblins who looked like birds and animals cooking food over fires. A woman with pure white skin, fiery red eyes, and a wild halo of white hair was making daisy chains beside an enormous woman with two heads. Fairies as big as humans tended flowers, mended clothes, and collected fallen leaves. Although Tamisin tried not to stare, everyone stared at her as if *she* were something extraordinary.

The farther they went into the forest, the prettier it became. Huge shade trees towered over a profusion of their smaller cousins, which in turn stood guard over such a variety of shrubs and flowers that Tamisin was amazed. Everything that could bloom seemed to be doing so at once, filling the air with a heavy perfume.

Tamisin was rounding an enormous group of rhododendrons covered in purplish-pink blossoms when Tobi, head down and muttering to himself, ran into her. The little goblin stumbled and fell flat on his back. Tamisin reached down to help him, but he brushed off her hand, declaring in an annoyed voice that people should watch where they're going. And then he looked at her face and his jaw dropped. "Tamisin!" he said even as his gaze darted from shrub to path to shrub again, as if looking for somewhere to hide. "Excuse, pardon, forgive me. I didn't mean to run into ya like that."

"Tobi!" said Tamisin. "What are you doing here? Did you come to see the queen?"

"Who? Me? Of course not! Why would the likes of me be visiting the queen, Her Majesty, Titania? No, I was just passing through, going by, in the neighborhood. Nothing to do with the queen. Sorry, I've, uh, got an important engagement, meeting, errand . . . Gotta run!" Tamisin stepped aside as Tobi scurried past, giving her one last furtive glance before disappearing behind the shrubs.

"I wonder what that was all about," Tamisin murmured. "He seemed awfully nervous."

Swooping around her in a brilliant, twinkling mass, the little fairies herded Tamisin into a mossy glade. She was halfway across before she saw the throne. Made of twisted branches still growing and in leaf, the back of the throne rose higher than her head and bore a crown of snow-white blossoms. Goblin and fairy women as well as a group of nymphs were gathered near it, fussing over the fairy standing serenely in their midst. While one brushed her golden hair with a nettle brush, others polished her nails with pink rose petals or held up dresses for her approval. She had turned away to stroke the sleeve of a misty gray dress when Tamisin approached.

"Why did you come back, Tobianthicus?" the fairy queen asked without looking up. "You already gave me your report." It wasn't until a group of Tamisin's fairy escorts broke away, darting toward the queen in an agitated frenzy of twinkling lights, that Titania turned her head. Seeing Tamisin, Titania waved her hand, dismissing her attendants and the tiny fairies.

"Come closer, my dear," the queen said in a voice as soft as a summer breeze and as sweet as the violets growing beneath her feet.

Tamisin approached the throne, drawn by her own curiosity as much as by the queen's command. The fairy queen was the most beautiful person Tamisin had ever seen. Her skin was flawless, her features were delicate and well proportioned, and her hair cascaded down her back in a river of curls. Although she was truly lovely, it wasn't her beauty that made Tamisin stop and stare.

Tamisin had been prepared for a lot of things when she met the fairy queen. She'd expected her to be beautiful, delicate, and otherworldly in ways she couldn't even imagine. Although Titania was all of those things, what Tamisin didn't expect was that looking at the fairy queen was a lot like looking at herself.

Like Tamisin, the queen had hair the color of sunlight and slightly tilted eyes of a brilliant turquoise. Although their noses were equally slim and straight, Tamisin's mouth was fuller, her chin not quite so pointed. The two faces might have been copies of each other, only Tamisin's was more substantial and . . . human.

"What . . . I mean, how . . . ," Tamisin began, pressing her hand to her cheek.

"Tobianthicus was right," Titania said. "The resemblance is remarkable. I couldn't deny who you are even if I'd wanted to. It's odd though. I never expected to see you again, but now that you're here I couldn't be happier. Welcome home, Tamisin, my very own little girl."

"What are you saying?" asked Tamisin. "I admit there is some similarity, but . . ."

"You're my daughter, Tamisin. Flesh of my flesh, blood of my blood. I gave birth to you . . . Who were those people who took you in?"

"The Warners," said Tamisin in a high, thin voice that she barely recognized as her own.

Titania nodded. "That's right. The human lawyer told us but it seems so long ago."

Tamisin wasn't thinking when she replied, "My mother says it seems just like yesterday."

"But I'm your mother!" Titania said, sounding annoyed. "I told you that. The Warners took care of you only because I couldn't. They weren't your real parents. Now that you're here with me I want you to forget all about those other people. Tell me, is there anything you want to know? Anything at all?"

"There's a lot, actually," said Tamisin. "If you were my mother, and I must admit, you look like you must be, why didn't you want me? Why didn't you raise me your-self? Did you give me away or did someone steal me from you? And if they stole me, why didn't you come looking for me?"

"Those weren't at all the kinds of questions that I meant. Don't you want to know about me? I am the fairy queen, after all. Very well then—if anyone is going to ask questions, I should be the first. How did you learn that you were not an ordinary human?"

"It was . . . everything. It was my ears and my spreckles and my dancing and the fairies and the way the goblins kept finding me and then it was my wings and . . ."

"Did you say wings?" said the queen, frowning ever so slightly. "I had no idea. You had no fairy qualities at all when I sent you away. No matter. Apparently your fairy side has come forth more than I anticipated. I sent you to the humans thinking you would fit in with them. I never intended for you to return to me. Weren't you happy there?"

"I was very happy," said Tamisin. "But I've always known I didn't belong, that I was different. I know a lot of girls feel that way, but my differences were bigger than most and a lot more obvious. And now I'd like to ask you a question if I may."

Titania sighed. "What would you like to know?"

"Why did you send me away? Didn't you want me here? Didn't you want me at all?"

"What you mean to say is, didn't I love you? A perfectly reasonable question, considering the circumstances. Yes, I suppose I did, but it was obvious from the start that I couldn't keep you. You were a red, squalling thing, unlike normal fairy babies, who are pink-cheeked and happy from the moment they are born. Yet even so I would have kept you by my side if things had been different. I had conceived you through my husband's trickery, and having you nearby kept me from forgiving him, which I needed to do for the good of our kingdom. We have our quarrels, Oberon and I, but we are strongest when we are together."

"So you sent me away so you could stop fighting?"

"In part, but also to keep you safe. Your father was a human, made to look like a donkey goblin on the night of your conception. I fell in love with him, or thought I did, through magic that was soon reversed. It was many months before I knew that I carried a child, but time passes differently in the human world, and your father had grown old and died by then. You would have gone to him had he still lived."

"That story sounds awfully familiar," said Tamisin.

"I believe a human named Shakespeare once included it in one of his tales. He took great liberty in the retelling, embellishing that which should not have been made public knowledge. I was not pleased, but he was only human and the fey rarely take humans' stories seriously."

"Why should it matter to them?"

"By the time you were born, much had changed in the human world, yet too much had stayed the same here. The king and I had conquered the goblins years before and they have been rebellious ever since. Most goblins abhor humans, which I regret to say is a common feeling among the fey. Should the goblins have learned that I had borne the daughter of a human, they would have seen it as just cause to take up arms against me. Even more so if they had known that the human had resembled a goblin when I knew him; they would have considered it a gross insult. Goblins would have killed you, or worse, had I kept you here. You can see that I sent you away for your own good."

"Yeah . . . ," Tamisin said. "You were thinking only of me." She sat down a few feet from the throne even though she was pretty sure she was supposed to remain standing in the presence of royalty. Somehow she no longer cared. Her real mother had just told her that she'd have been an embarrassment if she'd stayed . . . an inconvenience, a political disaster, a—

"I understand that this is a great deal to comprehend all at once," Titania said.

"Especially since I'm only human," muttered Tamisin.

Titania appeared to be relieved that Tamisin understood. "Indeed," she said, nodding.

"Except I'm not!" said Tamisin. "My life would have been so much easier if I were! You sent me to live with people who couldn't possibly understand what it was like to be part fairy. I had no idea what it meant when I changed and no one else did either. There've been times I was convinced that I was going crazy! Didn't it ever occur to you to care about what my life was like? You made me, then threw me away like I was a shoe that didn't fit!"

"The decision was not as easy as that, I assure you," said the queen.

"Sorry I made your life difficult," Tamisin said. She knew that she shouldn't talk to the queen of the fairies that way, but the woman was also her mother.

"You need not apologize," said Titania, "although your coming here was ill advised. Everything that I was hoping to avoid when I sent you away is coming to fruition. Your return could not have come at a worse time. Oberon and I have quarreled again. Even now he is on the shores of the Southern Sea. In his absence my forces are depleted, as he has taken half our troops with

225

him. There are rumors that the goblins are planning an uprising. I am certain that they know of Oberon's absence and hope to take advantage of it, especially now that you've fueled their anger with your presence."

"But the goblins brought me here!"

Titania reached out to pat her on the head. "Do not blame yourself. You had no way of knowing."

"I wanted to come meet you, but I think it would be best if I went home now. I guess I fit in there better than I do here."

"If only you had realized that sooner," said Titania, "but it is already too late. Many have seen your arrival and word has spread. My scouts tell me that goblins are looking for you even now. Should you leave this forest, you will be captured and used against me. I cannot let that happen. This will be your new home, Tamisin, for better or for worse."

Tamisin's jaw dropped. "You mean I *have* to stay here?"

"Don't say it as if I'm imposing a terrible sentence on you. I'm offering you a home that most girls would give anything for. You'll have the freedom to do whatever you want, provided you stay in the Old Forest. You'll have handmaidens at your beck and call to bring you the best of everything the fey can provide. Unlike in the human world, you'll never have to go to school, and you'll answer to no one but me."

"I can never see my friends or family again?"

"I am your family now, Tamisin. You have no need of anyone else."

Chapter 21

Jak was waiting at the head of the path when Leadless appeared to escort him into the forest. After the gnome left, no one spoke to Jak until Tamisin arrived with her fairy escort, who stayed long enough to circle Jak as if to remind him that he'd better mind his manners.

Jak took one look at Tamisin's expression and said, "Isn't she willing to help? I thought she might let you stay here until she gets it straightened out with the goblins."

"Oh, I'll be staying here, all right. Tell me, Jak, did you know she was my mother? Was I the only one who had no clue that—"

"Titania is your mother? You're joking, right?" When Tamisin shook her head, Jak's legs went weak and he had to sit down on the hollow log behind him. It made sense that the fairy queen was her mother. After all, they both could control the weather. He couldn't believe that he'd been traveling with Titania's daughter. Of course, he'd intended to kidnap Tamisin, and he would have if it hadn't turned into a rescue. He was in so much trouble . . .

"I look just like her," Tamisin was saying when Jak began to pay attention again. "Titania is the one those people were talking about at the inn. Tobi knew about it. He had to. Did you know that he's one of Titania's spies? He had given her his latest report just before I got there. He didn't want me to know about it and was awfully nervous when he saw me. Titania as much as admitted it, although I don't think she intended to."

Jak buried his face in his hands. "I had no idea she was your mother," he said. "I've never been to court before, or seen the queen during any of her travels. How was I supposed to know that you looked like her? And if Tobi's a spy . . . How did he . . . I mean, when—"

"You can ask him yourself when you see him. He's here somewhere."

"That would explain why he always knew so much about what was going on. He came and told me things . . . I thought he'd learned them from my uncle, but if he was really working for Titania . . . And to think that I trusted him!"

"He's still your friend, Jak. I don't think Tobi would do anything to hurt you."

"Not intentionally, maybe," Jak said, rubbing the scar on his forehead where the broken pottery shard had hit him in the Pit.

When he felt Tamisin sit down beside him, Jak glanced at her and said, "Was Titania happy to see you?"

"She said she was, but then she told me how all her problems are my fault."

"Why would she say that?"

"She didn't say it in so many words, but she did say that because I came to see her, the goblins know that she had a half-human child and that they're going to use the knowledge against her. Oberon is away and so is half her army, so she's got a real problem. So do I. She said I can't go home. I have to stay in her forest or the goblins will kill me, or worse, whatever that means."

"Do you want to go home?" asked Jak.

"I don't know what I want, but I do know that I don't want to stay here forever. I fit in here even less than I did in the human world. Have you seen how delicate these fairies are? Even the big ones look fragile. I feel like an elephant in a room full of baby chicks. One false move and I'll crush the lot of them."

"From what I've heard, I'd say that fairies aren't as fragile as they look. And I don't think you're being fair to yourself. You might like it here after a few days. I've seen worse places to live."

"I've been trying to remember why I ever wanted to meet my mother. I guess I expected too much. I was hoping she'd be this wonderful woman who loved me and missed me and couldn't wait to meet me and we'd ask each other all sorts of questions. Did you know that when I met Titania today, the only thing she wanted to know about me was how I'd learned that I was a fairy? I didn't really get to ask her much. I wanted to ask about my father. She did tell me that he's dead."

"I'm sorry to hear that," said Jak.

"She also said that the goblins would be even more stirred up if they knew that my father was a human who'd been made to look like a goblin, as if being human was a horrible thing and even worse if they thought he was mocking the oh-so-wonderful goblins. Then she said that everything she was trying to prevent is going to happen because I came here."

"You've forgotten that the goblins were looking for you even in the human world. I wonder if Titania knows how long they've been after you. Oh, yeah," he said, shaking his head. "Forget I said that. If Tobi knew, I'm sure she did, too."

"Was that goblin telling the truth when he said that you went to the human world to kidnap me?"

"I wouldn't put it that way, exactly," Jak said, choosing his words carefully. "I went to find you and persuade you to come back with me, but I had no idea who you were. All I knew was that you had seen goblins when no one else could and that you were a danger to goblin-kind, especially since you could throw lightning bolts as easily as most humans throw Frisbees."

"That's ridiculous!" said Tamisin.

"I had a feeling you didn't know you had the talent. You never seemed to do it on purpose. Haven't you noticed that there's thunder and lightning whenever you're upset?"

Tamisin shook her head. "No, there isn't!"

"Really?" said Jak. "What about my Halloween party?"

"That was a coincidence! How could lightning have anything to do with me?"

"That's what I wondered," said Jak, "although it makes sense now that we know about your mother. I had no clue, but I wonder if anybody else did. My uncle was awfully interested in you. I couldn't figure out why he would care so much that you could see goblins, or control lightning, for that matter, but if he had already made the connection and figured out who you were . . ."

"What do you suppose he wanted with me?" Tamisin asked.

Jak shrugged. "I don't know. Maybe he wanted to hold you hostage to get something from your mother, or maybe, if your mother was right, he wanted to use you as evidence for what she had done. I don't think he would have hurt you. He's an honorable goblin, not at all like Nihlo."

"Thank you, Jak, for not taking me to your uncle when I asked you to bring me here instead. I've probably gotten you in trouble—"

"A lot less trouble than you would have been in if we'd gone to see him!"

"But you didn't ask for any of this," said Tamisin.

"Neither did you," said Jak.

"Pardon me, but would you mind moving?" A three-headed troll had come up beside them and was pointing at their boulder. "I have to take this to the ring for extra seating. The older fairies like to sit down after the first dance or two."

Tamisin sighed and gave Jak a tremulous smile before

telling the troll, "We'll get out of your way in just a second." Turning back to Jak, she added, "I think we should look around. I want to see more of my new home, and I want you to go with me."

꩜

They explored the forest after that, watching the fairies who washed the flowers with dew, snipped the spent flowers off their stems, and polished the rocks until they gleamed. They saw goblin women baking bread in ovens made of clay and fairies mixing juice in a hollowed-out log. Nymphs stepped out of their trees to pick baskets of nuts and fruit while a troll woman made dainty pastries with her big, beefy hands.

An old wooden door had been placed atop two stumps, creating a table to hold the food. After filling plates made from tightly woven grasses, Jak and Tamisin wandered until they reached the ring where the fairies would dance that night. They chose a boulder set just outside the ring and sat side by side to watch the fairies trim the grass and decorate the surrounding trees with flowers.

"So what do you intend to do next?" Tamisin asked Jak between bites.

"I think I'd like to go back to your town," said Jak. "The people are friendlier there and they accept each other for who they are. Humans aren't very well liked here, and I'm tired of being told that I have 'tainted' blood."

"Not everybody is accepting in my world," said Tamisin.

Jak shrugged. "Of course, even if we could get there, you know we wouldn't be left alone. The goblins would come looking for you and probably me as well. Don't worry," he added. "I'll think of something. We'll both be going back there. Just wait and see."

"They told me I could find ya here," said a voice, and they looked up to find Tobi with a peach in his hand.

"Where did you go?" Jak asked. "The last time I saw you, Nihlo was trying to separate me from my hide."

"Ya looked like ya could handle yerself, so I took off. I didn't want to get in yer way."

Jak shook his head. "More likely you went to report to the fairy queen. We know you're her spy, Tobi. You don't need to pretend that you aren't."

"What? Me? I never . . . ," Tobi began, but then he shrugged when he saw the expressions on their faces. " 'Twasn't like it was my idea. She made me do it after she heard that a human girl had seen me. She wanted to know what ya looked like, Tamisin. When I told her that the girl looked just like her, she made me promise to tell her anything more I heard about ya. I didn't have anything to tell her until Targin wanted me to help Jak find ya. Now she wants me to tell her every little thing! She'd said I couldn't tell ya about her bein' yer mother, but when I heard that those goblins tried to kill ya . . ."

"Your Highness!" called a full-sized fairy from the other side of the ring. Her arms were cradling something blue and frothy that sparkled in the sunlight. Ignoring the outraged cries of the fairies who'd been meticulously grooming the center of the circle, she traipsed across it, scowling at Jak and Tamisin. "You should have told someone where you were going. I've wasted a lot of time looking for you. The queen says that you must wear this to the dance." The fairy handed Tamisin the blue dress she'd been carrying, then stepped back and shrank to the size of a dragonfly.

"Wait!" shouted Tamisin. "I'd like to talk to my mother."

The little fairy turned big again in a shower of sparkling lights. "Her Highness is busy with important matters and can't be bothered now," she said, looking annoyed.

"When can I talk to her again?" asked Tamisin.

"When she wants to talk to you," said the fairy. This time when she shrank, she darted away before Tamisin could say another word.

"What is it?" Jak asked, but Tamisin was already shaking out the fabric and holding it up at arm's length. A pair of shoes that had been wrapped inside the fabric fell to the ground, the light reflecting off pale blue crystals.

"Ohh!" she breathed. "It's the most beautiful thing I've ever seen!" It was a sleeveless dress made of fabric the same shade of blue as the summer sky on a cloudless day. Slender green vines twined across the bodice and over the shoulder straps, then encircled the back that had been cut low enough for wings. Tiny crystals matching those on the shoes were scattered across the dress, making it shimmer at the slightest movement.

"Very nice," said Jak.

"It's glorious!" she said. "But what about you? She didn't send anything for you to wear."

"I doubt they expect me to dance," said Jak.

"I'll dance!" said Tobi. "I'm real light on my toes."

"But you'll go, won't you?" Tamisin asked, reaching for Jak's hand. "I don't want to go unless you go with me."

"I will if you want me to," said Jak.

"I do!" Tamisin said, giving him a quick kiss on the cheek. "I have got to go try this on! Do you mind?"

"Go right ahead," he said.

Tamisin left and Tobi disappeared to find more food, leaving Jak staring blankly at the ground in front of him. Although Tamisin didn't want to stay with the fairies, Jak knew that at least for the time being it was the right place for her. Unfortunately, as far as he could see he had no place to go. As a goblin, he couldn't stay with the fairies much longer. He was sure that the only reason he had been allowed in their forest at all was because he had escorted Tamisin. His welcome was bound to run out soon, and when it did, he'd have to find somewhere to live. He would have gone back to his uncle's, but he doubted that Targin would want to see him after he'd messed up his plans, whatever they had been. And although he would have liked to return to Tamisin's school, it wouldn't be the same unless she was there.

He was still thinking about what he would do next when a voice called, "*Psst*! Hey, Jak!" It was Bruno, calling to him from a group of holly trees set back from the fairy ring.

"Bruno! How are you doing? Are you off duty now?"

"Shh!" Bruno whispered so loudly that the fairies

trimming the far side of the ring turned to look. Waving his paw in the air, the bear goblin gestured for Jak to join him. Curious, Jak followed Bruno deeper into the woods, away from the ring and the watching eyes of the fairies. They didn't stop walking until they'd left the last of the fairies behind and come to a part of the forest that wasn't nearly as well tended as the rest.

"Why are you being so secretive?" Jak asked when Bruno finally turned to face him.

"Because *he's* here." Bruno stepped aside so Jak could see Barth. "He came to see you," said Bruno, "but I had to sneak him in. He's not supposed to be here, and frankly, I'm not either. Make this fast. I have to be back at my station in a few minutes."

Barth nodded. "I won't be long. I had to come warn you, Jak. Word is out that your cousin is planning to kidnap that girl during some dance."

"The dance is tonight, but what can Nihlo do? There are guards at the entrances, and I'm sure they won't let any goblins get near Tamisin."

"Nihlo is tricky," said Barth. "I don't know the details, but I heard from a friend who has a friend who knows Nihlo, who said that there's a Gate to a Gate. I was hoping that you would know what that meant, because I sure don't."

Jak shook his head. "I don't either. Maybe your friend heard it wrong."

"Maybe," said Barth. "Anyway, I thought you should know."

"Thanks," said Jak. "I appreciate it."

"Come on, Barth, I don't know how I'm going to sneak you past Leadless a second time, but I'm going to try. See ya, Jak."

"Yeah," said Jak, whose mind was already somewhere else. Although Jak didn't know exactly what Barth might have meant by Gate to a Gate, something was nagging at him. It had happened the Halloween that he went to the city with his class, but he just couldn't . . . And then he remembered the Gates. He had arrived through one and left through another. Although the Gates at the school had been fairly close together, the Gates in the city had been miles apart. What if the reverse was also true if only one could find it? What if there was a Gate in the world of the fey that could take one to a Gate in the human world close to another Gate that would take them somewhere very different in the world of the fey? And what if that other Gate was within an enemy's territory, somewhere no one would expect it to be? "Gate to a Gate," Jak said out loud. "That has to be it!"

"Good for you!" said a voice only a few feet away. Jak spun around, but he already knew it was too late. Bruno and Barth were gone, and he was alone in the forest with Nihlo and the boar goblin, the last people he wanted to see. The guards had taken away his knife before he was allowed to enter the fairies' forest, so Jak no longer had a weapon with which to defend himself or the time to make one. "I knew you would figure it out," said Nihlo. "Tobi was right. You are smart, for a human that is."

"Bruno and Barth aren't—"

"In on this? No, I used those two berry brains to get

you here, that's all. It was easy to let Barth learn just enough of my plan that he would think he was really on to something."

"But why . . ." Jak turned his head as the boar goblin plunged a slim knife into his back. The poison worked faster this time, perhaps because it was closer to his heart. His cousin was waiting to catch him when his legs collapsed, then a hooded figure stepped out of the shadows behind Nihlo and turned toward the light shimmering between two trees. Remembering what it had been like the last time he'd been poisoned, Jak closed his eyes so they wouldn't dry out. Unable to see or move, all Jak could do was listen as they dragged him to the Gate.

⚘

Tamisin loved the dress. It fit her as if it had been made for her, which she thought was probably true. She loved the silky feel of it on her skin. She loved the way it rustled when she walked. But most of all she loved the way it looked when she saw her reflection in a small pond. The nymph who lived in the pond had been kind enough to still the water so Tamisin could see herself. At first Tamisin had thought it was a trick and that she wasn't looking at herself at all, but when she moved her hand and the reflection did, too, she began to see that maybe she *was* the beautiful creature looking back at her. *If only my mother could see me,* she thought, but it wasn't Titania she had in mind.

Tamisin was still admiring the image in the pond when a fairy in a fluffy pink dress and matching cap stopped by to fix her hair. The fairy brushed it with a nettle brush, shaking her head and clucking her tongue at the snarls. When she was finished, she looked pleased with her creation and even more pleased when Tamisin said how much she liked it. Tamisin's long blond hair was still loose around her shoulders, but now she had a dusting of mica specks to make it sparkle and sprigs of forget-me-nots tucked among the locks.

By the time Tamisin went to look for Jak, the entire forest was alive with creatures big and small hustling and bustling as they prepared for the dance. Fairy and goblin handmaidens hurried back and forth on errands for the queen. Some of the goblins ran on four feet and some on two, while some of the fairies flew and others walked. Tamisin had to keep watch in all directions so she didn't bump into anyone or get in their way. Their excitement was contagious and she found herself looking forward to the dance, if only she could find Jak—she couldn't find him anywhere.

Feeling lonesome and a little bit lost, she decided to go see Titania, regardless of what the fairy who had brought the dress had said. After finding a familiar part of the forest, Tamisin retraced her steps to where she thought she might find the mossy glade. She found what she thought were the same rhododendrons, but instead of a clearing behind them there were only more shrubs and trees. Confused, she stopped the next big fairy she saw. "I'd like to speak to the queen," she said. "Can you tell me how to find her?"

The fairy seemed irritated at first, but then she took a

good look at Tamisin, her eyes opened wide, and she gasped, "It's you! You're the one who released me when that awful boy had me trapped in a cup. I never thought I'd get the chance to thank you."

Tamisin smiled. "I'm glad I was able to help. Do you think you could help me now, though? I was sure the queen's throne was around here somewhere."

The fairy shook her mop of pale blue curls. "No one can find Titania unless she wants to be found, unless of course you're one of her guards or handmaidens. And don't ask one of them to take you because they won't unless she tells them to."

"But I was just talking to her a few hours ago, and her throne was right there," said Tamisin, pointing at the shrubs.

"It's not there now, is it?" said the fairy, not bothering to turn around. "I wouldn't keep looking for it if I were you. It would just be a waste of time. Speaking of time, I still have so much to do. Thanks again for help- ing me!" With a wave of her hand, the fairy scurried off.

Tamisin felt lonelier than ever. Whenever she got ready for a dance at home, her mother fussed over her. Although she'd found it irritating, she missed it now and wished she were home where people cared about her. Trying not to think about all the people she might never see again, she started back to where she had last seen Jak. She passed the spot where they'd eaten their lunch, but the boulder they'd sat on had been moved, and any sign that they had dawdled there had been swept away. Preparations were almost finished around the fairy ring.

Trolls were rearranging the boulders, which pixies draped with cloths in bright flower colors. Fairies placed bowls of fruit and nuts on the cloths while lady gnomes lugged out pot after pot of nectar, honey, and fresh cream.

When the sun began to set, fireflies lined up wing to wing on the branches of the neighboring trees, shedding a fanciful, flickering light. Tamisin thought the dance was about to begin when a pompous-looking gnome strutted into the center of the ring, but he was there to measure the height of the grass. When he found some that was too tall, he motioned for the fairies who had spent the day trimming it to trim it some more. While other gnomes inspected the flowers strung from branch to branch, and the mushrooms edging the ring, Tamisin walked around the entire circumference, trying to find Jak.

As the night grew darker and the fairies and their friends assembled for the dance, Tamisin felt more and more anxious.

"How ya doin', Princess?" said Tobi, suddenly appearing in front of her.

"Have you seen Jak? I can't find him anywhere."

"Not since ya went to change yer clothes. That's a mighty nice dress ya got there. Is it as soft as it looks?"

Seeing that Tobi was about to touch her dress with his sticky fingers, Tamisin twitched the fabric out of the way. "Don't you dare touch it until you've washed your hands!"

Tobi frowned as he examined his fingers. "What's wrong with 'em? Here, is this better?" he asked and licked them.

Tamisin shuddered. "No, it's not. If you'll excuse me, I have to find Jak."

"Why?" said Tobi. "He's prolly hiding so he don't hafta dance!"

"Jak wouldn't do that," she replied, her throat tight with anger. "He promised he'd come. Despite what you might think, Jak has never lied to me. He didn't take me anywhere I didn't want to go, regardless of what Nihlo said. And he wasn't spying on me to report to my mother like you were—and probably still are. I'd appreciate it if you'd stay away from me, Tobi! I have enough things to worry about without you reporting everything I say or do!"

Tobi looked stunned. "But I didn't . . . I wasn't . . . I wouldn't . . ."

Lightning flashed overhead as Tamisin turned her back and stalked away, leaving the little goblin sputtering.

Tamisin was furious—at Tobi for talking about Jak that way, at Jak if he really had stood her up. She was debating whether or not she should continue looking for him when Titania arrived with her handmaidens and everyone began to line up behind them. A goblin girl with a plumed tail like a squirrel's took Tamisin's hand in her own and led her to the front of the line, just behind Titania. The fairy queen was dressed in a shimmery silver gown that seemed to flow over her body like liquid silver. Covered with precious gems, it caught the light at a thousand points, making Tamisin's gown look dull in comparison. Titania smiled graciously at Tamisin, then proceeded to walk through the forest, leading the line that grew progressively longer as more of the fey joined in. Wherever they walked, Tamisin looked for Jak, hoping she might yet see him, but he seemed to have vanished entirely.

It was midnight when the dance began, and the moon shone down on the revelers, adding its light to that of the fireflies. Titania was the first to step into the ring, and then Tamisin and the handmaidens followed while the rest of the fairies stood outside and watched. With so many eyes on her, Tamisin felt close to panicking.

And then the music began and Tamisin no longer had time to think. Titania took a dozen steps, her movements so graceful that she seemed to float above the grass. Then the handmaidens followed her, copying her movements like shadows in a brightly lit room. When they turned to Tamisin, she knew that they expected her to do the same. She tried her best. Following Titania's lead, they danced across the ring, the others as light as butterflies while Tamisin was always one step behind. It wasn't until they reached a patch of moonlight that her dancing began to change. It was a full moon that night, and it affected her just as it had back in the human world. A few more steps and she'd lost herself to the dance, imagining herself in a world that was neither fey nor human, a world that reflected both, as well as much that was uniquely hers. She was so caught up in the dance that she never noticed the handmaidens leaving the ring, nor when Titania left a moment later.

Tamisin danced as she had for so many nights, only

this time something different happened. She twirled, and as she twirled, her wings opened behind her like buds unfurling into beautiful flowers. No longer wet or limp when they emerged, her wings were glorious from the moment the air touched them. And here in the land of the fey where magic was as common as moonlight, Tamisin's wings truly blossomed. Where her wings had seemed large in her human home, here they were twice as big. Their color was more brilliant as well, the blues more vivid and the violets richer. Unlike normal fairy wings that never changed hue from the day the fairy was born, Tamisin's wings shimmered as she moved, the colors rippling across them in silver-edged sparkles. As graceful and as fluid as the dance itself, her wings moved with her, enhancing her dance and enthralling her audience.

Tamisin would have danced all night if a cloud hadn't passed in front of the moon. As the light in the ring dimmed, she paused and for the first time realized that she had been dancing by herself. She glanced up, suddenly self-conscious, only to see the wonder in the fairies' eyes. The faces blurred together as she looked from one to the next, hoping to see Jak. He wasn't there, but at least now she felt as if the fairies might actually like her, even if it was just for a moment.

"Well done!" said Titania, and at that all the fairies cheered, a rousing sound that made Tamisin smile.

As the music struck up a lighter chord, the fairies outside the ring began to enter, some to congratulate her, others to dance the next dance. She saw Tobi looking sad as he kept his distance, but still no Jak. Although she hadn't felt tired while she was dancing, Tamisin was exhausted now and wanted nothing more than to find a seat and something cool to drink. Even so, she couldn't help but look through the crowd as she left the ring, wondering why Jak hadn't come to the dance. It wasn't like him to break a promise. Tobi couldn't be right, but if he wasn't, where was Jak? She couldn't imagine what might have happened to him. She was about to ask one of the guards to help her look for him when a goblin woman approached her.

"Your Highness," said the woman. "Might I have a word with you? It's of a personal nature." Glancing from Tamisin to the shadowy forest beyond the ring, the woman hinted at the need for privacy.

Tamisin hesitated, but only for a moment. The woman had a sweet face with the green eyes of a cat and the soft white hair of a grandmother. Dressed in the pastels of Titania's handmaidens, she looked like the kind of person Tamisin could trust. Although she didn't recall having seen the woman before, so much had been going on over the short time that she and Jak had been there that she was sure she had seen only a fraction of her mother's attendants. With a wave of her hand, Tamisin told the guard that she was all right and followed the woman into the woods.

"It's about Jak," the woman said once they were alone. "He's gone back to see his uncle."

"Why would he go without telling me?" asked Tamisin.

"He didn't want to, but he was called away. His uncle is furious with him because the boy defied him by coming here."

"But it wasn't his fault," Tamisin said. "He came only because I asked him to." She felt awful now. Not only had she been angry with Jak for something he didn't do, but he was in trouble for something she'd asked him to do.

"I'm sure you're right, Princess, but Jak's uncle, Targin, is awfully stubborn. The goblin is known for his temper, so there's no saying what he might do to Jak unless . . ."

"Unless what?"

"Unless someone intercedes with his uncle. It would have to be someone who cares about Jak enough to travel to his uncle's den and talk some sense into the goblin. I would do it myself, only I doubt Targin would listen to me."

"I could go," said Tamisin, "but Titania thinks that the goblins want to use me against her. Wouldn't I be putting myself in their hands so they could do just that?"

"Your mother has been misinformed," the woman said. "Someone would have to be terribly foolish to do something that would incur her wrath. Targin may be many things, but no one has ever called him foolish. They say that humans are capable of great loyalty and compassion. However, if you'd rather stay here where you feel safe . . ."

"No," said Tamisin. "I'm not going to let Jak bear the consequences for something I made him do. Can you tell me how to get there?"

"I'll do better than that. I'll take you myself. I know a shortcut that will get you there safely in no time at all. We can leave right now if you'd like."

"Why do you care so much about Jak?" Tamisin asked, still not sure if she should trust the woman.

"Because I'm his great-aunt, Lurinda. His grandmother is my sister. Surely the dear boy has mentioned me to you?"

"He didn't tell me much," Tamisin said, trying to remember if he'd mentioned his aunt's name at all. She glanced down at her delicate gown and slippers. "Shouldn't I change my clothes before we go?"

"There isn't time," said the woman. "If we don't get there soon, it may be too late."

"But my mother . . ."

"If we take the shortcut we can be there and back before anyone knows you're gone. Trust me, this is the best way."

At first the light of the moon was enough to let them pick a route through the forest, but when they reached an older, less-cared-for section where the trees met overhead, preventing the light from reaching the ground, the woman took a handful of dust from her bag and blew on it. Light flared, allowing Tamisin to see the roots that would have tripped her and the branches that would have blocked her way.

"Where are we going?" she asked.

"We're almost there," the woman said.

Tamisin was beginning to have doubts when they stepped between two trees and a pale light shimmered

247

around her. A chill caused goose bumps to prickle her arms, then suddenly they were in full daylight with the summer sun warming her skin. Tamisin squeezed her eyes shut as the bright light made her eyes tear. "What just happened?" she asked. Peeking through her lashes, she turned to look behind her. The fairy forest was gone, replaced by a meadow awash with wildflowers. Tamisin glanced up at the sound of a jet flying high overhead. Somewhere a radio was playing music with a lively beat. It was obvious that they were no longer in the land of the fey. It took her a moment before she recognized the field where she had picked flowers the day she went on a picnic with Jak.

"It's the shortcut," the woman said. "Follow me."

They passed the waterfall where Tamisin and Jak had had their picnic, then hiked through the woods, forsaking the path that ran alongside the stream. Cutting through a backyard, they reached a street lined with sycamore trees. A woman glanced up from weeding her garden while a little girl playing hopscotch on the sidewalk pointed at Tamisin and said, "Look! It's Cinderella!"

"How can it be summer here?" Tamisin asked Lurinda as they crossed another street. "Jak and I have been gone only a few days and it was autumn when we left."

"Didn't Jak tell you that time passes differently here than it does in the land of the fey? It never passes at the same rate from one day to the next, which is why we have to hurry. Who knows how long we'll have been gone while Targin decides Jak's fate?"

"Where are we going now?" asked Tamisin.

The street was vaguely familiar with its meticulously maintained older homes. A truck belonging to a lawn service was parked in front of one of the houses, and the men unloading the mowers stopped to stare as Tamisin and Lurinda passed by. "Must be a party," said one of the older men.

"This way," said the woman, leading Tamisin behind the only run-down house on the street.

Tamisin had the feeling that they were being watched as they walked through the yard. It wasn't until she glanced at the porch that she recognized the house. "This is where Jak lives!" she said. "I came here for a party."

A face appeared at one of the windows, but was gone before Tamisin was able to get a good look. "I wonder if that's his grandmother," she said. "Maybe I should stop in and tell her about Jak."

Lurinda frowned and hustled Tamisin past the house. "There's no time for that now. Whoever is in that house wouldn't be able to do Jak a bit of good. Here we go, right between these two trees."

"This is the Gate Jak and I fell through the night of his party. We didn't end up anywhere near where he thought we would."

"That was a fluke," said her companion. "The Gate wasn't working right because of a storm. It corrected

249

itself the very next day. I came through it just a few hours ago in fey time."

Herding Tamisin in front of her, the woman took her to the hazy patch of air that marked the Gate.

"I don't understand," Tamisin said. "Did my mother send you here?"

"Don't worry, my dear," said Lurinda as they stepped from one world to the next. "It will all become clear very soon."

Chapter 22

Lurinda swore under her breath when they stepped through the Gate between the worlds and found that it was night in the land of the fey. "Be as quiet as you can," she whispered into Tamisin's ear. "The lamia have been more active of late, and loud noises attract them."

"Really?" said Tamisin. "Lou never mentioned that."

Lurinda gave her an odd look, but didn't say anything more as she escorted Tamisin through a meadow, past a copse of trees, and down a steep slope to a stout door set in the hillside. After pressing a square of metal set in the door, she stepped back to wait, her eyes scanning the darkness around them. Leaves rustled in a nearby shrub, making her jump and turn around; she seemed relieved when the door finally opened. Taking Tamisin's arm, she hurried her through the doorway.

A man closed the door the moment they stepped through, then locked it with an odd-looking key. When he turned to face them, Tamisin saw that he wasn't a man at all, but a goblin with eyes like a cat's and black hair so thick it might have been called fur. A scar ran the width of his cheek, nearly reaching the base of one of his catlike ears, making him look quite ferocious. He eyed Tamisin as if she were something he might have found stuck to the bottom of his shoe, then glanced at Lurinda and nodded before walking away.

"Who was that?" Tamisin whispered to Lurinda.

"That was Targin, Jak's uncle."

"But isn't he the one I need to talk to?" asked Tamisin.

"He'll talk to you when he wants to, and not before."

"I thought we hurried to get here so I *could* talk to him."

"That's true," said Lurinda, then she, too, turned to walk away.

"Wait!" Tamisin put her hand on the woman's arm, inadvertently pulling up her long sleeve. "I need to . . ." Tamisin's voice trailed off when she glanced down at Lurinda's hand. The goblin woman's long, thin fingers had a dusting of white fur on the back and bore a single ring. Although the ring was unfamiliar, Tamisin had seen those hands before. "I know you!" Tamisin said, looking up into Lurinda's eyes. "You were there when that goblin woman bit me. I was just a baby, but I've had the dream so many times . . . It was you, wasn't it? You tucked my blanket around me. It was a kind act after those women were so cruel."

"I'm surprised you remember," Lurinda said, shaking off Tamisin's hand. "I was certain the old crone's magic didn't work when I heard that you had come back. Yes, it was me. I was your mother's favorite handmaiden. She came to me when she knew that she was pregnant and I helped her hide it from the court. I was there at your birth and I saw how difficult you were going to make your mother's life. I loved her then; she was my queen and I wanted only what was best for her."

"What about the goblin woman who bit me?" Tamisin asked.

"When I knew that you were going to be taken away, I paid her to use her magic on you. I thought she could keep you from coming back. Unfortunately for you, her magic wasn't strong enough."

"What about Jak? Where does he fit in all this?"

"Nowhere now. The boy was a useful tool, but he isn't smart enough to get out of the way when his betters want to take over. The boy doesn't know his place. The stories Nihlo has told me about Jak are disgraceful. Targin should never have let his sister leave her halfling here. I wouldn't have been so charitable."

The goblin woman's words made Tamisin feel sick to her stomach. When Lurinda turned on her heel and strode off down the hall, Tamisin had to swallow hard before calling after her, "Can I see Jak?"

"If you can find him!" Lurinda replied without looking back.

Tamisin wasn't sure what to do. It was obvious that neither Lurinda nor Targin had any intention of helping her and could probably be very nasty if they chose to be. Tamisin could only assume that Jak really was there somewhere, but she had no clue where she should start looking. A long corridor stretched before her with doors leading off on either side. She was debating whether or not she should start opening doors in the hope that she would find the right one when she realized that many of them were open just enough that the goblins inside could peek out. As a door clicked shut behind Lurinda, the goblins began to emerge from the rooms until a crowd had gathered around Tamisin. Some looked as if they might be members of the cat-goblin clan, but the rest looked like humans who had been given features from other animals. Tamisin saw long doglike faces, the tusks of wild boars, short, sharp beaks, and long bushy tails.

While she stared at the goblins, they were just as interested in her, acting as if they had never seen any-thing quite like her before. She put up with their poking and prodding, but when one with a snout pinched her arm, Tamisin slapped the goblin, making it squeal and back away. The rest of the goblins were grumbling when a tiny woman with long gray and white hair, catlike eyes and a kindly, wrinkled face pushed through the crowd, knocking goblins with her cane when they didn't move.

Reaching Tamisin's side, she smiled up at her, saying, "Don't you remember me? I'm Jak's grandmother Gammi. We met at the Halloween party."

Tamisin nodded slowly. She had seen Jak's grand-mother only briefly, but this could be that woman.

"Don't pay them any mind," Gammi said, jerking her thumb at the goblins. "They don't mean anything by it. Come with me. I've got a nice cozy room where we can

sit and visit. I can't believe she brought you here, then
left you to your own devices."

"Do you know where Jak is?" asked Tamisin.

"Of course not," Gammi said in an overly loud voice.
"But come with me anyway."

Puzzled, Tamisin followed the old goblin woman
down the hall to a room that was indeed cozy. Although
it was only one room, it had been set up as two with
shelves down the middle separating a bed on one side
and a small table on the other. So many colorful pillows
were piled on the bed that Tamisin didn't see any space
to lie down, but the chairs next to the table were big and
cushy, just right for curling up in for a nap. Even the
floor was padded with a thick rug that sank beneath her
feet when she walked.

Once Tamisin looked at the walls, she didn't notice
anything else. Every inch from the ceiling to the floor was
covered with pictures. Some were paintings, some were
sketches, some were little photographs like the ones shot
in photo booths. Most of them were goblins, although
there were also fairies, gnomes, humans, and at least two
trolls. Tamisin saw a photograph of a little boy who
might have been Jak alongside a beautiful woman of the
cat clan. She had the same dark hair as Jak, but her eyes
were more slanted and her cheekbones more prominent.

"That's his mother," said Gammi. "My youngest
daughter and the most headstrong. Takes after her aunt
Lurinda that way. Jak was just a kitten when I took that
picture with his father's camera. I was visiting them in
the human world at the time. I liked his father, but don't

255

tell Targin I said that. Jak's father was a good human, and my daughter loved him to distraction. Then he disappeared and she went crazy looking for him. He was gone for a year before she got any clue as to where he might be, so she brought Jak here and left him with Targin. She thought it was better if her brother believed that she was out wasting her life on frivolous things, but she went looking for her husband. She still is as far as I know. I haven't heard from her in years."

"Does Jak know all this?" asked Tamisin.

"He has no idea," said Gammi. "I didn't want him to think he should go looking for them. It's bad enough that I lost his mother that way; I didn't want to lose him, too. That sounds selfish of me, I know, but that boy means a lot to me. And that's why I'm going to tell you where you can find him."

"So you *do* know!"

"Of course I know! There's very little that goes on around here that I don't know. Jak is down with his hipporines. Targin locked him down there, thinking that he'd be as scared of those monsters as the rest of them are. But I know better. My Jak is the bravest one here, though there's many that are too foolish to see it. Now, what we're going to do is sit here and have a nice cup of catmint tea while you tell me all that you and Jak have done since the night of his Halloween party. Then, after everyone has quieted down for the night, I'll show you where he is."

"What time is it now?" asked Tamisin. "It was after midnight when Lurinda took me from the fairies' forest, then daytime when we cut through the human world."

"It's night now, just past supper, and I daresay it's a few days later than you remember. Now, you have a nice rest and I'll get that tea, and maybe some supper for you besides. I doubt you've eaten . . . Uh-huh, I thought not. Lurinda isn't the type to think of such things. Go ahead—you sit in that chair. It's the softest."

After Gammi left the room, Tamisin curled up in the chair, sitting so she could see the pictures on the walls. Her head was nodding when Gammi returned, but she jumped up to help the old woman set the tray on the table. During the next few hours while Tamisin ate berries in cream and drank tea, they talked about all sorts of things, including Jak's parents, Gammi's other children, Tamisin's human family, the friends Gammi had made in the human world, Tamisin's visit with the fairy queen, and how much Tamisin wanted to go home. After a while Tamisin started yawning, but she sat up straight when Gammi mentioned Lurinda.

"She was the firebrand of the family, always ready to fight for a cause. Then the fairy queen's people came to get her and we didn't see hide or hair of her for years. We did get letters though, and at first she sounded truly happy. It seems she was the queen's favorite, not surprising considering how beautiful she was and how sweet she could be when she was getting her way. Then something happened, she never did tell us what, and Lurinda fell from the queen's favor. Her letters changed after that. She still said she was happy, but I could tell the difference. It wasn't until she came home that I learned how bitter she'd become. She felt as if she'd been wronged. Now it seems she has a new cause, though she won't tell me what it is. I hear things though, so I know it involves your mother."

"What do you think she intends to do?" asked Tamisin.

"I'm not sure, but I have a good idea. She and Targin have both been brimming with secrets lately. I think she's the one who told him about you. It was after she returned home that Targin came up with his grand plan for Jak to go to the human world. Bert and I went along to help, but Jak probably would have done fine on his own. None of us had any notion that Titania was your mother. My Jak is a good boy and never meant you any harm."

"I know that," said Tamisin.

"There are some of us who wouldn't care that the fairy queen has a half-breed daughter, but there's others who would get all riled at the notion. I think Lurinda and Targin are betting on that to stir up support for a revolt, though they each have their own reasons. My son thinks he's helping our people, whereas Lurinda . . . Let's just say that my sister is a bad person to cross. I've known her to bear a grudge for years. I bet kidnapping you was her idea, too. She was the one who planned all our escapades when we were young. This whole thing is right up her alley."

Gammi glanced at the pictures on the wall and sighed. "It's been bothering me no end that members of my own family are causing all this trouble, so I decided it was up to me to stop it. I think my son wants to be king of the goblins, a noble enough cause if it didn't mean that so many people would have to die to get him there. But Lurinda . . . I think she has her sights set on something grander, although what it is I just don't know. She always did want to be at the top of the heap. Whatever they're planning is going to happen in the next few days. This place is crawling with goblins, with more coming all the time. So now that I've talked your ear off, I'm going to tell you what you really want to know. In just a few minutes I'm going to walk you down that hallway and show you a door, but there can't be a peep out of you or Lurinda will stop us. When she brought you here, she never intended for you to see Jak again. She told you all that fiddle-faddle just to get you here so they'd have a hold over your mama."

"My mother warned me that might happen. I can't believe how stupid I've been!"

"You haven't been stupid. Lurinda's good at what she does. She can persuade a bird to fly upside down if she's got a mind to. I should know. I'm her little sister and she talked me into doing more addlepated things when we were girls than I care to remember.

"Hand me my cane and we can get started," said Gammi as she struggled to her feet. "That's it. Now I'll just wrap this cloth around the bottom to muffle the noise. There we go. Wouldn't want my tap tapping to tell everybody what we're doing. Here, put on this cape so they'll think you're a goblin if anyone does see you. Now follow me and don't make a sound. If you have any questions, now's the time to ask them."

Tamisin was so confused that she just shook her head.

"No? All right then. I'll unlock the door, and I'll leave it that way. Here, take this torch." Gammi handed Tamisin a short stick with wooden prongs at the top. The prongs held a transparent cube that glowed with an inner fire. "Don't worry, it won't burn you. The gnomes make these things and you won't find any better. It doesn't look very bright now, but it'll work just fine in the dark. Once you're in the hipporines' cave, find Jak and bring him back here. I would have gone myself before this, but there are some things these old bones can't do. Come first light I'll let you both out the front door before anyone else is stirring. You'll have to find your own way after that, but Jak's a smart boy and will figure something out."

"Thank you, Gammi," Tamisin said, kissing the old woman's cheek. "I don't know what I would have done without you."

"Neither do I," chuckled Gammi. "Now be off with you, and take care of my grandson!"

After sticking her head out of her room and looking both ways, Gammi led Tamisin down the hall. It was much longer than Tamisin had thought, and she kept expecting someone to pop out of one of the rooms and catch them. Nothing happened, however, and when Gammi opened the door at the end and stepped aside to let her pass, Tamisin mouthed the words "thank you."

Then, stepping into the darkness beyond the door, she held up the torch and tried to see.

⚜

Jak was delighted when his uncle threw him in the cave, although he was careful not to let it show, which was easy because he was still sluggish from the antidote to the poison. Knowing how the animals would react when they saw him, he kept his distance until he was sure his uncle and the other goblins were gone.

The greenish-white glow had spread farther across the walls, making the cavern even brighter than he remembered. The hipporines refused to settle down until he walked among them, petting and scratching and getting reacquainted with his old friends. Although the foals born in his absence were rough and wanted to take a bite out of him, Jak knew just how to handle such young ones. Once the hipporines quieted, Jak crawled onto the shelf where he'd often gone to rest.

The next morning when he woke, sunlight was pouring through the opening in the cave ceiling. He hurried over the wall so the hipporines' caretakers would still believe that he was afraid of the animals; he was certain that if they thought he liked being with the beasts they'd find something truly awful to inflict on him instead.

Every morning the goblins came to feed the hipporines around the same time, leaving a plate of food or a crust of bread for Jak as well. He was forced to drink from the pool at the base of the wall, but the water was clean, for it had yet to flow into the hipporines' trough.

Jak filled his day with taking care of the beasts. There was so much to do that he slept soundly at night; nothing short of the hipporines acting up could wake him.

On the third night, Jak was asleep dreaming of his life in the human world when the hipporines began to scream. He woke with a start, afraid that he'd overslept and the goblins had already come to feed the beasts. Halfway to the wall he realized that the sun wasn't shining through the hole in the ceiling and that it was still dark enough to be the middle of the night.

Through the noise of the hipporines, Jak heard someone calling his name. He watched as a faint light bobbed down the tunnel, bursting into a glowing ball when it entered the cave, banishing the darkness for twenty feet in every direction. It was Tamisin.

Whooping loudly, Jak vaulted over the wall. "I thought I'd never see you again," he said, walking toward her.

Tamisin laughed. "You're not getting rid of me that easily. Not after all we've gone through."

A scuffle broke out among the hipporines, raising the noise level on the other side of the wall and reminding Jak of where they were. He frowned at Tamisin. "How did you get in here? This is the last place you should be. What are you doing here anyway?"

"I've come to rescue you," she said. "Lurinda found me during the dance. She said your uncle was mad and you needed someone to speak on your behalf; it was really just a ploy to get me here. I don't know how well you know her, but she isn't a good person, Jak. She's trying to use me to get at Titania. I think she may have been the one to send Nihlo after me. And she told me some things about my mother . . . I might have misjudged her—my mother, I mean."

"I know all about Lurinda," said Jak. "She was there when Nihlo's friend stuck me with a poisoned knife in the fairies' forest. I closed my eyes, so they must have thought I was unconscious, but I heard everything they said and then I figured out the rest. Lurinda told my uncle, Targin, about you so he'd get you here. When I wasn't fast enough to suit her, she offered the reward. She didn't care what shape you were in when she got you, so it didn't matter who brought you to her. When that didn't work, she sent Nihlo. I think she'd gone with him to the edge of the Sograssy Sea; she just stayed in the woods so no one would see her.

"My uncle is interested in goblins' rights; Lurinda's goals are more personal. I think she started the whole thing because she wanted revenge against Titania, but it's gone beyond that now. Lurinda wants what Titania has—respect, power and control—and she's willing to do just about anything to get it."

"And then I came here on my own," said Tamisin.

"Lurinda is a master at manipulating people. She would have gotten you here one way or another if you'd refused to come."

"That's pretty much what Gammi said. We had a long conversation. I like her a lot."

"Good," said Jak, smiling into her eyes. "So do I. But that still doesn't explain how you got down here."

"Gammi unlocked the door and we're supposed to go back to her room. She'll hide us until morning and let us out before anyone is up."

"It sounds as if you two have it all figured out."

"We do. So if you're ready . . ."

Jak had just taken Tamisin's hand when he heard voices echoing in the tunnel. This time there was no mistaking who they were. "Quick," he said, pulling her toward the wall. "The goblins are coming. They're early today. You'll have to hide on the other side. I don't want to find out what they'd do to you if they discovered you here."

The hipporines had also heard the goblins; the sound of their voices had sent the beasts into a rage.

"But what about them?" Tamisin asked, gesturing toward the hipporines.

"If we hurry, I can get you to a place where you'll be safe." Jak linked his fingers together and crouched down. "Step on my hands and I'll help you up."

"I don't think I—"

"There isn't time to argue. Don't worry. I know what I'm doing. We'll climb the wall now. Once we're on top, we have to jump. I'll go first, then I'll catch you. The hipporines won't hurt me, but they don't like strangers. You'll be all right as long as I stay between you and them. There's a ledge on the back wall where the goblins won't see you and the hipporines can't reach you. We have to be fast." Jak braced himself against the stones while Tamisin slipped her foot onto his hand and reached for the top of the wall. He waited while she scrabbled at the stones. A moment later he was crouched beside her, looking down over the other side. He had to admit that the hipporines looked frightening with their ears back and their fangs bared as they milled just below the wall.

"Hey, you miserable excuses for monsters!" called a goblin from the tunnel. "It's time for breakfast!"

At the sound of the goblin's voice, the larger hipporines screamed so loudly that Tamisin put her hands over her ears. Jak pointed at the far wall and waited until she nodded. He gave her hand a quick squeeze, then jumped off the wall, landing lightly on his feet. The hipporines moved to surround him the way they always did, but he pushed them back and held up his arms for Tamisin, catching her as if she weighed nothing at all. Jak set her down while the hipporines surged around him, trying to get to Tamisin, craning their necks to snap at her. She was running beside Jak when one of the beasts caught the back of the cape in its mouth and yanked her off her feet. Jak kicked the hipporine, forcing it away from Tamisin while she struggled to stand. She was moving again when the light went out and she realized that she'd dropped it. Tamisin stopped to look behind her. Scooping her into his arms, Jak picked her up and ran. And then they were at the far wall and once again Jak boosted her up. Only this time he didn't follow.

After gesturing for her to stay down, Jak ran back, hoping to retrieve the gnome light, but it had been trampled to dust before he could reach it. Without slowing his pace, Jak vaulted to the top of the wall, then jumped down to the ground on the other side.

A moment later, three goblins entered the cave lugging grisly sacks of raw, dripping meat. "I hope you're hungry, beasties!" shouted the goblin who was carrying a pointed hook strapped to a long pole. "Snarp, it's your turn to feed them."

"Who made you my boss?" cried Snarp.

"Your mother, when she made you a moron! Now get up there or I'll use this on you!" the goblin said, waving a hook in Snarp's face.

Grumbling, Snarp jumped to the top of the wall and began cursing at the snarling, snapping hipporines. Once he'd emptied his sack onto the heads of the beasts, the other two goblins tossed their sacks up to him and he threw that meat as well. When the sacks were empty, two of the goblins left while the third stayed long enough to toss a crust of bread at Jak. The goblin cackled when the crust landed on the ground, then hurried after his companions, shouting at them to slow down.

Jak waited until he could no longer hear their voices before going over the wall. Moments later he was bending over Tamisin where she lay curled on the ledge. She jerked away when he set his hand on her shoulder, and he remembered that she couldn't see in the near dark. "The goblins are gone," he said. "You can get down now. The hipporines won't bother you while they're eating."

"I can't see a thing," said Tamisin. "I don't suppose you have a light with you?"

"No, but then I haven't needed one. Cat goblins can see when it's this dark." He heard a scraping sound and a quick indrawn breath. "Let me help you. Here's my hand. Lean this way . . . That's it. Now put your feet over the side." Jak guided Tamisin as she crawled off the ledge, catching her when she slid the last few feet. He held her hand as they walked to the wall, then helped her over that as well.

"I wish I could make light the way the full-blooded fairies do," said Tamisin. "All they have to do is beat their wings fast."

"Have you tried it?" asked Jak.

"No, but I will now," she said, taking off Gammi's cape. "There's plenty of room here. Stand back and let me see what I can do."

Jak was amazed when Tamsin's wings unfurled behind her. They were much bigger and more powerful than he'd imagined. The breeze they created when she moved them stirred up a small dust storm, making Jak's eyes sting.

"Nothing's happening," Tamisin said eventually. "I didn't really think I'd . . . Wait, did you see that?" she asked, suddenly sounding excited. "There was a glimmer, I'm sure of it! Hold on. Let me see . . ." Tamisin was panting now, her breath coming in short, sharp gasps as she beat her wings faster and faster. "There! I can see you. You don't need to look so surprised."

"I'm not. I just didn't expect it to work so well." He coughed, squinting at her through air now thick with yellow-brown motes. "You don't have to beat your wings that fast. It's too bright, and the dust . . ."

"Oh, sorry," Tamisin said, slowing her wings to a less frenzied pace. She glanced at the entrance to the cave. "Do you suppose the door is still unlocked?"

"I hope so," said Jak. "Otherwise we're both trapped down here."

Tamisin walked up the tunnel, beating her wings more slowly as she learned just how fast she needed to move them to create light. Jak followed, seeing the tunnel with real light for the first time. It seemed shorter that way, and they reached the end before he knew it.

While Tamisin stood to the side, still beating her wings, Jak tried the latch. It was locked. "Do you think you can change it like you did that door back at the inn?" she asked.

"I tried that before you got here. It didn't work. The gnomes probably made the lock just like they did the one on the front door. Nothing can open that lock except the key that goes with it. But I'll try again anyway." After setting his hand on the door, Jak closed his eyes to focus on the lock and what he wanted it to become. *A glob of raspberry jelly,* he thought. *That wouldn't keep anything out.* He could feel the tingling sensation, so when it grew strong enough, he pushed with his mind. Nothing happened except he got a pounding headache and the taste of raspberry jelly in his mouth.

"I didn't think it would work," he said. "We're both trapped now. We should return to the cave in case someone comes back. My uncle must be up to something if he had his goblins feed the hipporines so early."

"Are you sure there isn't any other way out?" Tamisin asked as they turned around. "Could there be another door that the goblins don't use very often?"

"Nothing that we can use," said Jak. "Believe me, I've looked."

Tamisin sighed. "I wish I hadn't told Tobi to stop following me. If he had seen me leave the dance with Lurinda, he could have told my mother. At least then they'd have some idea where to look for me. If only I had some way to let them know . . ." Tamisin stopped near the end of the tunnel and stood so still that even her wings weren't moving. "That's it!" she cried. "All I need to do is dance!"

"If that will make you feel better," Jak said.

"It's not about how I feel," said Tamisin, giving him an exasperated look. "Whenever I dance in the light of a full moon, fairies come to see me. They find me wherever I am. My parents thought they were fireflies and made me dance inside because they'd always show up."

"But there isn't a full moon now. Look!" Jak pointed toward the pool of water. Sunlight was streaming through the hole in the ceiling, making the water glint and sparkle beneath it. The sun had come up while they were in the tunnel.

"That doesn't matter," said Tamisin. "The moonlight taught me the dance, but I know it by heart now."

"Don't you need music?" asked Jak.

"The music is in my head," she said, and she began to dance.

Jak watched as she twirled and spun, gesturing with her arms like a willow tree in the wind. With her body swaying, her wings fluttered like petals carried on a breeze one moment, then undulated like pond grass the next. Jak could see how fairies would be attracted to her dancing. It was the essence of nature, the heart of what gave the fairies their magic.

Tamisin danced with her eyes closed, but when she stopped she opened them and looked around expectantly. "They didn't come," she said, sounding disappointed. "I must have been wrong; it does work only when there's a full moon." Tamisin sighed and glanced up at the hole in the ceiling. "You know, there is another way. I wonder how big that hole is."

Jak shrugged. "You'd have to be in the water and look straight up to see it."

"Or fly," said Tamisin, beating her wings. She rose above the water, making the surface dimple with the breeze her wings created. "I think it's big enough," she called back to Jak.

"Then you should go," he said. "Maybe you can get word to someone that I'm down here."

"I'm not leaving you," said Tamisin, coming back to land beside him.

"If you're thinking of carrying me, forget it. When fairies are full sized their wings aren't strong enough to support their own weight for more than short distances. You'd never be able to fly up there with my weight, too."

"You're forgetting one thing, Jak," said Tamisin. "I'm not like most fairies." Wrapping her arms around his waist, she looked up at the hole in the ceiling. "That isn't too far. We'll be out of here in a minute provided that hole is big enough for the both of us. I've never carried anyone before, so put your arms around me and hold on tight. You can close your eyes if you get scared."

Jak laughed as he slid his hands under her wings just below her shoulder blades. The wings felt warm against the back of his hands and almost as smooth as her skin. "Why would I be scared?" he said when Tamisin began to beat her wings. "We're not going anywhere." And then they were off the ground and flying over the pool. Jak looked down. Heights had never bothered him, but then, he'd never flown before. As the pool receded below them and the hole in the ceiling drew closer, he tightened his arms around Tamisin and took deep breaths, trying to slow the pounding of his heart.

The walls of the hole were as smooth as if someone had carved them. Although the opening was about twelve feet wide when they entered it, it soon began to narrow. Soon Tamisin was struggling; the higher she flew, the less room there was to beat her wings. The walls couldn't have been more than nine feet apart when her wings began to brush the sides of the hole. Her flying became more erratic, and the effort it took was obvious in the perspiration beading her forehead and the near-frantic look in her eyes. Jak wasn't sure they were going to make it when he looked up. Although they were only a few yards from the opening at the top, the hole was closing in so much that soon Tamisin wouldn't be able to move her wings at all.

Jak looked up to check the width of the hole. A group of small objects blocked the light around the edges, making the hole seem narrower and more irregular than it had from below. When the objects moved, Jak realized that cats were peering over the edge.

The walls were less than six feet apart when he said, "Now it's my turn. I should be able to brace my body across the opening, and we can chimney-walk out of here."

"What . . . are you . . . talking . . . about?" panted Tamisin, her muscles shaking with fatigue.

"It's how I learned to climb up vertical shafts. You brace your back against one side and your hands and feet against the others. Then you work your way up the shaft by moving your back, then your feet. My friends and I had races at school, and I got pretty good at it."

"I'll try . . . anything."

"When I give the word, you let go of me. Ready, set, now!"

When Tamisin took her arms from around him, Jak let her go as well and in the same movement flung himself against the wall. He slipped for a terrifying second before he braced himself. When he was comfortable with his position, Jak reached down to Tamisin, who was already losing height. He pulled her up beside him. "Close your wings!" he ordered and she did, snapping them shut and folding them away.

With Jak's help, Tamisin climbed to the wall above him, bracing her body just as he told her to. Then, moving ever so carefully, they ascended the wall a few inches at a time. When Tamisin reached the top, she wasn't sure what to do, so Jak situated himself so that she could use him as leverage. Tamisin was soon up and over and a moment later so was Jak.

Weak with relief, they were rubbing their aching muscles and congratulating each other when Jak saw the sparkle of fairy lights among the trees. He was still watching when the lights flickered and turned into full-sized warriors.

"I think we have company," said Tamisin.

"I know," said Jak. "Your dance worked!" Excited, he glanced at her, then turned around to see where she was pointing. "Oh!" he said, spotting the fierce-looking goblins entering the clearing.

With fairies on one side and goblins on the other, Jak and Tamisin had come out of the hole in the middle of a battleground.

Chapter 23

The first goblin spear flew so close to Jak's cheek that he could feel the air move. "Watch out!" he shouted, reaching for Tamisin, but the goblins had already snatched her away and were dragging her back to their side.

Before Jak could go after her, a tiny fairy buzzed around his head, shouting, "Get down, you fool." A thick vine hit him in the back of the legs, making him stagger and fall to his knees. He would have tumbled into the cave, but the vine clung to his ankles and hauled him toward the trees.

"Jak!" Tamisin screamed as the goblins pulled her farther behind the goblin lines.

The vine dragged Jak until he had passed the first of the fairy warriors. "Let me go!" he shouted, but none of the warriors answered. While tiny fairies flew overhead, the full-sized warrior fairies stood shoulder to shoulder, facing the goblins on the other side of the clearing. Raising hollow reeds to their lips, they blew small, golden darts at the goblins. Jak wondered why the darts buzzed as they flew until one reed misfired and the dart fell to the ground and walked away. The darts weren't darts at all, but golden bumblebees that stung the goblins they hit and chased the ones they didn't.

When the vine finally went limp, Jak jumped to his feet and shouted, "Why did you do that?" at the warrior who seemed to be in charge. "You let them take Tamisin!"

"No, we didn't," said the fairy, a tall slender man with hair the same shade of silver as his eyes. "You did. The vine would have brought her to us if you hadn't been in the way."

A blue-haired warrior who had been listening to a swarm of fairies no bigger than the bumblebees nodded, then turned to the silver-haired fairy and announced, "Colonel Silverthorn, Fifth Platoon reports that the goblins are retreating!"

"Mugwort, Crabgrass, Sumac, have your platoons follow them in air formation with dust ready for deployment at your discretion. The rest of you, reload your reeds and arm yourselves with wands. We're going after the princess before they can take her underground. And remember, today the only good goblin is a sleeping goblin!"

"What about me?" asked Jak.

Colonel Silverthorn looked annoyed at the interruption. "You don't count. You're half human."

"I mean, where do you want me to go?" said Jak. "I want to help get the princess back."

"Just stay out of the way, halfling," the colonel said. "This is a job for fairies."

As far as Jak could tell, all the fairies had done so far was let Tamisin fall into the hands of the goblins. Even so, he would help the fairies if it meant he could keep her safe. He didn't care why else the fairies and the goblins were fighting; all he was concerned about was Tamisin. "I'll stay out of your way if you stay out of mine," he said. "And my name isn't Halfling. It's Jak!"

While some of the fairies made themselves tiny and flew with their platoons after the fleeing goblins, the rest re-armed themselves even as they ran. The fairies were fast, but Jak was faster and reached the bottom of the hill before any of the full-sized warriors. At first he thought that no one was there. The shrubs at the base of the hill weren't thick enough to hide anyone, and the trees were too spindly for anyone to have climbed. But then he began to hear voices so close by that he could have sworn they were all around him.

"Uh, oh! There are the fairies! Quick, we have to hide!"

"They're going to get us if we're not careful."

"I'm afraid! What do you think they'll do to us?"

Then the fairies were there searching the area and looking puzzled when they couldn't find anyone. "I can hear them, but I don't see them," said the colonel. "They must have found a way to make themselves invisible."

"No, they haven't," said Jak. "It's a trap. They aren't here at all. They're throwing their voices to make us think they're here, only I'm not sure why."

"No one is this good at voice projection," said Colonel Silverthorn. "They have to be somewhere close by."

"I tell you, they're not here. We have to leave," said Jak. "Don't you hear that?"

"It sounds like thunder," said one of Silverthorn's lieutenants.

Jak shook his head. "Look!" A dark shape was approaching from the far side of a neighboring hill. Jak couldn't tell what it was until he saw the tossing heads and the shape resolved into individual beasts. "They're driving the hipporines this way!"

"Hippowhats?" asked Colonel Silverthorn. "I've never heard of such a thing. If you were sent here to mislead us, I'll deal with you myself, you . . ."

"There," said Jak, pointing at the beasts. A hipporine screamed. While Colonel Silverthorn watched the animals with disbelief, Jak dashed to the nearest hillside and climbed until he was higher than the hipporines could reach. Rearing and bucking, the hipporines charged at the fairies.

"Run!" Jak shouted to the colonel, who was still watching, dumbstruck. The first of the hipporines was almost on the colonel when he made himself small. The tiny fairy darted out from under the rearing hipporine. A moment later the colonel was standing beside Jak, full-sized once again. The few fairies who'd been slow to change were nearly overrun and came away from the encounter dazed. One fairy was struck with a hoof and flew erratically when he finally made himself smaller.

"I've never seen anything like them before," said Colonel Silverthorn.

"The goblins were probably counting on that," said Jak. "My uncle has been keeping them hidden for years."

"Your uncle?" the colonel asked, eyeing Jak with suspicion.

"Targin, my mother's brother."

When the hipporines discovered that the fairies had taken refuge on higher ground, some of the animals screamed in rage as they scrabbled up the hillside, stopping only when it became too steep. The rest paced back and forth just below the fairies, waiting for them to come down.

"We'll have to neutralize those beasts somehow," said Colonel Silverthorn. "We can't have them running loose like this."

"Don't hurt them!" Jak said. "We can take them away from here—to somewhere they won't hurt anyone."

"On my way here I saw a valley that might work," said one of the lieutenants. "It was a dead end, so if we could get the beasts to go in . . ."

"You could close off the other end. That's a great idea," said Jak. "I think I know the valley you mean."

"And how do you suggest we herd these animals?" Colonel Silverthorn asked.

"Leave that to me," said Jak. "If I can get the head stallion to go, the rest will follow him. Just make sure you close them in once I get them in the valley."

Putterby, the stallion, and half a dozen other hipporines were still raging at the fairies when Jak started down the hill. They lunged at him, rearing up and pawing the air while he tried to soothe them with his voice.

"Look at those monsters," said the colonel as the hipporines pawed the ground, tearing up great clods of dirt. "That boy will never be able to control them."

Jak slipped among the hipporines, deftly avoiding their teeth and hooves until he reached the stallion, who turned an intelligent eye to his old friend and stood, sides quivering, nostrils flaring. Putterby snorted as Jak ran his hand down the stallion's neck. Then in one smooth movement the boy leaped onto the hipporine's back and squeezed the animal's heaving sides with his legs. The hipporine turned his head and tried to bite Jak's foot, but his neck was too short to reach. Slipping his hand into the beast's coarse mane, Jak got a good grip and held on. Furious, the beast tried to buck him off. The other hipporines scattered as Putterby gyrated from hillside to path and back again, but Jak's legs were too strong and his hold was too tight.

With one last toss of his head, Putterby started to run. Although he protested every time Jak kicked his side, the stallion turned where Jak wanted him to go. From the thunder of hooves behind them, Jak didn't have to turn around to know that the other hipporines were following, but he was relieved to see the twinkle of lights as two platoons of fairies kept pace on either side.

❦

The goblins had made it plain right away that they wouldn't hesitate to hurt Tamisin if she didn't do what they wanted. That hadn't been a surprise, considering who had grabbed her. Nihlo had been sent with the patrol to watch for approaching fairies. Having captured the princess, he'd been given the job of watching over her, which seemed to make him angry. Tamisin's jaw ached where Nihlo had hit her when she tried to talk to him as he dragged her down the hill to Targin's den. The grizzled cat goblin who stood at the door sent them to join other goblins in an already crowded room. At first Tamisin thought that a goblin named Wulfrin was in charge. Lean-bodied and with flowing gray hair, he had the air of a predator about him. Then Targin arrived to look out the hidden opening in the side of the hill and everyone's attention switched to him. Tamisin didn't know what happened, but whatever Targin saw made him angry, and he left in a hurry after snarling at the goblins to await further orders.

"I can't see the hipporines any more," said a baboon-faced goblin, his nose pressed against the wavery glass.

"How many fairies do you see?" Wulfrin asked.

The baboon goblin scratched his backside and shook his head. "Don't know. They move around too much to count."

"He probably can't count that high," snickered another goblin.

"Shut up!" snapped the baboon goblin.

"Stop your squabbling and tell me what the fairies are doing now," Wulfrin said.

Trying to see out, the smaller goblin rubbed his face

along the glass, leaving a dirty smear. "Can't see 'em from here. Maybe they left, too."

Suddenly the door slammed open and one of the cat goblins stuck his head in the room. "Targin is outside," he told Nihlo. "He wants you to bring the fairy girl to him."

"Move it," said Nihlo, shoving Tamisin toward the door. She kept her eyes lowered, afraid that Nihlo would consider anything, including eye contact, to be a direct challenge.

Thunder rumbled. Remembering what Jak had told her about her connection to thunder, Tamisin raised her head to listen. She decided to try a little experiment, so she took long, deep breaths in an effort to calm down. When the thunder stopped, she ducked her head so no one could see her smile.

Tamisin was determined not to do anything to attract Nihlo's attention. She might be able to escape if he was distracted. Now that they were in the hallway, he wasn't watching her as closely as he had been and seemed more interested in what everyone else was doing. His head turned every time a goblin passed them as if he was looking for someone. Tamisin didn't think anything of it until a figure in a hooded cloak stopped to speak to Nihlo. The newcomer's face was hidden, but when she reached up to pull her hood farther forward, her sleeves fell back and Tamisin could see her hands. It was Lurinda, which didn't make sense. Why would the goblin woman try to conceal her identity in her very own home?

Whatever Lurinda said to him, it must have had something to do with Tamisin because Nihlo glanced in her direction more than once during their conversation. When Lurinda finished talking, she turned to walk away, but Tamisin cried out, "Wait, Lurinda! I need to talk to you."

The hooded figure paused and glanced back. "What is it, halfling?"

"I don't understand why you're working against Titania. From everything you've told me, I thought you were her friend. You've kept her secret all these years. Why have you turned against her now?"

Lurinda closed the gap between them in two long strides. When she spoke, her whispered voice shook with anger. "I was her servant and her confidant, but I was never her friend, although I tried to be. I consoled her when she fought with Oberon and I was by her side when you were born. You were the offspring of the fairy queen and a human who had been changed by magic into a parody of a goblin. Do you know how degrading that would have been for goblins everywhere, and how much they would have hated your mother? I couldn't let that happen, not to Titania, not then. I was the one who convinced her that she needed to give you up. When you were taken away I thought that everything would be as it had been. But it wasn't. Titania said that she couldn't bear to look at me because it made her think of you. She gave me a lesser post where she rarely saw me. I would have been better off if she had released me from her service, but I was stuck there until they thought I was too old to be of any use. I'm free now and it's time she paid for the way she treated me."

Whirling on her heel, Lurinda strode away, leaving Tamisin speechless. This was the woman who had stolen her from her mother only days before. She was also the woman who had talked her mother into sending the infant Tamisin to the human world.

"Move it!" growled Nihlo, shoving Tamisin so that she stumbled toward the door.

The den was in rolling countryside, forested except for the paths and clearings that the goblins had created over centuries of use. Nearby hills concealed other dens, also belonging to members of the cat clan. What was normally a quiet forest whose only sound was birdsong and the creaking of branches in the wind had become a battleground filled with goblins herding flocks of battering rams ready to knock down the enemies' defenses, strategically placed goblins hefting spears as they waited for the fighting to begin, and goblins camouflaging themselves in the trees.

Nihlo was prodding her toward a large group of goblins when the fairies began their attack. A platoon of tiny fairy warriors zoomed low to sprinkle yellow dust on the heads of the goblins herding the rams. Two of the goblins sneezed, and they all looked up as the last of the drifting dust settled on their heads and shoulders.

"Fairy dust!" shrieked a goblin, slapping at his clothes. The first goblin to fall asleep settled to the ground with a sigh. The second fell in a boneless heap, snoring before he hit the dirt. With their shepherds asleep, the rams ran wild, butting everything in their way. By then the goblins were aware of what had happened, so when the fairy platoon approached another group of goblins, they were met with waving spears that swatted them aside like flies.

Over on another hillside, a group of big fairy warriors was building a barricade of rocks. Spear-carrying goblins ran toward them, but a swarm of tiny warriors zoomed into the air, carrying heavy sacks from which they sprinkled dust on any goblin who came too close. This time it was blue dust that made the goblins' feet grow so enormous that they slapped the ground like paddles, making walking almost impossible. Then there was purple dust that made their noses grow so long and heavy that the goblins had to struggle to hold up their heads. Some goblins were coated with dust of both colors.

It wasn't long before the fairies building the barricade were finished. Gathering behind it, they aimed their wands and shot bolts of icy air at the goblins. They were so intent on their larger targets that they didn't notice a small rat goblin who, scurrying from stone to tree to shrub, stayed hidden until he reached the barricade. After placing his hand on the rock wall for only a moment, he squealed with delight when it turned into a clump of pointy-topped mushrooms, leaving the fairies exposed.

The rat goblin was running back toward goblin lines when an angry fairy pointed a wand at him. A blast of cold air shot from the wand, turning the goblin into an ice-covered statue. He made a pitiful keening sound as he froze, drawing the attention of every goblin around. Hundreds of goblin eyes turned toward the fairies. A moment later, a flood of roaring, barking, snarling goblins descended on the fairies, who suddenly became small, making the air sparkle as they flew away. A few remained behind to freeze the oncoming goblins.

When it looked as if these last few fairy warriors were about to be overwhelmed, a goblin with a horsey face howled, "Lamias!"

Nihlo jerked his head toward the top of the hill where a group of older goblins were gathering and told Tamisin, "We'll go up there. That's probably where my father is anyway."

They had climbed partway up the hill when a goblin ran screaming past the spot where they'd been standing. Tamisin looked back as a lamia with long golden hair slithered after the goblin. Nihlo hustled Tamisin up the hillside, glancing back over his shoulder to make sure there weren't any lamias following them, too.

When they reached the top of the hill, they found a large group of goblins clustered at the edge of a clearing. Wulfrin was in front beside Targin, but Lurinda, still wearing her hooded cloak, was in the back behind the taller goblins. Titania stood on the opposite side of the clearing, the air sparkling around her as warriors of all sizes stood guard over their queen. Tamisin glimpsed the small, masked figure of Tobi peeking through the branches behind the fairy warriors, but she didn't see Jak anywhere. She'd last seen him being dragged toward the fairies when the goblins recaptured her, but now that she didn't see him with them she feared that he had been injured or worse.

Targin and Wulfrin were busy arguing when a hush settled over the assembled fairies. They were all watching as Titania raised her hand, her fingers outstretched, her palm taut. At first nothing seemed to happen, but then Tamisin felt something move beneath her feet, forcing its way from the earth. She hopped onto a large rock as roots erupted through the grass, whipping the air as they reached for something, anything. Thick tendrils wrapped around Nihlo's leg, making him swear and reach for his knife, but they tightened their grip and dragged him downward. Staggering, he stepped back into the clutches of another thick root that wound around his knees and yanked him off his feet completely. When the other goblins tried to run away, roots tripped them and wrapped themselves around their squirming bodies. The goblins who could still move their hands pulled at the roots with their fingers, or tried to cut them with knives, but only a few could free themselves.

"Transmogrification!" bellowed Targin, and they all seemed to know what to do. One after the other the goblins bent down and closed their eyes, and when they opened them, the roots were roots no longer. The goblin in front of Tamisin turned them into morning glory vines, which he ripped out of the ground. Another changed the roots into hair that he clipped as neatly as a barber.

Then tiny fairies descended on the goblins, flinging pink dust. Only a few goblins fell asleep before Targin again signaled to his warriors. They raised reeds to their mouths and shot thorns at the fairies, piercing the tiny bodies so that they fell to the ground, still and silent. As their fellow fairy warriors bellowed, Titania called up a breeze that whisked her fallen soldiers back to her side of the clearing. Nymphs emerged from the trees to tend to the injured warriors, while the few tiny fairies who had not been injured straggled back to await the orders of their queen.

The wind grew stronger, blowing into the goblins' faces, making their eyes tear and their noses stream, plucking the reeds from the goblins' hands, rending the spears from their grips, and leaving them without any weapons but their wits. While the other goblins watched, Targin reached down and picked up a stone. His eyes were closed and his brow was furrowed as he turned the stone into a buzzing, straining wasp nest, sealed shut from the outside. Pulling back his arm, he hurled the nest into the midst of the fairies, where it hit the ground and exploded in a shower of dry powder, releasing the furious insects. Fairies shouted, slapping at their clothes, their hair, and their skin as other goblins followed his lead and threw wasp nests of their own. And then Titania's lips moved and the wasps turned to fly straight back at the goblins who had sent them.

At the wasps' approach, Tamisin pulled her sleeves down and covered her face with her arms, but the insects seemed to shy away from her, attacking the goblins around her instead. The goblins were still flailing at the wasps when Titania spoke once more and the ground beneath them stirred as springs bubbled through the soil.

Although the rock upon which Tamisin stood gave her firm footing, the goblins near her staggered as the ground turned mushy beneath them. Goblins sank into the soil up to their knees, crying out to their comrades for help, while Titania raised her voice, calling on a colder wind that circled the goblins and froze the ground, trapping their feet in the hardening, freezing mud.

Targin picked up another stone, cupped it in his hands, and dropped a red-hot coal onto the ground. Steam rose from the soil, inspiring the other goblins, who found stones and bits of twig on the ground near them and turned them into glowing embers or flaming logs. But no matter how hard they tried, the ice refused to thaw, and they remained trapped.

When it looked as if the goblins had nothing else they could do, Titania motioned again. The ground rumbled and suddenly the air seemed to be tinged with gold. "Name yourself, goblin," Titania said to Targin in a voice as clear as if she were standing only feet away.

Although he was sunk in the frozen ground up to his knees, Targin kept his back ramrod straight and crossed his arms. "I am Targin, head of the cat clan," he said. "I am ready to negotiate."

"And why would I negotiate with you?"

"Because my goblins captured your daughter," said Targin.

"Yet you don't seem able to grasp that you have lost."

"But I haven't. You'll get your daughter back as soon as we've reached an agreement. My people are unhappy with your rule," Targin said. "They yearn to return to a time when goblins ruled goblins and answered to no one else."

"You and I both know that isn't possible. I'm not parceling off my kingdom for anyone."

"Either you do what we want or we'll give your halfling to the lamias."

"And do you really think I'd stand for that?" asked the queen.

"What would you do, call lightning down on our heads?" asked Targin. "Make us half donkeys like the princess's father? Wait! It was Oberon who perpetrated that travesty. You just fell in love with the man who mocked goblins." The goblins behind him became restless, muttering to each other in lowered voices.

Nihlo sneered at Tamisin. "Did you hear that? My father wants to feed you to the snake women." Tamisin tried not to flinch when he pinched her arm hard enough to leave a bruise. These creatures were willing to let her die to get what they wanted; they didn't know that Lamia Lou was her friend. If only there was something she could do . . .

Titania was talking to Targin again, but Tamisin couldn't hear her over Nihlo's taunting. She held on to her anger, adding to it her memories of all the cruel things people had ever said or done to her. When she pictured Lurinda telling her how she'd talked Titania into sending Tamisin away, thunder rumbled over the forest, growing louder the angrier Tamisin became.

Lurinda turned toward Nihlo and gave him a signal with her hand. Nihlo nodded and glanced at Tamisin. When she saw his knife, she suddenly understood. Everything Gammi had said about her sister came back to Tamisin—how she held on to grudges and how she was a bad person to cross. Keeping her eyes on Nihlo's knife, Tamisin let her anger and fear grow, knowing it was the only way she was going to get out alive. Goblins shrieked as lightning struck a tree at the edge of the clearing and thunder crashed overhead.

Targin pointed his finger at the queen. "Your theatrics won't work with us. You can bring lighting down on our heads and we still won't change our minds."

Titania glanced up at the sky and made a calming motion with her hand. When the thunder didn't subside, she looked puzzled. Turning to the fairy warriors beside her, she said something that only they could hear. Then they, too, began to look confused.

Nihlo was hauling Tamisin closer with one hand while brandishing his knife with the other when Jak pushed his way through the goblins. Tamisin gasped when Jak appeared at her side, but he didn't look at her. Pulling back his fist, he struck his cousin with such force that Nihlo let go of Tamisin and fell against the goblin behind him.

"Don't ever touch her again," Jak snarled.

"And who's going to stop me?" Nihlo asked, feeling his swollen lip.

Jak pulled a knife out of a sheath on his belt and said, "Who do you think?"

"Jak, are you—," Tamisin began.

"I'm fine," he said, sparing her a quick glance. He must have noticed that she'd opened her wings partway, because he added, "Get out of here while you can."

Thunder boomed as lightning ripped the sky again. A fierce wind thrashed the branches of the forest; a soaking rain pelted everyone until hair, fur, and feathers were wet and bedraggled. Targin gestured for his goblins to bring Tamisin forward, but her wings were already spread wide behind her, and her feet were leaving the ground. Unlike that long-ago Halloween when the wind had slowed her down while she fled the goblins, this time it acted as her ally, enveloping her in a pocket of calm as it pushed the goblins away. Targin's goblins fought to take hold of her, but Tamisin beat her wings once, twice, and then the wind carried her high above the ground, leaving the goblins, her mother, and everyone else watching her in astonishment. Full-blooded fairies couldn't really fly when they were big because their wings weren't strong enough, but then, she wasn't really a fairy. Tamisin Warner was something much better. She was a halfling.

❦

It wasn't hard to find Lamia Lou. All Tamisin had to do was wait until the screaming goblins ran past and see who was chasing them. When she found a lamia with long dark hair, she flew low enough to see her face, then landed on the ground beside her. "Hi!" Tamisin said. "I have a favor to ask of you, but before I tell you, can I ask why you're chasing the goblins? I thought you didn't like eating them anymore."

"I don't," said Lamia Lou. "They thay that goblins tathte like chicken, but they're wrong. If you athk me, chicken tathte much better. But we aren't chathing the goblinth becauthe we want to eat them. We jutht want them to thtop being tho noithy. Everyone in my family ith very thenthitive to noithe. It hurth our earth."

"You mean you come here to make them stop being noisy, then they see you and get even noisier, so you chase them?"

"That'th it," said Lamia Lou. "Now what about that favor?"

"It's really very simple . . . ," said Tamisin.

When Tamisin returned to the top of the hill, she found Titania and Targin still arguing and everyone else looking wet and miserable. The ground had thawed, releasing the goblins. Lurinda and Nihlo were gone. To her relief, Jak was still on his feet.

The storm had died down while Tamisin talked to Lamia Lou, leaving the ground so soggy that it squelched under her feet when she landed. Everyone seemed surprised to see her, but she couldn't decide if it was because they had been unable to believe their eyes the first time or because they thought she had gone and wasn't coming back.

"Hello, Mother, Targin," she said, nodding to each in turn. "I see you haven't settled your differences yet."

Targin glared at her, obviously angry that she hadn't been the bargaining tool he'd wanted. It was her mother who spoke up first, and even she sounded angry with Tamisin. "Why are you here? I was proud of you for escaping from this lout on your own, but I see no reason for you to return."

"I came for you, Mother. And for him," Tamisin said, gesturing toward Targin. "I wanted to give you some advice. You need to stop threatening each other. You'll never get anywhere that way. I want you two to sit down and work things out like responsible adults. I know you want to be a good queen, Mother, and do what's best for your subjects. And you," she said, turning to Targin, "want what you think is best for your people. It seems to me that you already have similar goals."

"We don't need your advice," said Targin.

"That's too bad," said Tamisin. "Because my friends and I aren't going anywhere and neither are you until you reach an agreement, no matter how long it takes."

"What friends?" Targin asked with a sneer. "If you mean my nephew, that boy's a traitor and deserves to be whipped for letting you go."

"I think the princeth meanth uth," lisped a voice from the woods as four lamias slithered into the clearing to the horror of everyone except Tamisin. "My name ith Lamia Lou and I'm a good friend of Princeth

293

Tamithin. That maketh her a friend of my thithterth, too. Unh, unh," she said, rattling her tail at a goblin who looked as if he were about to run away. "You heard the princeth. No one leaveth until we thay they can."

Tamisin was enjoying herself immensely. "Thank you, Lamia Lou."

"Your threat won't work on me, Tamisin," said Titania. "I could leave any time."

"That's true," said Tamisin. "But some of your fairies might get hurt and you wouldn't want that."

Titania glanced at the nymphs who were still tending to the fallen fairies. She turned to Targin. "What exactly are your demands?"

"We want to control what goes on in our territory. We'll obey your laws when we're elsewhere in your kingdom, but we want to make our own laws inside our forest. And we don't want our children taken from us to serve at your court indefinitely. We want a set period of time and we want their service to be voluntary."

Titania frowned. "That's ridiculous. There would be chaos if every group of fey made its own laws. I can't possibly consider it!"

"Isn't there something you could do, Mother?" said Tamisin. "If the goblins are really so unhappy . . ."

Titania sighed. "Perhaps you can write your own laws regarding some matters, but there are others that must stay the same throughout the kingdom. Travelers must be able to pass through your forest in safety, so the laws against killing and eating them cannot change."

Targin nodded. "And as to the children serving at the royal court?"

"I must discuss it with my advisers, but I don't think your request is too unreasonable."

Titania and Targin were still talking when Jak came up behind Tamisin trailing a dozen cats. "Are you all right?" asked Tamisin. "What happened with you and Nihlo?"

"Nihlo didn't have the stomach for a real fight once he saw that his poison no longer affected me. I guess he'd already used it on me too many times, plus his father gave me the antidote a few days ago. Nihlo took off when I didn't collapse after he pricked me," Jak said, showing her a hole in his sleeve. "How are you?"

"I'm fine now that you're back."

"If you two are finished," said Titania, "we'd like to go."

"Is everything settled?" asked Tamisin.

"Her Royal Majesty will be convening a meeting of the heads of all the goblin clans," said Targin. "She assures me that we will be able to work out something."

"Good," said Tamisin. "And I want you both to give me your word that neither fairy nor goblin shall bother us should Jak and I return to the human world."

"So be it," replied Titania. "No fairy under my command shall follow you or cause you mischief or harm in the human world."

"And I give my word for my goblins," said Targin.

"Oh, there's one other thing," Tamisin added after glancing at the lamias. "You should know that loud noises hurt the lamias' ears. It tends to make them angry. I don't think you want to make them angry, do you?"

"No! Of course not!" said Targin. "I never knew . . ."

"I thank you for your help, ladies," Tamisin told the lamias. "You may go now." The collective sigh of relief from fairies and goblins sounded like a breeze passing through the clearing.

"It's 'bout time!" Tobi said as he climbed down from the tree and hurried over to join them. "I thought ya'd keep us here till morning. Uh-oh!" Tobi scurried behind Jak and Tamisin as the lamias slithered closer. The cats hissed and drew nearer to Jak.

The goblins were already disbanding when Herbert trotted out of the forest. "Lamia Lou," he called. "Are you ready to go? You said you wouldn't be long. I've missed my slithering sweetie."

"I've mithed you, too, Thtud Muffin!" replied Lamia Lou. "Come over here and let me introduthe you to my thithterth. Thith ith Lamia Lee and thith ith Lamia Lynn and thith ith Lamia Thlamia, my baby thithter. Girlth, thith ith Herbert!"

"Ladies!" Herbert said, whuffling his lips in admiration.

"Tamisin, I'd like to talk to you," said Titania. "That was clever of you to dance the way you did down in the goblins' cave. I don't know why, but your dancing draws my fairies like no one else's can. Unfortunately, it took longer to locate you when you were underground. My warriors were unable to find you until the cats showed them the hole in the clearing. Thank goodness the cats like you so much, Jak."

"Yeah," said Jak, nudging a persistent cat away with his foot. "It's great."

"Are you really returning to the human world now?" asked Titania. "You're both welcome to stay with me for as long as you'd like."

Tamisin glanced at Jak, then back at Titania. She wanted to answer her mother without hurting her feelings, but she wasn't quite sure how to do it. "That's kind of you," she finally said, "but you were right when you told me that I belong in the human world. I have family and friends who care about me there, and Jak's family . . . well, he'd be better off there, too."

Titania nodded. "It's probably just as well. You'll be safer in the human world, at least until I've met with the heads of the clans and things have calmed down. But even there you'll have to be careful. I meant what I said about my fairies leaving you alone. However, there are some fairies who don't listen to me. And I've only just learned that my former handmaiden Lurinda stole one of my most valuable rings. Shortly before she left my service she made it appear as if another handmaiden had taken it, but I've always suspected Lurinda. She's proven her guilt by taking you the way she did, which she couldn't have done without the ring. It's a ring of power that can open any Gate, at any time, which is how she brought you here, Tamisin, and how she got away. I have to find her and get the ring back. Lurinda has already used it more in the last few days than I did over all the years I had it in my possession. The ring shouldn't be used lightly. Using it too frequently will weaken the fabric that divides the human and the fey, with potentially disastrous consequences. I don't know what she hopes to accomplish, but I doubt it will benefit anyone but her. Remember, she can use my ring to go anywhere she pleases, so be careful, whatever you do. I just hope that the human world is safer for you than this one has proven to be."

"We'll keep our eyes open," said Jak.

"If you're going back today, I have it on good authority," Titania said, darting a glance at her fairy warriors, "that a Gate is open across the Sograssy Sea at the edge of Deep Blue Lake. Ordinarily it would take you a day to reach it and you wouldn't get there before it closes, but considering who your friends are . . ."

"That sounds perfect," said Tamisin.

Targin had joined them while they were talking to Titania. "I wanted to apologize to you, Jak. You were doing what you thought was best, and since I never told you what I was doing or why . . . Let's just say that things might have gone differently."

Jak nodded, but didn't say anything.

"What about me, Princess? Are ya still mad at good ole Tobi?" the little goblin asked, peeking out from behind Jak.

"That remains to be seen," said Tamisin.

"Herbert and I would be happy to take you acroth the thea," said Lamia Lou. "We're going acroth anyway. I want Herbert to meet the retht of my family."

"How many are there?" Tamisin whispered to Jak.

"I don't think anyone has ever counted them," Jak whispered back. "And I doubt anyone really wants to."

Chapter 24

Once again Lamia Lou gave Jak and Tamisin a ride across the Sograssy Sea, this time with the lamia telling endless tales about her family. Only Herbert seemed genuinely interested.

"... And then there wath Great-Grandma Lamia Zalina. That old woman wath a real hoot! Thhe filed her teeth to pointth tho thhe'd look thcarier, but it made her teeth rot and they all had to come out. Without her teeth her face collapthed and thhe had to gum her food. No one thought thhe looked thcary after that."

"That's too bad," murmured Herbert.

"You would have liked my grandmother Lamia Mia. Thhe perfected the art of thlithering through the grath without dithturbing a thingle blade. That woman thcared more people to death than anyone elthe in the family."

"She sounds delightful," Jak said through gritted teeth.

"I bet none of them were as beautiful as you are, Sweet Lips," said Herbert.

"That'th true," said Lamia Lou.

After what seemed like half a day, Tamisin had heard enough stories. Since Lamia Lou had assured them that she and Jak could come and go freely across the sea, she was ready to try it without an escort. "We're not taking you out of your way, are we?" she asked. "Which direction would you go to see your family?"

"That way," Lamia Lou said, pointing at a right angle to the way they were traveling.

"Then I think this is where we part company," said Tamisin. "If you wouldn't mind stopping . . ."

Lamia Lou slithered to a halt. "Are you thure? The other thide'th thtill an hour away. We really wouldn't mind taking you there, would we, Herbert?"

"Not at all," said the unicorn.

"We'll be fine," Tamisin said. "I'm sure you have other things to do than spend the day helping us."

"If you inthitht," said Lamia Lou as Tamisin and Jak climbed off her snaky tail. "But you're mithing a lot of great thtorieth."

"We'll be back to hear them some other time," said Jak.

The lamia had already started telling Herbert about another relative when they disappeared into the shoulder-high grass. "Thank you," Jak told Tamisin. "After riding a hipporine this morning I wasn't sure that I'd ever sit again. I don't think I could have stayed on Lamia Lou's tail much longer."

"You mean you didn't want to get off because of her stories?" asked Tamisin.

"That, too. And I thought my relatives were strange!"

"Gammi's not. I really like her," said Tamisin. "I'm glad she's going to join you soon. I didn't know she liked living among humans that much."

"Neither did my uncle, Targin. She nearly took his head off when he tried to forbid her to go back. I'd never seen him look browbeaten before."

Tamisin laughed. "She is his mother. I don't think he would have turned out to be such a strong leader without her."

"It's amazing how much of an impact mothers can have on their children, even when they're not around. At least now you know who your mother is and that she really does love you."

"I suppose," said Tamisin. "I mean, I want to go home and everything, but I was a little disappointed that she didn't say anything about seeing me again."

Jak laughed. "Oh, but she did. She kissed you good-bye right before we left, didn't she? When the queen of the fairies kisses you, it means that you'll have to return to her someday. Even people who want to stay away are compelled to go back eventually. They have no choice, and neither will you."

"She could have just asked me back for a visit," said Tamisin.

"Aren't you ever satisfied?" Jak said, laughing again.

They had made good time crossing a patch that was no more than waist high when they entered the last of the taller grass. Tamisin considered opening her wings and rising into the air to see where they were going, and it even crossed her mind that they could get to the other side much faster if she were to fly them there, but Jak wanted to stretch his legs, and she was enjoying their conversation now that Lamia Lou and Herbert were gone.

"Tell me something," she said as Jak took the lead. "When we get back to the human world will everything still be the same between us?"

Jak's back was to her as he worked his way through the taller grass, so she couldn't see his face when he said, "I don't know. Are you still going to want to see me? After all, you are a princess and I'm just a halfling."

"The important word there is 'halfling,'" said Tamisin. "Who else can understand what it's like to be a part of two different worlds and not really belong in either? And who else can see the things that I can see and know that they really exist? And who else can I show off to when I want to fly?" Laughing out loud, Tamisin threw her arms in the air and twirled just as she did when she was dancing. She was on her fourth spin when she heard a sound like a strangled cough. "Jak," she said, stopping in midtwirl. "Are you all right?"

Jak wasn't where she thought he'd be, so she turned around, thinking she'd gotten disoriented. "Jak?" she called again, but there was no answer. There was no one around and nowhere he could have gone. She forged ahead, pushing the grass aside, and tried again, louder this time. "Jak!" When there still was no response, Tamisin felt a twinge of fear. This wasn't right. He had to be there, didn't he?

Tamisin retraced her steps, examining the flattened grass. This was where she had walked. This was where she had twirled. And over here... Tamisin's breath whistled between her teeth when she saw where the grass had been flattened to one side. Someone else was here, and something was very wrong.

Opening her wings with a whoosh, Tamisin took to the air. It was easy to see the trail from above; although it was straightening, the grass that had been trampled caught the light differently from the grass around it. There was a hill and a dip and... Tamisin gasped when she finally saw Jak. He was on his feet, with his fists raised, and he wasn't alone. Nihlo had found them again.

※

When Tamisin's shadow passed over Jak, he shouted, "Stay back, Tamisin," without taking his eyes off the knife in Nihlo's hand.

Jak had no knife, or anything he could readily turn into one. When Nihlo lunged, jabbing with his knife, Jak danced aside, then kicked with his opposite foot, knocking the weapon out of the goblin's hand. Nihlo was on his hands and knees rooting through the trampled grass when Jak shaded his eyes from the sun and called to Tamisin. "Give me your hair clip."

The emerald green clip was made of plastic and looked like two interlocking sets of claws. He caught it as it sailed through the air, then quickly looked to see what Nihlo was doing. His cousin had found his knife and was just getting up off his knees.

"What do you think you're going to do with that?" Nihlo asked when he saw the clip. "Pinch me to death?"

"Actually," said Jak, "I had something else in mind." He knew it was risky when he closed his eyes because Nihlo might take advantage of it and throw his knife, but he was hoping that curiosity alone would stay the goblin's hand. Jak thought about the clip, then pictured what he wanted it to become. He felt the tingling and when he pushed, he no longer held the clip.

"Hey!" exclaimed Nihlo. "What's that?"

"It's a cage to keep you in," said Jak. Made of steel, the cage was thirty feet across and enclosed both Jak and Nihlo. The sides rose for ten feet, then arched together to form a ceiling over their heads.

"How did you do that?" asked Nihlo. "Everybody knows that halflings can't transmogrify anything."

"Then everybody must be wrong," said Jak.

Nihlo sneered and took a step closer. "You think you're so smart, but that was the dumbest thing I've ever seen. You made a cage for me and put yourself in it."

Jak nodded. "That was really stupid, wasn't it? Although you have to admit, it is a nice cage." While his cousin watched, Jak reached up to run his hand over one of the bars. "Good quality metal, too. It should last a really long time." Jak's back was turned when he closed his eyes again. When he opened them, a door had appeared in the cage. He stepped through before the goblin could react and closed the door behind him. Nihlo started running, but Jak had the bars changed back before his cousin was even close.

"You son of a sea witch!" Nihlo shouted. He lunged at

Jak, hitting the bars with his chest and shoulder, but Jak was already well out of range.

Jak waited for Tamisin to land beside him. When she took his hand, he squeezed hers, then turned to Nihlo and said, "What I don't understand is why you're here at all. You must have heard about your father's promise that no goblin would come after us."

Nihlo looked as if he'd tasted something foul. "I've forsworn my father. I don't follow his orders anymore."

Jak nodded. "You follow Lurinda's orders now, don't you?"

A rustling in the grass announced the arrival of Lamia Lou and Herbert. Nihlo swore and stepped away from the side of the cage.

"I heard the thouting. Ith thomething going on?" asked the lamia. She clasped her hands in front of her chest and gazed at the cage in delight. "Thay! Thith ith nice! What'th it for?"

"It's here to hold this piece of trash until Targin can come get him. I'm sure my uncle will know what to do with his son. Would you be able to get word to Targin that Nihlo is here?" Jak asked Lamia Lou.

"It would be my pleathure!" she replied.

"But first, why don't you share with him some of the stories you were telling us," said Jak. "Tell him about your grandmother who could slither up to a victim without making a sound."

"And the one with the filed teeth," added Tamisin.

"I'd love to!" said Lamia Lou, smiling so broadly that her fangs glistened in the sunlight.

"I wonder what day of the week it will be when we get back to the human world," said Tamisin. The edge of the Sograssy Sea was in sight, and just beyond it sparkled the waters of the Deep Blue Lake.

"Does it matter?" asked Jak.

"Not really," said Tamisin. "It's just that admission to the movie theater is cheaper on Tuesday night. I thought we could go if something good was playing."

Jak pretended to be surprised. "Are you asking me out on a date?"

"I sure am," said Tamisin as she turned to face him. "And it's going to be indoors, where no fairies or goblins can surprise us."

"Goblins surprised us in my house during the Halloween party," Jak reminded her. He took her hand in his and pulled her toward him.

"True," said Tamisin. "But then everybody knew about the party. We're not inviting anyone else on our date."

"Not even Tobi?" Jak asked with a grin.

"Especially not Tobi," said Tamisin. "This time everything is going to go right."

"I think it already is," said Jak. And he kissed her.

This fairy adventure isn't over yet!

Read on for a sneak peek of E. D. Baker's
new fairy book.

Chapter 1

Tamisin had to dance. Although the sky was overcast and the full moon was hidden behind the clouds, the moon still called her to raise her arms, twirl on her toes, and move to music only she could hear. Her long blond hair floated around her, brushing the wisteria blossoms each time she twirled by her parents' back porch. Her bare feet left imprints on the grass as she stepped around the bird-bath in the center of the yard. Her eyes, raised to the concealed moon, didn't seem to notice what was around her but shone as if she had glimpsed something far more wonderful than anything either the human or fey world could offer.

When Tamisin Warner danced, she was as graceful as a woodland creature, her movements as fluid as water rippling over unseen stone. Each step, each gesture, evoked the essence and mystery of the fey world. Anyone who had ever seen her dance could tell that it was as hypnotic for the dancer as it was for the spectator.

That night, Tamisin had been dancing for only a few minutes when the fairies arrived. They came in a cloud of sparkling lights to hover around her, watching silently until her very last gesture. When Tamisin's arms fell to her sides and she took a long, shuddering breath, the fairies fled.

Fairies were nothing new to Tamisin; she had been a child in a human family the first time she felt the urge to dance under a full moon and had seen fairies every month since. Even so, she had been shocked when wings sprouted from her own back and she learned that she might not be as human as she'd always assumed. In fact, no sooner was she whisked off to the fairies' land than she learned that she was adopted and her birth mother was Titania, the queen of the fairies. According to Titania, her birth father was a human named Bottom who had died centuries before. She also learned that the fairies were very strange, so she had found her way home to the human world again. Still, it seemed neither place felt right.

After the first month back in the human world, Tamisin began to feel restless. She started going for short walks around the neighborhood and one day ended up in the woods behind the school, standing in front of the two tall trees that formed a gate to the land of the fey. There were no shimmering lights between the trees, which meant that the gate wasn't open. A few days later Tamisin went for another walk, purposefully heading in a different direction, and ended up in the same place. She tried it again over the weekend and wound up standing in front of the still-closed gate.

Tamisin arrived at school early the next morning to wait by her boyfriend Jak's locker. He was a cat goblin and had visited the land of the fey with her. "What's up?" he said as he walked down the hall. He gave her a quick kiss and added, "You're never here before I am."

"I just wanted to talk," she said, leaning against the next locker as he started his combination.

"Is something wrong?" he asked, frowning.

"Not wrong, exactly. Just odd. You've been busy with basketball practice and, well, I've been really restless lately and have started taking walks. The weird thing is, no matter where I go, I end up in the woods behind the school. There's a gate near that waterfall you took me to last autumn."

Jak's frown deepened. "You've been going to a gate to the land of the fey?"

Tamisin nodded. "Yes, but it's never open. And I'm not *trying* to go there. I just end up standing in front of it somehow."

"Do you want to go back to the land of the fey already?"

"Not really. I'm sure I will someday, but not yet. I hated that so much time passed here while we were there for only a few days. We missed Thanksgiving and Christmas and Petey's birthday. I really wanted to be here for my little brother's birthday party; I was going to put it on for him this year."

"What about Titania?"

"I don't have any burning desire to see her again, if that's what you're asking. She is my birth mother, but I don't think I'll ever feel as close to her as I do to Mom. Janice is the only mother I've ever known. She took care of me whenever I was sick, she read me to sleep when I was little, she taught me how to tie my shoes . . . She's *Mom*, and I guess she always will be. Titania is beautiful and exciting and pretty amazing. But I feel more like she's a really cool aunt I didn't know I had until now. What about you? Do you ever think about visiting your old home?"

"You mean my uncle Targin's cave? All the time," said Jak. "And then I'm grateful that I don't have to. You have no idea how much happier I am here in the human world. I have friends here, and family who care about me. Gammi is the only relative I have who showed me any kindness, and she lives here now. And Bert is like a big brother who would do anything for me. He may be a bear goblin, but I'm closer to him than I ever was to my cousin Nihlo. I still have nightmares where Nihlo is chasing me through the corridors, threatening to lock me outside at night so the lamias will eat me. You can't imagine how scary that was for a little kid. At least here there aren't trolls, or manticores, or other creatures that would want to eat you."

"That's true," said Tamisin.

"I couldn't go back now, anyway," said Jak. "I'm sure all the cat goblins hate me for siding with Titania against my uncle Targin. Given half a chance, they'd probably skin me alive and serve me for dinner."

Tamisin shifted the books she was carrying. "You wouldn't have to see your relatives. The land of the fey is a pretty big place."

"Why would I want to go back? I have everything I need right here. Including you."

Tamisin smiled. She was glad she'd talked to Jak. Just telling someone about it made her feel better. She really didn't want to go back to the land of the fey, at least not for a good long while.

Although she tried to put the gate and the land of the fey out of her mind and stopped going for walks, the desire to visit the gate continued to build inside her. A few weeks later she couldn't stand it any longer and returned to the woods behind the school. There were still no shimmering lights between the trees. Nor were there any the next time she went, or the time after that. She no longer tried to fight the urge to go to the woods, but every time she went, the gate was closed, and she became increasingly frustrated.

"Is something wrong?" Jak asked one day at school after she had snapped at her friend Heather.

"Yes, but you won't want to talk about it," Tamisin told him, slamming her locker door.

"What is it?" he asked. "Did someone do something?"

Tamisin shook her head. "Nothing like that. It's just that . . . I went to the gate yesterday, but it's closed—again!"

"How often have you gone there?"

Tamisin looked away. "At least twice a week for the last two months. But don't worry, it's been closed every time."

"Are you trying to go to the land of the fey?" he said, sounding incredulous.

"Yes . . . No . . . Maybe . . . I don't know what I'm trying to do!" she said. "I guess I just want to see if I *could* go back. If I wanted to, I mean."

"Why didn't you tell me?"

"Because I know how much you don't want to go back!"

"So you'd go without me? Tamisin, do you know how dangerous that would be?"

"Not if I went through the gate behind the school. It goes directly to Titania's forest."

Jak put his hands on her shoulders. "There is no completely safe place in the land of the fey. Promise me you won't go alone."

"I can't promise anything," she said, pulling away.

"It's Titania's kiss. It makes you want to go back to her."

"Then it was a pretty powerful kiss! I can't sleep most nights, and when I do, I dream about the land of the fey. I went flying last week, but the urge to go through the gate kept me flying in circles above it when I saw it was closed again. I can't fly or talk to fairies or dance without wanting to go through the gate even more, so I've stopped flying, and I've yelled at the fairies so often that they come around only when I dance. The one thing I can't do is stop dancing, and believe me, I've tried. I've barricaded my bedroom door with my dresser, and I've tied my ankles to my bed, yet I still find myself outside dancing with my hair a tangled mess and my feet bare and half frozen. I don't know what to do, and it's driving me crazy!"

"I've heard that no one can withstand the compulsion

of the fairy queen's kiss," said Jak. "But I didn't know it was this bad. I guess you don't have any choice about returning to her."

"Well, I'm not going, am I?" said Tamisin. "She kissed me, but she must not really want me there if the gate is always closed. Unless . . . Do you know of any other gate that leads directly to Titania's forest?"

Jak shook his head. "Sorry, I don't."

Tamisin leaned against the locker behind her and closed her eyes. "It's probably just as well. I'd have to tell my family before I left, and I don't know how they'd take it."

Although Tamisin didn't mention the gate to Jak again, she had no intention of quitting. She continued to visit the gate every few days but never did find it open. Then one night Jak invited her to his house for dinner. Knowing how much his grandmother liked mice and raw meat, she wasn't sure she wanted to go. When she arrived, she was relieved to learn that Bert was cooking dinner. He served panfried trout, biscuits with honey, and berries that he'd bought frozen and weren't quite thawed.

"Dinner was delicious," she told the bear goblin as he licked berry juice from his fingers.

"Glad you liked it," he said. "We had fish last night, too. Catfish," he said, grinning at Gammi.

"Odd name for a good fish," said the old cat-goblin woman. "We had it 'cause my cousin Sulie came for a quick visit," she told Tamisin. "The gate between the cat-goblin clan home and our backyard was open, so she stopped by. Didn't stay more than a few hours, which is just as well. For some reason the gates are slow to open but close mighty fast. We had a good visit, though. I liked catching up with all the goings-on back home."

"If she was here for a few hours," said Jak, "I wonder how long she was gone from the other side."

Gammi shook her head. "There's no saying. Time passes differently here and there from one visit to the next. Why, I remember when—"

"Excuse me," Tamisin said, turning to Jak. "Do you mean to say that the gate behind your house was open and you didn't tell me?"

Jak saw the look on her face and his expression turned serious. "I didn't think it mattered. You wouldn't want to go through it anyway. It leads to the center of the cat-goblin clan!"

"Just because you don't want to go that way doesn't mean I can't! I could fly from there to Titania's forest."

"And have a dragon pluck you from the sky? Or a flock of harpies mug you? Or a goblin shoot you down with poison-tipped arrows? Flying can be just as dangerous as walking in the land of the fey. I don't want you going there by yourself, and *I* don't dare go through that gate."

"Or any gate, apparently!" said Tamisin. "You know I want to go back, and you haven't even looked for another way to get there."

"I didn't know it was that important to you," Jak began.

"How can you say that?" Tamisin pushed her chair back and stood. "I told you I was checking the gate every few days to see if it had opened. If it wasn't important to me, do you honestly think I would have kept going back? It's gotten so bad that when I go to the woods and the gate is closed, my heart pounds, my stomach hurts, I break out in a sweat, and I can barely breathe. I'm having anxiety attacks just because that gate is closed, and I'm having them every single time I go there. This isn't like wishing I could go to a party and being disappointed because I can't go. This is like needing to swim to the surface of the water because I'm at the bottom of the pool and running out of air! Thank you for dinner," she told Bert and Gammi. "I hate to eat and run, but I really need to go now."

"Tamisin . . . ," said Jak, but she had already left the room. A moment later she was out the door and hurrying down the sidewalk.

Tamisin was furious. Jak knew exactly how important this was to her. He was the one who had told her about the effect the fairy queen's kiss had on people in the first place! He was afraid to go back, so he didn't want her to go either. Well, forget him! She didn't need him, or Titania either, for that matter. If the fairy queen had wanted her to return to the land of the fey, she would have made sure Tamisin could get back. Tamisin had heard somewhere that fairies were known to be fickle; her mother had probably already changed her mind about having her half-human daughter around.

As days passed, Tamisin's resentment grew. The desire to return to the land of the fey became her constant shadow. Short of living beside the gate and waiting for it to open, there wasn't much she could do, so she did her best to focus on being human.

One day her mother passed by the bathroom while Tamisin was putting on makeup. Tamisin looked up when she realized that her mother was watching her.

"Why are you covering your spreckles?" her human mother asked. "I thought you stopped doing that a while ago. And you're wearing your hair down over your ears. I think it looks so cute pulled back into a ponytail."

Tamisin shrugged. "I'm trying to look more human, and that's really hard with pointed ears like mine, or glittery freckles on my cheeks."

"Is everything all right? Your father and I have noticed that you don't smile as much as you used to, and we hardly ever hear you laugh. You know you can talk to us if something is bothering you."

"Nothing is bothering me," Tamisin said, forcing herself to smile. She loved her parents and didn't want to hurt them; she was sure that hearing how much she wanted to return to the land of the fey would upset them.

That night, Tamisin was on her way to bed when she passed her parents' room and overheard them talking in quiet voices. She couldn't hear much other than her name, but they sounded worried. Although it made her want to run into the room to reassure them, there wasn't anything reassuring about the way she felt, and she really didn't know what to say.

Tamisin continued to visit the gate, her frustration growing each time she saw that it was still closed. She would have had plenty to say to Titania about the kiss, the closed gate, and the confusion that she felt over going to the land of the fey, but with no way to talk to Titania, she turned her anger on Jak.

"Tamisin!" he called down the school corridor one day after she'd spent weeks ignoring his phone calls and avoiding him at school. "We need to talk."

"No, we don't," she said, turning away so she wouldn't have to see the hurt in his eyes that was reflected in the pit of her stomach. She knew she was being unreasonable, but seeing him just made her angrier. Not only had he not told her about the gate, but he was half cat goblin, and reminded her all the more of the land of the fey. It was harder to feel human when Jak was around.

A tree frog called from her neighbors' lily pond, sounding like a chick in a henhouse; the noise brought Tamisin fully back to the present. When she saw that she was standing in the yard in her nightgown once again, she shook her head and sighed. Tugging her fingers through the snarls that twirling had whipped into her hair, Tamisin started toward the back door, hoping she had come out that way so the door would be unlocked. (Once, she'd climbed out her bedroom window to dance and had to climb back through in the middle of the night.) She had almost reached the steps to the porch when she sensed movement behind her and glanced back. A human-sized fairy stood in the trees at the edge of the yard. Tamisin gasped. Usually the fairies who watched her were tiny—and harmless.

The fairy stepped out of the shadows and into the light cast by the carriage lamp beside the door, revealing his narrow face; his thin, pointed ears; and the tilt of his bright green eyes. He was taller than most full-sized fairies and wore the subdued browns and greens of a warrior. Sweeping his peaked cap off his head, he bowed in a courtly manner. "I am sorry to startle you, Your Highness. My name is Mountain Ash. You're Princess Tamisin, are you not?" he asked.

"I am," she replied.

"I had heard of the pull fairies feel when you dance, but I did not know how strong it was until I experienced it for myself. I am glad the rumors were true, for it helped me find you. I've come to give you news about your father."

Tamisin frowned. "My birth father died hundreds of years ago."

"Someone has lied to you," said Mountain Ash. "Your father is very much alive. If you come with me, you will see that I'm telling the truth." The fairy held out his hand as if to grasp hers.

Tamisin took a step back. This was too much like the stranger danger they taught little kids about in school. "There's no way I'm going with you," she said. "I have an English final in the morning, and I need to get some sleep."

The fairy warrior sighed and moved toward her. "I had hoped it wouldn't come to this," he said, and raised his hand toward her cheek.

Tamisin slipped out of reach, but before she could take another step, his hand was touching her shoulder, and an instant later, everything began to change. She started to run, but her entire body felt fizzy, as if bubbles were popping inside her. Tiny lights exploded around her; she could see them even after she shut her eyes. When she opened her eyes again, the trees, the house, and the birdbath all seemed to be growing until they towered above her. Soon the grass itself was higher than her head. She cried out when an enormous hand closed around her and squeezed just enough to pick her up. Then she fell into the gaping mouth of a brown sack and was engulfed in darkness and stale air. She landed on her side with a gasp as her breath was forced from her lungs.

"Oberon thinks it's time you met your real father," Mountain Ash's voice boomed as the opening over her head shrank to a tiny circle, then disappeared altogether, cutting her off from light and any hope of fresh air.

Tamisin rolled over and tried to stand, staggering when the bag rose and the bottom curved under her feet.

Small bits of dried leaves crunched beneath her, releasing the scent of mint. She could tell that she was rising by the way she suddenly felt heavier. There was a rushing sound in her ears, and Tamisin passed out.

E. D. BAKER

made her international debut with *The Frog Princess*, which was a Texas Lone Star Reading List Book, a Book Sense Children's Pick, a Florida's Sunshine State Young Readers List book, and the inspiration for the hit Disney movie *The Princess and the Frog*.

Ms. Baker has written eight books in the Tales of the a Frog Princess series, as well as *The Wide-Awake Princess* and the sequel to *Fairy Wings, Fairy Lies*. She lives on a small farm in Maryland, where she and her family breed horses. They also have dogs, cats, goats, and two ducks named Quackers and Fromage.

www.edbakerbooks.com
www.talesofedbaker.com